# DEATH UNDER A FULL MOON

DIANNE SMITHWICK-BRADEN

BLACK ROSE writing™

First printing



ISBN: 978-1-61296-650-2

PUBLISHED BY BLACK ROSE WRITING

www.blackrosewriting.com

Printed in the United States of America

Suggested retail price $17.95

*Death Under a Full Moon* is printed in Palatino Linotype

*This book is dedicated to my parents and my maternal grandparents. Their stories and the memories of visiting Rayland were part of the inspiration for this tale.*

*I'd like to thank my family and friends for allowing me to "borrow" their names for this book series.*

# DEATH UNDER A FULL MOON

# CHAPTER 1

It was a peaceful mid-September evening in Wilbarger County, Texas. The setting sun painted the sky with ribbons of orange, pink, and gold. The temperature was mild, and the air was still…a welcome relief after several days of hot, dry wind.

Brian Flynn shut down the engine on his tractor and sat quietly surveying the land that he and his family loved. The farm house sat near the center on the northern boundary of their two-hundred-acre farm. The land was divided into three fields. He had just finished preparing the east field. It needed to be planted with wheat in the coming week. The center field of alfalfa had given its last crop until spring. The west field was C.R.P. land.

He watched as his ten-year-old son Hunter and his six-year-old daughter Chloe played on the tire swing he had made for them. He smiled as the sound of their laughter floated to his ear. They both had golden hair like their mother, but they had his brown eyes. Kelly opened the back door, waved to him, and called the kids inside. Brian's stomach grumbled as he started the tractor and drove back to the house.

Inside the house, the Flynn family sat at the kitchen table enjoying their supper. As was their nightly ritual, they discussed the events of the day. Brian listened while the children and Kelly talked. When they had finished, it was his turn.

"I saw some deer tracks near the pond at the edge of the field."

"Can we go see them, Daddy?" Chloe asked.

"We'll go to the pond Saturday."

"Your dad and I will clean up the kitchen. It's time for you two to get your homework done," Kelly told them.

Hunter and Chloe reluctantly obeyed. Homework was the worst part of the day as far as they were concerned.

"You're quiet tonight. What's wrong?" Kelly whispered.

"Nothing," Brian answered, pretending to concentrate on the dirty dishes.

"Brian, look at me," Kelly urged.

Brian looked at his wife silently for a moment. Finally, with a heavy heart, he said, "Jim is going to put his place on the market. He doesn't have any more work for me."

Kelly put her arms around her husband. "What are we going to do?"

"I don't know. It will take a lot of rain to save the farms around here. It may be too late. Water wells are drying up all over this part of the country. Ours isn't producing the amount of water we need to water the crops. If this drought doesn't end soon, we're going to be in serious trouble. I've been trying to decide whether we should plant the wheat next week or take the seed back and put all of our land into C.R.P."

"What's C.R.P., Daddy?"

The couple rolled their eyes and grinned at each other. Chloe was always listening, particularly when the conversations were whispered. Kelly shrugged her shoulders and said, "We may as well tell them."

"It stands for Conservation Reserve Program," Brian told his daughter. "The government will pay us if we put our land in that program for at least ten years. It's supposed to control soil erosion and make a place where wild animals can live."

"Dad, what will we do if you don't farm?" Hunter asked.

"I'll have to find a full time job and drive to town everyday like your mother."

"What about Mr. Jim?"

"Mr. Jim doesn't need my help right now," Brian reluctantly told his son.

The family sat in silence for a few moments pondering the turn their lives were about to take. Finally, Kelly said, "We're going to weigh all of our options before we make such a big decision. Your dad and I will talk about this more later. Finish your homework."

When the homework and evening chores were done, the young couple tucked their children in before going to bed themselves.

"Brian, I'm concerned about the kids. They're too young to have to worry about such things."

"I know. I'm glad they heard it from us rather than someone else. A lot of folks are having the same decisions to make. You know that one of their friends is bound to say something."

"That's true. I guess it's best they know there will probably be some big changes coming. Do you think that we might have to sell out and move to town?"

"I hope not," Brian said as he turned off the light and held his wife close. "We won't even discuss that unless there's no other choice."

Outside the house, the full moon glowed proudly in the evening sky. A small herd of mule deer grazed contentedly in what remained of the alfalfa field. A few of them watched the lights of the farm house blink off as its occupants settled down for their nightly dreams. The deer grazed contentedly, unaware that something else watched and waited in the cover provided by the tall native grass of the C.R.P. land.

A young healthy doe slowly wandered away from the herd as she grazed toward the tall grass. Startled, she raised her head and looked at her surroundings. She turned and began to trot back toward the herd. She had taken only a few steps before she broke into a run. Suddenly, she felt a sharp pain in her shoulders. She struggled to free herself from the pain and the weight bearing down on her. The noise she made while battling for her life alarmed the remainder of the herd. They ran in terror as strong jaws delivered the killing bite, breaking the unfortunate doe's neck.

The large animal dragged the deer into the tall C.R.P. Once satisfied that its catch was safe from other predators, it began to feast on its kill. Using its claws to open the flesh, it ate the heart, lungs, and liver first. When the beast was finally satisfied, it buried what remained and gracefully moved through the native grass, leaving little of its prey behind.

The following morning Brian waved goodbye to his family as they left for the day. He felt good about the decision he and Kelly had made about their future and was eager to get started. He would find a full-time job and continue to farm during his off hours for the time being. There wouldn't be a lot of farm work to be done until spring. They had decided to plant the wheat as planned. It would be a dry land crop depending on Mother Naturc for its needed moisture. In doing so, they hoped they would be able to conserve enough water for irrigating the alfalfa in the spring and summer.

Brian knew it was only a temporary solution. If the drought continued, the water would run out, and the crops would fail. Since neither he nor Kelly could see into the future, they were gambling on one more year to keep their home.

Brian drove into town to see his friend Drew Clifton. Andrew Clifton was vice president at one of the local banks. He had mentioned a job opening the last time they had seen each other. Brian hoped he still had that opening or at least knew of another one. He had made a ten thirty appointment for that morning so that he could be sure to see Drew. He arrived ten minutes early and paced restlessly while he waited.

"Brian, how are you?" Drew asked extending his hand to his friend.

"Hi, Drew. Doing okay," he lied. "How are you?"

"Good. Come in. Would you like some coffee?"

"That sounds good. Thank you."

"Sit down. Make yourself comfortable." Drew watched his friend while pouring the coffee. "What brings you into town today?"

Brian took the coffee and sighed. "I suppose you know this isn't a social call."

Drew nodded as he sat down. "I figured as much since you made an appointment. What can I do for you?"

"I need a job, Drew, a full time job that I can depend on. I thought you might know of someone needing help. My crops weren't good this year, and Jim told me he's going to sell out. I need something other than farming so that I can support my family."

"Are you planning to sell?"

"We decided last night to give it one more year. I've lived on that place all my life. It's the only home I've ever known. I can't stand the thought of selling. Kelly doesn't want to sell either. We're going to try farming on the side and conserving as much water as we can. If things don't improve, we may put it into C.R.P. Selling would be our last resort."

"Do you need a loan? I'd be happy to loan you some money or cosign for a loan."

"Thanks, Drew. I appreciate it; I might have to take you up on that offer later. Right now, what I need is a job. Any job will do as long as the pay is steady."

"There aren't any openings here at the moment. I did hear a rumor that there has been some turnover at the state hospital. I'll call over there and see what I can find out for you."

Brian waited patiently as Drew turned to his desk phone and dialed a number.

"Paul Randolph, please," Drew said when someone answered. He waited a few minutes before saying, "Paul, this is Drew Clifton. Doing well. How are you? Good, good. Are there any job openings over there? Well, I have a good friend here in my office, and he's looking for a job. You probably know him; it's Brian Flynn." Drew smiled as he listened and made notes.

"There's a security guard position open. Can you be in Paul Randolph's office at one o'clock this afternoon?" Drew asked Brian as he covered the mouthpiece of the telephone.

Brian nodded, relieved.

"He'll be there. Thank you, Paul."

Drew handed Brian the note paper.

"Thank you, Drew. I really appreciate your help."

"What are friends for? I hope this helps."

The two friends shook hands. Brian left to find some lunch and a place to wait until time for his one o'clock appointment.

After meeting with Paul Randolph, Brian drove to Kelly's office.

"How did it go?" Kelly asked.

"I start orientation Monday morning," Brian answered. "I'm going to be a security guard. It's going to mean working some nights."

"We'll make it work somehow," Kelly assured him.

Brian drove home feeling as if a tremendous weight has been lifted.

• • •

The sun rose to chase away the dreams of the night. Its light illuminated a landscape which would soon be trimmed with the orange, red, and amber colors of fall. The last Saturday of September promised to be a beautiful day.

Lizzie Fletcher woke to the song of a meadowlark. She lay in bed listening to its song while relishing the comfort of her bed. It was a simple pleasure, one that she seldom had the opportunity to enjoy.

All was quiet at the Paradise Creek Inn. It was the beginning of a temporary lull in a steady and oftentimes booming business. The coming holiday season would keep her family busy into the New Year. Lizzie had made plans to enjoy the downtime.

The Fletcher family owned and operated the inn. As the managing partner, Lizzie lived at the inn and saw to the daily tasks. Her parents and grandmother helped as they were needed.

It was located on the Fletcher family farm in Wilbarger County, Texas. The house had been built by Lizzie's great grandfather. It had been her grandmother's suggestion to renovate the old house into an inn.

Looking at the clock, Lizzie decided she had lain in bed long enough. She had things to do before Wade arrived.

She showered and dressed quickly in her favorite jeans and t-shirt. She brushed her shoulder length red hair back from her face and applied a little cosmetic enhancement that showed her vivid blue eyes to the best advantage. Satisfied with her appearance, she went to the kitchen.

Lizzie thought of Wade as she prepared a picnic lunch. She felt a little silly, but she was excited about the day. They had both been so busy that she had not seen him in weeks.

Wade Adams was the Wilbarger County sheriff. They met in April of 2012 when Wade and Doctor Hughes came to her rescue after a storm had practically dropped an injured man on her door step.

He was at the inn daily after the bodies were discovered. He had asked her to have dinner with him after the cases were closed. It was hard to believe that it was already nearing the end of 2013 and that they had been seeing each other almost a year-and-a-half.

Lizzie shuddered at the thought of those who had died and who had been responsible for their deaths. It was still hard at times to believe it had all been real instead of a storyline in a movie. She was startled from her reverie when her mother came into the kitchen.

"Something sure smells good in here," Ellen commented.

"Hi, Mama," Lizzie answered as she hugged her mother.

"Fried chicken?"

"Yes, ma'am."

"I guess it's a good thing I didn't plan that for supper tonight. You're planning to be back for supper aren't you?"

"We will. I promise."

"Good. Here's the basket you wanted. I brought this old blanket that Daddy and I always took with us. You can use it if you want."

"That'll be great! Thanks."

"Where are you going for your picnic?"

"I thought I'd take him to the spring."

Ellen smiled wistfully. "We used to love going to the spring. We haven't been in years."

"I hope it's still a nice place to go," Lizzie replied. "I haven't been since I moved home."

"What are you going to do it if it isn't?"

"I have a backup plan, but I really want Wade to see the spring."

The phone rang in the office, interrupting the conversation.

"I'll get it."

"Thanks, Mama," Lizzie said as she began packing food into the picnic basket. She went to the pantry for a few finishing touches. As she closed the pantry door, she heard her mother calling her. She hurried back to the kitchen to find Wade smiling down at her and holding three long stemmed yellow roses tied together with sheer white ribbon.

"Look who I found hanging around out front," Ellen teased.

Lizzie stood smiling up at him for a moment before saying, "Hi stranger."

"Hi, beautiful. I'm sorry I'm late. I had to stop by the flower shop," he said, handing her the flowers.

"They're my favorite."

"I know," Wade grinned.

"Thank you," she replied as she took the roses and kissed him.

It was a long, passionate kiss. One that said much more than the mere words "I've missed you" could convey. It was the kind of kiss that held a world of meaning to the participants.

Ellen was both pleased and uncomfortable. She felt like an intruder in a very private moment. She wanted to leave, but the young couple blocked her exit. In an attempt to give them some privacy, she began rummaging in the refrigerator. After several minutes, she gave up and loudly cleared her throat.

"Ahem." No response. She tried again, "Ahem." Finally, Ellen said, "You two had better get moving before your lunch gets cold".

The couple broke the kiss and moved aside.

"I'm sorry, Mama. Are you trapped?"

Ellen hurried from the room calling "You kids have a good time, but don't be late for supper."

"We won't," Wade answered grinning.

"Watch out for the poison oak," she called as she closed the door.

"I'll put these in some water before we go," Lizzie said as she went to the cabinet for a vase.

"Where are we going?"

"Have you ever been to the spring at Rayland?"

"No, I didn't know there was a spring there."

"Daddy used to take me there when I was a kid. I'd like for you to see it. We can have a picnic there and enjoy the afternoon."

"It smells great, and I'm starved."

"We should probably take my jeep. Getting there will involve a little off-roading."

"We can take my truck. You're providing the meal; I'll provide the transportation."

"Okay, but don't say I didn't warn you."

"Where is the spring," he said grinning at her.

"I'll show you. Are you ready?"

Wade picked up the picnic basket. "Lead the way," he said.

Lizzie followed him carrying the blanket. Wade put the picnic supplies in the back seat of his Ford F-150 super crew before helping Lizzie inside.

"Rayland, here we come," he joked as the motor roared to life.

# CHAPTER 2

Rayland, Texas was located in the northeastern corner of Foard County and less than one-half mile from the Wilbarger county line. It had once been a thriving community. There had been a school, two stores, other businesses, and a church. Now, all that remained was a farm store, a few houses, and the decaying remnants of the cotton scales and gin.

The natural spring located between Rayland and the Pease River was hidden by trees and brush. It was difficult to reach by car or truck. The best way to get there was with an off-road vehicle or on foot.

Lizzie directed Wade to the road that led to the spring. They bounced along until the path was impossible for the truck to pass.

"We can walk the rest of the way. It isn't far from here," Lizzie told Wade.

They climbed out of the truck. Wade assessed the situation as he reached for the picnic supplies.

"There's no way I can turn around. I'll have to back out," he said as he followed Lizzie.

Lizzie picked her way carefully down the gentle slope. She stopped a moment to let a snake slither across the path. She glanced back at Wade and noticed his hand searching for the butt of his gun.

Realizing that he wasn't wearing his gun, he mumbled under his breath, "I hate snakes."

Lizzie turned to hide her grin and said, "We're almost there. That gap in the trees just ahead is where we're going."

Lizzie led the way through the trees. She stood aside as Wade passed through.

"Wow," was all he could say.

They stood silently taking in the scene. Surrounded by the trees was a pond no more than eight feet long and six feet wide. It appeared to be a natural depression in the land that filled with water cascading from a small waterfall beneath a rock formation slightly above the pool. The trickling of the water had a soothing effect.

"It's beautiful isn't it?"

"It was definitely worth the trip."

Lizzie smiled happily and said, "This is one of my favorite places on earth. Few people know it's here".

"Why haven't you shown me this before?"

"We've been so busy that it didn't occur to me until I was reminiscing with Granny last week. I haven't been here since I moved back from Chicago."

"It looks like this is a favorite watering hole for local wildlife," Wade said indicating a variety of tracks near the pond. "This one is a deer. Over here is a bobcat and a coyote. There's a wild hog over there." He paused for a moment then asked, "Lizzie, do you know what this one is?"

Lizzie looked closely. "No, but it's bigger than the rest of these. What is it?"

"I'm not sure, but the game warden will know," he said frowning. He took his smartphone from his pocket and snapped a photo. He stared at the animal's track until his thoughts were interrupted by a low rumble.

"I think we'd better eat," Lizzie laughed.

"I'm ready," Wade said while rubbing his belly.

Lizzie spread the blanket on the ground under a tree, and Wade helped unpack the food from the basket.

"You've outdone yourself, Lizzie. I was expecting sandwiches, not fried chicken, coleslaw and," he hesitated as he opened another container, "potato salad." He looked at her in amazement.

"I hope you like it," Lizzie smiled with satisfaction.

"No doubt about it," he said as he bit into a drumstick.

As they ate, they told each other everything that had happened since they had last seen each other. Lizzie told Wade about upcoming events, and Wade told her that he had not yet found anyone to fill the job opening at the jail.

The physical conversation begun by the kiss at the inn demanded to be continued when they had finished eating. There in that beautiful place accompanied by the music of nature, the young couple expressed their love. They clung together for a while in silence until their reverie was broken by Wade's grumbling stomach.

"I brought apple pie if you want dessert," Lizzie told him.

"My favorite."

"I know," she grinned.

They ate their pie and decided to explore the area around the spring. They hiked to a small cliff formed over centuries as the Pease River carved its way through the land. The couple stood arm in arm as they surveyed the river.

"Don't you think we'd better start back?" Wade asked. "I don't want your folks to be upset with me for making you late for dinner."

"They wouldn't be upset with you, but you're right. We should start back," Lizzie replied reluctantly.

It had been a beautiful afternoon that both Wade and Lizzie hated to see come to an end. But it was getting late, and they still had to maneuver their way back to the main road. They returned to the spring and reluctantly packed the remains of their picnic before hiking the twenty yards back to the truck.

Wade carefully backed his truck toward the main road. They had almost reached their goal when they heard a loud pop as the right rear of the truck seemed to fall into a hole. Wade swore under his breath as he got out and walked around the truck.

Lizzie rolled down her window and asked, "What happened?"

"Nothing serious. Something cut the tire. It's as flat as it can get."

"Do you have a spare?"

"Yep, but I can't change it here."

"Do you think we can make it to the store over there?"

Wade looked at the tire and toward the store. "That's probably the only option."

Wade climbed back into the truck and slowly backed onto the main road. He then drove the short distance to the Rayland Farm Store, commonly called The Store.

Wade parked his truck in front of the open garage. A large sign above the door declared "Flats Fixed Here."

A round man with a bald head had been leaning back, balancing his chair on two legs. He was dressed in greasy, striped bib overalls and a blue work shirt with the sleeves rolled up to his elbows. He lowered his chair and pulled the cigar he had been chewing from his mouth.

"What can I do for ya, young fella?"

"Is it alright if I change my tire here?" Wade asked.

"Help yourself."

Thank you, sir."

Lizzie got out of the truck and called, "Hi, Mack!"

"Well, I'll be damned. If it ain't little Lizzie! How the hell are ya?"

Lizzie grinned at the man. "I'm great. How are you?"

"Fair to middlin', fair to middlin'. Who's that with ya?"

"Come meet him."

They walked to where Wade was grumbling beside his truck. He looked at Lizzie and said, "You were right. We should have brought your jeep. I forgot that this flat tire is the spare."

"Well, I bet we can get ya fixed up," Mack declared.

Lizzie stifled a giggle and said, "Mack, this is Wade Adams. Wade, this is Mack Carson."

"Pleased to meet ya," Mack said extending his hand.

Wade took his hand and said, "Good to meet you."

"Say, ain't you the new sheriff in the next county?"

"Yes, sir." Wade had been the Wilbarger County sheriff for six years. His predecessor held the job for thirty years. He knew he'd be considered the new sheriff for years to come.

"Ain't you out of your jurisdiction?" Mack said grinning and pointing toward the "Wilbarger County" sign a short distance away.

Wade grinned at the man and answered, "This is a pleasure trip."

Mack laughed a loud hearty laugh that made his round belly bounce with merriment. "That's what I figured. Ya'll been down to the spring I guess."

"Yes, sir."

"Well, let me have a look at that."

Mack studied the tire for a few minutes before saying, "I don't think I have a seventeen in the garage here. I can probably fix this one. It may take a while. You two go on inside and say howdy to Pearl. She'll be put out if she don't get to see ya."

With that, the man put the cigar back in his mouth and carried the damaged tire into the garage.

Wade and Lizzie opened the wood screen door and went inside. It took a minute for their eyes to adjust to the dim lighting. The Store was a cross between an old fashioned general store and a modern day convenience store.

The front half of the building was lined with shelves of grocery items and coolers for milk, lunch meat, and beer among other things. The back half of the store held a variety of hardware necessary for repairs on a working farm. Locals shopped there for anything from a ten penny nail to a loaf of bread.

An old fashioned, chest-type Coke machine, complete with attached bottle opener stood near the front door. The wood floor creaked as Wade and Lizzie moved toward a flat top display ice cream freezer. They were perusing the ice cream choices when they heard the old wood floors squeak and a voice nearby.

"Oh my word! Is that Lizzie Fletcher?" The voice belonged to Pearl, Mack's wife and co-owner of the store.

Pearl Carson was of average height and build with a mass of died black hair piled on top of her head. Her voice was loud and raspy. She had a distinctive laugh that could be heard all over the store and possibly the county Wade thought.

Mack and Pearl Carson looked exactly as they had when Lizzie was a child. They seemed to be ageless.

"Hi, Pearl. How are you?" Lizzie smiled and asked.

"Just fine, honey. How're you? You look so good," Pearl replied as she hugged Lizzie. "Who is this good lookin' fella with ya?"

When Pearl paused for a breath, Lizzie introduced her to Wade.

"Have ya'll been down to the spring?"

"Yes, ma'am."

"Fewer and fewer folks know about it. It's a shame somethin' so pretty is so little used."

"It might not stay pretty if lots of people are coming and going," Wade suggested.

"Well, that's probably true. I can't get over seein' ya again after all these years, Lizzie. You've grown into such a pretty gal. Don't you think so, Wade?"

"Yes, ma'am," Wade answered smiling at Lizzie as she blushed.

"And ain't you just the handsomest fella. He's a sight for sore eyes ain't he, Lizzie?"

Now, it was Lizzie's turn to enjoy Wade's obvious discomfort. "Yes, ma'am," she replied.

"I declare you must be the handsomest couple for miles around." She paused for breath before asking, "When's the weddin'?"

Before Wade or Lizzie could reply, the screen door slammed and Pearl automatically smiled a greeting to the new arrivals.

"Well, look who's here. Dara, you know Lizzie don't you?"

"Lizzie?"

"Dara?"

The two women hugged.

"I haven't seen you since high school. What have you been doing since then, Lizzie?"

Lizzie gave Dara an abbreviated version of her history and introduced her to Wade.

Dara Preston was slender and petite with a brilliant smile. Her sandy brown pixie cut hair seemed to emphasize her golden brown skin. Her eyes were a warm, friendly brown.

Dara informed Lizzie that she had married Kent Preston and now lived in his family home nearby. They both worked from home and farmed on the side.

While the women visited, Wade took in his surroundings. He saw a man standing in the corner that he recognized. He approached the man, extended his hand, and said, "Hello, Paul."

Paul Randolph jumped, looked around nervously, and shook Wade's hand. "Hi, Wade. How are you?"

"Doing alright. Are you okay? You don't look well."

"Oh ya," he replied nervously. Just having a bad day I guess."

"Maybe you should go home and take it easy," Wade suggested.

"I will in a bit. The wife sent me in here for a few things. Her folks are at the house. I'm kind of enjoying the peace and quiet," he said in a conspiratorial whisper.

"I won't give you away. Take it easy though."

"Thanks, I will."

Paul Randolph was a tall, thin man with prematurely gray hair and sad brown eyes. He wore glasses that tended to slide down to the end of his nose. He continually pushed them back into place. He had a long face that blended with his neck giving him the appearance of having no chin. His hair was unkempt, and his clothes more often than not appeared to have been slept in.

He was a nervous and whiney type of man. He had no self-confidence. He was easily talked into doing things that were seldom in his best interest. He worked in the personnel office at the state hospital and worked his wife's family farm near Rayland on weekends. He was competent in the personnel office, but he knew nothing about farming, a fact that this wife and father-in-law would not let him forget.

His wife April was a loud, boisterous, dominating kind of woman. She was a bit overweight with dark hair, fiery green eyes, and a frequently bad attitude. She tended to bully her husband as did her family. Friends and neighbors often wondered how long the marriage would last.

Wade noticed that Pearl had gone to the back door of the store and seemed to be talking with someone there. He walked back toward Lizzie in time to hear Dara say:

"We're having a little get together in a couple of weeks. Why don't the two of you come?"

Lizzie hesitated and glanced at Wade. "It will depend on Wade's schedule," she answered.

"Give me your address. I'll send you an invitation. If something comes up and you can't come, just let me know," Dara said expectantly.

"We'll do that," Wade said.

Lizzie gave Dara her address as Mack called from outside, "You're all set to go."

Pearl returned to the counter with a basket of fresh eggs. "How's your Mama and Daddy, Lizzie?" she asked.

"They're doing great. We're supposed to have supper with them in a little while," Lizzie replied, glancing at the clock on the wall behind Pearl.

"And how's your granny doing?"

"She's great, too."

"Tell them all howdy for us will ya?"

"I will."

"And don't be such a stranger. Stop in and say howdy once in a while."

"Okay."

Wade paid the bill, the couple said goodbye to their new friends, and they drove back to the Fletcher farm.

# CHAPTER 3

Lois Fletcher opened the front door of the house she shared with her son and daughter-in-law, James and Ellen Fletcher. She was petite like her granddaughter with brown eyes and brown hair streaked with gray.

"Come in here so I can hug your neck," she smiled at the young couple.

"Hi, Granny," Lizzie said while hugging her grandmother.

"Did you two have a good afternoon?"

"We did," Wade replied as he shook hands with James.

"It's good to see you again, Wade," James said.

Wade was about to answer when Ellen called from the dining room, "Supper's ready!"

"You made it just in time," Lois said chuckling.

"Is Dan coming for supper?" Ellen asked James.

"His truck is out back. I'll go tell him it's ready."

"Mind if I tag along?" Wade asked.

"Suit yourself."

As the two men closed the door, the women busied themselves with putting the meal on the table. Wade took out his phone to show James the photo he had taken.

"Do you happen to know what animal could have made this track?"

James ran a hand through his red hair and studied the photo for a moment. "No, I've never seen one like that around here. Where did you find it?"

"It was at the spring. The animal must be going there for water. I'm planning to send it to the game warden, but I thought you might know."

"Maybe Dan will know what it is," he said nodding toward the man approaching them.

"Wade," Dan said extending his hand. "Maybe I'll know what?"

Wade shook Dan's hand and showed him the photo. Dan Hayes worked for the Fletcher family on the farm and at the inn. He studied the photo for a minute before he said, "The shape looks like a bobcat, but it would have to be a huge bobcat."

"That's what I thought," Wade replied. The three men stood in silence for a few minutes staring at the photograph.

"Supper's ready. We'd better get inside before they start fussing at us because the food is cold," James said with a grin and a twinkle in his brown eyes.

The men walked inside. They sat down to a meal of meatloaf, mashed potatoes and gravy, fried okra, and cherry cobbler for dessert.

The group sat at the table discussing the events of the day while letting their meal digest. They discussed farm and inn business. They gossiped a bit about what was happening with the neighbors. Wade and Lizzie told them about the spring and their unplanned visit to The Store. Lizzie told them that Pearl had invited them all to come by once in a while.

The older Fletchers told stories about the Carsons and the good times they had had together. The story of getting into poison oak at the spring left Wade laughing and scratching his arms.

"Wade, have you found a new deputy yet?" Ellen asked.

"Not yet. I've had two applicants, but their background checks disqualified them. I need to find someone before Maddie goes on maternity leave. Do you folks know of a woman who'd be qualified?"

"Does it have to be a woman?" Dan asked.

"Yes, I need someone to oversee any female prisoners we might have. Since Ruth Sanders retired, Maddie is the only woman in the department. I'll be in a jam if we have to arrest any women while she is on leave."

"Why are you scratching, Lizzie?" Lois asked.

"I don't know, Granny. I guess it was that story about poison oak. I've been itching since I heard it," Lizzie answered scratching her neck.

"Let me see that," Ellen said. "Oh no! It looks like you got into the poison oak."

"I don't see how. We looked all around before we put the blanket down."

"Let me see that arm, Wade," Ellen demanded. "You have it, too."

"I'll get the calamine lotion," Lois offered.

"Do you have it anywhere else?" Ellen asked.

"If I do, it isn't itching yet," Wade replied.

"Same here," Lizzie added.

"What blanket did you use?" James asked with a strange expression on his face.

"I loaned them our picnic blanket," Ellen answered as she applied calamine lotion to Wade's arm.

"Uh oh! Ellen, I used that blanket to get over a fence covered in poison oak a few days ago. I forgot to wash it."

"There must have been some of the oil on the blanket," Lois suggested.

The group joked about where Wade and Lizzie might start itching next. The young couple blushed as they looked at each other. They were both hoping there would be no more rashes but knew that there would be.

When the rashes had been tended to, Ellen asked, "Do you have anything for the itch at home?"

"No, ma'am," Wade answered

"Take this with you just in case. Lizzie, do you have anything?"

"Yes, I do," Lizzie answered trying not to scratch.

"Now that that's settled," Ellen said, "What were you men in such serious conversation about before supper?"

James grinned at his wife. He didn't know why he ever tried to keep things from her.

"Wade, show Ellen and Mama that photo. They might know what

it is," James suggested.

Wade took out his phone and showed the photo of the unknown animal track to the two women. They looked at it for a moment.

Ellen brushed a strand of brown hair back from her face. "Could it be a bobcat?" She asked with concern in her blue eyes.

"It was bigger than any bobcat track I've ever seen," Wade answered while scratching his leg.

"It might be a cougar track," Lois replied solemnly. "There was one in this area years ago. My daddy showed me some tracks when I was a young girl. It either moved on or was killed. I haven't heard of one being around here since then."

"I'd better call the game warden and send this picture to him," Wade said excusing himself from the table.

The table had been cleared and the dishes put in the dishwasher when Wade returned.

"What's wrong?" Lizzie asked.

"Stan Porter said the track is most likely cougar. He says a calf and a horse have been killed in this area in the last month."

"What are they going to do about it?" Ellen asked.

"He said trapping may be an option. He's monitoring where signs have been sighted, hoping to narrow down its territory. The problem is that cougars are shy and are seldom seen. They hunt from dusk to dawn and eat whatever they can catch. They prefer deer but will hunt cattle, horses, sheep, and small rodents. Even pets aren't safe if they are outside at night. Luckily, cougars rarely attack a human."

"Do you think it could turn up around here?" Lois asked.

"It's possible. Stan said they could have a range anywhere from ten to three hundred seventy square miles."

"We'd better keep our eyes open for signs around here then," James told Dan.

"I don't know what to look for. I don't know anything about cougars," Dan replied.

"Stan has some information posted on his website. That would be the best place to start," Wade suggested.

The group discussed cougars and their habits until Wade's cell phone rang. He was summoned to work. Reluctantly, he kissed Lizzie goodbye, thanked her family for the meal, and hurried back to town.

• • •

Lizzie picked up the invitation to the Preston's party and stared at it before looking at the clock in her kitchen again. It was to be a potluck dinner tonight, October 12th, at seven thirty. She smiled to herself when she thought about a conversation she had had with Wade earlier in the week.

"Lizzie, if I'm expected to wear a costume to the Preston's get together, I will definitely have to work that evening." He had told her. She still wished she could have seen the relief on his face when she told him the invitation was for a pot luck dinner.

She stood in the kitchen, still holding the invitation, and smiling as she thought about Wade. He was at least six feet of lean muscle. She liked how she had to tiptoe to kiss him. She loved to play with the little curls of dark blonde hair around his ears and his shirt collar. His green eyes and warm friendly smile always stirred her soul.

A loud beep from her phone interrupted her thoughts. It was five o'clock. She hesitated for a few minutes before making a casserole and putting it in the oven to bake. She had already showered but waited to get dressed.

Wade had been called into his office that morning. She had spoken with him earlier in the day. He promised he would try to make it, but she hadn't heard from him since noon. If she didn't hear from Wade by the time the casserole was done, she would let Dara know that they wouldn't be able to attend the party.

Lizzie had kept herself busy and tried not to wonder if she would see Wade. She glanced outside and noticed that the sun had already set. Promptly at six thirty, the oven timer beeped. Lizzie took the casserole from the oven and set it out to cool. *I'll just wrap this up and freeze it to be eaten another time,* she thought to herself. She sighed as she reached for the phone to call Dara. It rang when she touched it, startling her.

"Hello."

"Hi, Darlin'."

Lizzie smiled at the sound of Wade's voice. "Hi, how are things going?"

"Better. I'm sorry I wasn't able to call you sooner. It's been a wild day. I'm wrapping things up here. We may be a little late, but we'll make it to the Preston's. I'm going home to clean up. I should be at your place by seven thirty."

Lizzie hung up and quickly got dressed for the party. She didn't want to make Wade wait for her.

• • •

Kent and Dara Preston lived on the Preston family farm near Rayland. Kent was taller than Dara, but otherwise, they looked more like siblings than husband and wife. They worked the farm together and had their own businesses that they operated from home. He ran an internet business while Dara worked as a medical transcriptionist. They often had small parties in order to socialize with their friends and neighbors.

Wade and Lizzie arrived at the Preston's fashionably late. Most of the guests were already there enjoying appetizers and drinks. Dara wasted no time leading them around the room and introducing them to her other guests.

"Lizzie Fletcher and Wade Adams, I'd like you to meet our neighbors Nick and Emily Brinkman. Do you and Nick already know each other, Wade?"

Wade nodded and shook Nick's hand before shaking Emily's.

Wade had met Nick a few times in the past. He was a deputy sheriff in Foard County. Something about the man had always bothered Wade.

"This is Kent's Grandma Gail," Dara said continuing the introductions. "She's staying here with us for a while. Of course, you already know our friends and neighbors Maddie and Drew. This is my cousin Brian Flynn and his wife Kelly. I'd also like you to meet Alex and Morgan Dylan. They've just moved into the place across the road from us."

Dara paused and looked around for a moment. She smiled as she led the couple across the room. "This is my husband Kent. Kent, this is one of my high school friends, Lizzie Fletcher, and her friend Sheriff Wade Adams."

Kent smiled warmly at Lizzie and extended his hand to Wade. "It's nice to meet you both. I'm glad you could make it. Please, make yourself at home. Help yourself to a drink and some appetizers. We're waiting for Paul and April to arrive before we start to dig in."

"No need to wait on us. We're here," April Randolph proclaimed as she entered the house. "Paul was having trouble as usual getting things done today. He's been jumpy as a bullfrog on hot pavement today. I swear I don't know what I'm going to do with him."

Paul said nothing as he meekly stood holding the door open for her. He was visibly shaking and seemed to be looking at something in the distance. Wade couldn't help feeling sorry for the man and walked over to say hello.

"Hi, Paul. How are you tonight?"

"Did you hear that?"

"What?"

"Just as April went inside, it sounded like a woman screaming."

"I didn't hear anything. Was it close by?"

"Not real close. It sounded like it might have come from that direction." Paul hesitated a moment, staring and pointing toward the river before saying, "or it might have been…"

"What might it have been?"

"Oh, it was probably nothing. Just my imagination I guess. I've had a rough day."

"Paul, are you coming in or not? Make up your mind," April bellowed from inside the house.

Paul hurried inside, leaving Wade holding the door open. He stepped outside onto the porch for a moment and listened. Hearing nothing unusual, he shook his head and went inside.

"Why don't you men go out to the barn?" Dara suggested after dinner. "There's a new tractor out there that Kent has been dying to show off. You can smoke while you're out there if you want. Besides, Maddie doesn't need to breathe your second hand smoke in her condition," Dara added as she watched her very pregnant friend waddle to the restroom.

The men obeyed the request and dutifully admired the Preston's new equipment. Nick smoked his cigarette outside the barn door. He suddenly dropped his half smoked cigarette and stepped on it before hurrying inside.

"Did you boys hear that?"

"Hear what?" Kent asked.

"It sounded like a woman screaming."

"I heard it when we got here," Paul said.

"Could you tell where it came from?" Wade asked.

"No, not really. It sounded pretty close though."

The conversation was interrupted by a beat up old Chevy pickup driving up to the barn.

Carl Ellis stepped out of his truck, scowling and holding a machete. He was a big, muscular man with a square jaw and small, close set eyes. His thinning blonde hair was combed from just above his left ear over the top of his head. His overalls were old, worn, and dirty.

"Howdy, Carl," Nick said in greeting.

Carl ignored him as he scowled at the group. "What are you looking at my place for?"

"We weren't looking at your place. We heard something we

thought might have come from the river," Kent answered.

"Stay away from my place and stay off my land," Carl threatened. "Somebody's parked over on my land; I want that vehicle moved right now."

"I'm sorry. I didn't realize. I'll go move it," Paul squeaked and hurried to move his pickup.

"You do that," Carl said raising the machete menacingly.

"There's no need to get nasty, Carl," Nick said.

"Mind your own business. You have no jurisdiction on this side of the county line."

Kent stepped between Nick and Carl who were glaring at each other.

"What can I do for you, Carl?"

"You and your friends stay off my land."

"I hope you'll extend me the same courtesy."

"Another thing. Control that woman of yours."

"Excuse me?"

"Keep her away from my wife. She don't need to be filling my woman's head with her silly notions."

"I think you'd better go now."

"I'll leave when I'm damned good and ready."

"Mr. Ellis, I do have jurisdiction here. You have been asked to leave this man's property. It would be in your best interest to do so."

Carl Ellis stared at Wade defiantly for a moment. Then, he reluctantly turned and climbed back into his truck. "Remember what I said," he pointed at Kent as he drove away.

"Thanks, Wade. He's been trying to stir up trouble for months now. He wants this place and isn't happy that I won't sell it to him."

"You're welcome. I don't know if I've helped the situation. Maybe he won't bother you any more tonight."

"We should probably go back to the house. If I know Dara, she saw Carl and already has twenty questions for me."

The men quietly walked back to the house, each lost in thought.

"You boys are all mighty serious," Grandma Gail observed as the men came in. "Are you all suffering from tractor envy?"

"No, Grandma. Nick and Paul have been hearing things out there," Kent joked, trying to shake the bad feeling he had.

"Are you seeing things, too? Maybe a young woman in a torn dress?"

"No, why?" Nick answered curiously.

"I thought it might be Ruby's ghost," the old woman said, eyes twinkling.

"What is Ruby's ghost?" Emily asked.

"You've never heard of Ruby's ghost?"

Everyone shook their heads.

"It's a long story. Do you have time to hear it?"

"You have us all curious now. We'll make time to hear about Ruby," April answered.

"Well, alright then. Make yourselves comfortable."

"I haven't heard this story before, but I can guarantee it will be a good one," Kent smiled lovingly at his grandmother.

Everyone found a seat and waited expectantly for Grandma Gail's ghost story.

# CHAPTER 4

"I suppose I should start from the beginning," she said. "It was before the depression in the early twenties. Rayland was a lot different back then. Lots of people lived around here. There was a school, businesses, and churches. There was even a post office.

Dorothy Scott was a beautiful young woman. Many folks said she was the most beautiful woman to be found for miles around. She was only five-feet-two-inches tall and slender. Her hair was black, straight, and so long that she could sit on it. Her dark brown eyes held warmth and kindness. Every young man in Rayland admired her.

Woodrow Lawrence was handsome, tall, and lean. His hair was brown and seemed to have a mind of its own. His eyes were hazel and danced when he was happy. He was the kind of man that people were instantly drawn to. Everybody called him Woody. He lived across the Pease River in Hardeman County near Chillicothe.

One weekend in the spring, Woody's cousin invited him to attend a church social with his family. Woody agreed, and that was where he first saw Dorothy. I don't know if you believe in it, but it must have been love at first sight for them. They fell head over heels for each other that night.

Woody would ride his horse across the river every weekend to visit Dorothy. It wasn't long before they decided to marry.

Most of the local boys weren't happy about the wedding, particularly George Parker. Although she was unaware of it, he had made plans to make Dorothy his bride. He couldn't deal with the fact that she had chosen to marry someone from across the river.

The newlyweds began their lives together near Chillicothe. They were as happy as any young couple could be. That's where the children were born. Alfred looked like his father but had his mother's eyes. Ruby was a miniature version of her mother. Jack appeared to be a mixture of both his parents. His hair was black and straight, but he had his father's dancing hazel eyes.

I'm sure you've heard that times were hard during the depression. In the fall of 1933, Woody was offered the chance to work on a farm near Rayland. It wouldn't pay much, but he would have a house for his family. Dorothy could raise a garden to help keep them fed.

The farm that the Lawrence's lived on was right near here. The western boundary of their farm was on the Foard county line.

The trouble began shortly after. George Parker had been fired from the job and evicted from the house where Woody now lived. The fact that Woody was married to the woman George had wanted to marry added insult to injury. An intense hatred toward Woody and all he had, including Dorothy, grew. As far as George was concerned, Woody had three strikes against him. He wouldn't let it go and caused as much trouble as he could for the young family.

When school wasn't in session, the older Lawrence children did chores. Alfred helped Woody in the fields. Ruby looked after her little brother while Dorothy did her chores. Ruby's time to play came when Jack went down for his afternoon nap. She played with Naomi, a girl about her own age from the neighboring farm.

The girls generally met between the two farms. They would play in the trees near the river. Sometimes, they would walk to Rayland to visit one of the stores. On really hot days, they would walk to the natural spring to enjoy the shade and taste the cool clear water. Play time would end when they were called in for supper.

One night, in late August of 1934, Ruby slipped out of the house after bedtime to meet her friend Naomi. They had planned to go down to the spring and try their hand at frog gigging. They had heard some of the older kids talking about it and thought their families would be happily surprised at their ability to bring home something for the next day's meal.

While Ruby waited in the field for Naomi, four men arrived at her house on horseback with torches. She was watching the house when her friend arrived and stopped next to her. The two girls thought it would be great fun to spy on the grownups. They crept closer, being careful not to be seen. Ruby was fascinated by the way the shadows danced across their faces in the torchlight.

One of the men was yelling toward the house. 'Lawrence! I want to talk to you! Get out here!'

As the first man called her father, the other men slid off their horses and started toward the house. The girls couldn't see what was happening. They heard screaming and yelling from inside the house. Ruby watched as her parents and her brothers were dragged into the yard. Naomi nudged Ruby. 'I'm going to get Poppa. Come with me.' Ruby only shook her head, afraid to move.

By the time Naomi returned with her father, Ruby was in shock. Her house was ablaze, and the four men were gone. Naomi's father went to check on the fallen family. He could do nothing but cover their faces. He walked back toward his wife and shook his head. Then, he knelt down by Naomi and hugged her tight as he said, 'This is a terrible thing, a terrible thing. Naomi, I know you're scared, but I need you to do something for me.'

Naomi wiped the tears from her face and answered in a trembling voice, 'Ok, Poppa.'

'I'm going to stay here and watch over Ruby's family. Your mama is going to take care of Ruby. I need you to go get help. Will you be a big girl, and do that for me?'

Naomi nodded.

'Go over to Mrs. Hopkins' house. She has a phone. Tell her to call for help because the Lawrence's house is on fire, and they're hurt. Don't tell her that Ruby is okay. We don't know who did this or why. Do you understand?'

Naomi sniffled and nodded.

'Be careful. We don't know what's going on. Try not to let anybody see you. Now get going,' he said as he hugged her tight.

Naomi went obediently on her way to Mrs. Hopkins' house.

'Polly, take her back to our house. Try not to be seen. Don't let anyone know she's with us. She may be in danger.'

'John, who would do such a thing? What possible reason could they have to do something like this?'

'I don't know, Polly. It all seems like a horrible nightmare.'

Ruby had seen it all. The entire scene was replaying in her head as Naomi's mother carried her and patted her back. She was hidden by Naomi's family until her own relatives could be found. Her father's sister agreed to take her in. She lived with her Aunt Mabel and her much older cousin Marie near Muskogee, Oklahoma. Mabel's husband had died two years earlier.

Ruby had nightmares almost every night at first. She was never able to see the faces of those horrible men in her dreams. They were replaced by the dancing shadows made by the torches.

Slowly, over the years, the nightmares subsided, and the memories began to fade. Ruby lived happily in Muskogee until her aunt became ill and passed away. Marie, who had never liked her young cousin, didn't offer to take her in. Fortunately, her father's brother, Ward, came to the rescue. He and his wife, Charlotte, had never had any children. They were excited about her coming to live with them. Ruby was now sixteen years old and had lived in Muskogee most of her life. In July of 1944, she packed up her few belongings and found herself once again a resident of Rayland.

Ruby looked almost exactly like her mother had looked at that age. She became reacquainted with people her family had known. Mrs. Hopkins had been one of her favorite people to visit when she was a child. She soon discovered that the elderly lady remembered her and looked forward to visiting with her again.

There was a strange man that looked at her oddly every time she saw him. Ruby couldn't really describe the look. It seemed to her to be a mixture of curiosity and fear.

One early September evening, Aunt Charlotte became ill. She insisted that Ruby try to find Uncle Ward. The moon was full, and Ruby had no trouble finding her way. Her uncle had been helping a neighbor make repairs on a barn. She thought that he might still be there. Ruby could hear voices as she approached. She stood in the open barn door and peered inside.

Suddenly, she heard a loud scream that made her freeze where she stood. She was trying to process what she heard when the strange man staggered to the middle of the barn, obviously drunk. He pointed at her, screamed in terror, and ran out the opposite door. Ruby heard the screeching of tires and a thump. She ran through the barn to see what had happened. The drunken man had run out of the barn directly in front of an oncoming hay truck. The driver couldn't possibly have stopped in time.

Ruby looked at the man closely. His face was difficult to see at first. The head lights from the truck and the shadow of truck driver moving in front of them made it difficult to see. Slowly, his face became visible. Ruby realized that he had been one of the men responsible for her family's death. Suddenly, the memory of his face was perfectly clear but only his face. She still couldn't remember who the others were.

She walked back to her aunt and uncle's house in a daze. Her mind was replaying the scene over and over again. Uncle Ward had returned to the house in her absence. He was concerned at her appearance. She told him that she was fine but that a man had died just down the road. She didn't tell him who the man was. She didn't know his name, only his face.

The unfortunate man had been drinking heavily ever since Ruby had arrived in Rayland. He was convinced that she was the ghost of Dorothy Lawrence. He told the three other men that she had come back for vengeance. They had laughed at him the first time he told them about what he'd seen. They had all seen her since that day. She was always in the background of a crowd or alone in the distance.

The three remaining men seemed to see Dorothy's ghost everywhere. They became more and more afraid.

On Halloween night, Ruby and her friends were escorting some of the young children from church while trick-or-treating. She would stand in the background while the children got their treats. At one house in particular, the sight of Ruby smiling, standing behind the children, and illuminated by the full moon, shook the man of the house to his core. He hung himself in his own barn that night. The note he left said, 'I'm so sorry.'

No one knew what he had been sorry about. They presumed he was sorry for committing suicide. At the man's funeral, Ruby looked down on his face and recognized him. He was one of the men who had killed her family.

Ruby realized that her presence in Rayland might be disturbing to the men responsible for her family's death. Somehow that gave her a great deal of pleasure. It wasn't in her power to make them pay for what they had done. Making them uncomfortable enough to kill themselves would be sweet revenge. Unfortunately, she didn't know who she was making uncomfortable. She wondered if they would come after her. Ruby didn't know who those men were, but they knew her. She decided it would be wise to tell her uncle everything.

Uncle Ward and Aunt Charlotte were concerned when they heard Ruby's story. They had not known that Ruby had actually witnessed the murder of her family. They were concerned for her safety. They made her promise that she would never go out alone again.

Weeks went by, and Ruby kept her promise. One November evening, her aunt and uncle were at the church helping to decorate for the holidays. She had decided to stay behind but was terribly bored. She thought it would be safe enough to walk around the house and get some fresh air. Wrapped in a warm sweater, she reminisced about her days as a child while she walked. She wondered if the playhouse that she and Naomi had built was still there.

She had unconsciously started down the short path to the river when she was startled by a noise in the nearby brush. She looked up and saw a man standing in the moonlight. Ruby couldn't see his face. The full moon overhead cast his features in shadow. He had a rifle in his hand and appeared to be out hunting. She raised her hand and waved at him. The man took a few steps back and then turned and ran leaving Ruby to wonder what was wrong. She turned to look behind her but saw nothing. A little frightened, she hurried back to the safety of her house. She realized that the man could have killed her quite easily had he chosen to.

The man was found dead in his truck the following morning. He had apparently taken his own life with a hunting rifle during the night. Ruby recognized the dead man at the funeral. He also was one of the men responsible for the death of her family.

Now there was only one man left from that terrible night. Ruby didn't know who he was, but she feared him the most. She stayed close to her house and her family from that day forward. Ruby felt as though she were being watched anytime she was out with her family or friends. She thought it was probably her imagination, but she couldn't shake the feeling.

Sunday was Christmas Eve. Ruby was looking forward to the church luncheon after the worship. During the service, she listened to the Christmas hymns and thought about the last Christmas she had spent with her family. She could remember only bits and pieces. She had played with the gifts Santa had brought and with her brothers. She could see her parent's smiles as if it were yesterday. She remembered that her mother had made a delicious meal. A tear rolled down her cheek as she realized she couldn't remember how it had tasted. Uncle Ward hugged her tight. 'I miss them, too,' he whispered as he wiped her tears away.

At the luncheon, a man watched her from across the room. She stayed near Uncle Ward rather than eating with her friends. She was afraid of him, but she didn't know why. She was relieved when the meal was over, and they returned home.

One evening later that week, Ruby was startled by a loud bang on the front door. She waited quietly while Uncle Ward answered the door.

'Where is she? I want her out here right now!'

'Who do you want to see, George?'

'That girl! Get her out here now!'

Aunt Charlotte hurried Ruby into the kitchen while Uncle Ward blocked the front door.

'Hurry, Ruby. Bundle up and find a place to hide. I don't know what George Parker wants, but I have a feeling it isn't good.'

'I know it isn't. I recognize his voice. He's one of them. What about you and Uncle Ward?'

'You let us worry about that. You just find somewhere safe to hide,' Aunt Charlotte said as she pushed Ruby out the back door.

Ruby hurried out the back. Her skirt snagged on a shrub, leaving a scrap of pink fabric behind. She had no doubt who the man was. His voice brought back memories of the man screaming for her father from horseback. She wouldn't let him destroy those she loved again. She crept around the front of the house and stood in the shadows, waiting for her opportunity. He was clearly drunk. His words were slurred and his stance wobbly. He swung at Uncle Ward, missed and fell to the ground.

Ruby couldn't take it anymore. She knew that the full moon would give just enough light that she would be able to see. She just needed to get him to follow her. She was sure she could out run him in that condition. She stepped out of the shadows and into the moonlight.

'Why did you kill my family?' she asked holding her hands out in front of her.

The man stared at her as he tried to push himself up. 'Who are you?' he asked.

'What did they do to deserve to die like that? Jack was only two years old.'

The man was up on his knees now. 'Who are you?' he bellowed.

'You sat on your horse screaming orders to the others. Why? Why my family?'

The man was clearly frightened when he realized the girl had seen everything. She knew what happened.

'I don't know who you are, but I know you're no ghost,' he said as he stood up. 'At least, not yet.'

Suddenly, he was moving toward Ruby. She turned and ran into the shadows. She could hear her aunt and uncle calling her name as she ran. She could hear the man's labored breathing behind her. She had to out run him. She ran toward the river and the secret place where she and Naomi had played. The man was gaining on her. Her sides ached, and her legs burned. She had to keep going. She had to get away from him.

Ruby reached the edge of a cliff that formed part of the river bank just as George Parker grabbed at her. The edge of the cliff crumbled. They both fell, screaming as they tumbled toward the river.

George Parker was found with a broken neck in the river at the bottom of the cliff. In his hand, he was clutching a scrap of pink fabric. Ruby's body was never found.

It is said that, when the moon is full, Ruby returns wearing the torn pink dress she was last seen in. Some folks believe that she comes back to seek justice for those who have been wronged."

Grandma Preston looked around the room at the stunned faces before her. She smiled broadly, "How's that for a ghost story?" she asked.

The guests applauded.

"I told you it would be good didn't I," Kent said with pride.

Everyone paused as a low moan was heard from the corner of the room.

"Okay, who's pretending to be Ruby?" Dara joked.

"I'm not pretending to be anything. I think I'm in labor," Maddie said before moaning again.

The party hosts and guests sprang into action. Wade and Lizzie helped Maddie out of her chair and toward the door. Drew hurried outside to start the car with the rest of the men right behind. The women followed Maddie with her belongings and told her repeatedly to breathe.

Drew ran around to the passenger side of the car. He was shaking nervously as he held the door open with one hand and called Doctor Hughes with his cell phone in the other. Wade and Lizzie walked

Maddie to the car. When she was safely in, Drew slammed the door and ran to the driver's side. Tires screeched and dust flew as he stomped on the accelerator.

The remainder of the guests were smiling and laughing when they heard it. A loud scream pierced the stillness of the night. It was the kind of scream that caused a primal response. Chills ran down their spines; the hair on the back of their necks stood on end.

"That's what I heard earlier," Paul said to Wade. "I told you."

"Yes, you did," Wade replied obviously concerned.

"That's what I heard out by the barn, too," Nick added.

"What on earth is that?" Emily asked.

"It can't be good, whatever it is," Dara said as she moved closer to Kent.

Wade stood listening for a few minutes.

"What is it Wade?" Lizzie asked.

"I'm not sure, but I agree with Dara. It can't be good. I think it's time for us to leave. I have some phone calls to make."

# CHAPTER 5

Paul Randolph wasn't sleepy. He knew that if he went to bed now he would toss and turn, listening to April snore until he could take it no more. He thought about making his bed on the couch but walked outside instead. He sat down in the rocking chair on his front porch and thought about recent events.

It had been almost a week since the Preston's party. Maddie and Drew Clifton were the proud parents of a healthy baby boy. Wade had contacted the game warden and shared what he had learned with the community. The eerie screams were most likely those of a female cougar looking for a mate. It was probably the same cougar that had been killing livestock in the area.

Paul hadn't heard the scream since the night of the party. The story of Ruby's ghost and the memory of those screams in the night shook him to his bones. He wasn't sure why.

He stared at the full moon as his thoughts drifted to Carl Ellis. He was disgusted with himself for letting Carl intimidate him. They had been friends once. Paul realized that he found most people intimidating. He promised himself that he would try to change that.

A loud snore came from the direction of the bedroom. He shook his head. *I should probably start with my wife.* He sat quietly contemplating his marriage and the direction his life had taken.

He was startled from his thoughts by the now familiar but still unnerving scream in the night. Frightened, he stood and went inside. He paused for a moment deep in thought. His mind whirled. He knew he wouldn't be able to sleep. He wanted to sit on the porch a while longer, but that scream had frightened him. He squared his shoulders and went in search of his rifle. He returned to the rocking chair, sat with his rifle across his lap, and let his mind race. Eventually, his mind quieted, and he dozed in his chair.

Paul jumped up, sending his rifle clattering onto the porch. *Have I been dreaming? Did I really hear someone say my name?* He didn't know how long he had been sleeping. He wasn't sure how long he had been sitting on the porch. He stood and stretched. He decided he should go to bed. Shaking, he reached down to retrieve his gun and noticed that something wasn't right.

The pasture gate was standing wide open. He could wait until morning to close it. He sighed. *If the cattle get out, I will never hear the end of it*. He hesitated for a moment. *Why am I so afraid? How am I going to make a change in my life if I can't walk that short distance to close a gate?* He took a deep breath and stepped off the porch, carrying his rifle with him.

He closed the gate and started back toward the house. Something was moving in the moonlight beside the barn. He circled the barnyard and walked over to the side of the barn to investigate. Propping his gun against the building, he pulled a piece of cloth away from a nail. As he stood examining it in the moonlight, he heard a footstep behind him. He turned quickly and gasped. He took a step back in terror before falling to his knees, clutching his chest.

• • •

April Randolph woke to the sunshine streaming in her bedroom window. She noticed that her husband was not beside her as he usually was on a Saturday morning.

"Paul?" she called. When he did not answer, she got up and went to the kitchen. The coffee was not made. "Paul, why haven't you made the coffee?" Still he did not answer.

"Oh, that man!" April fumed as she searched the house for her husband. When she did not find him in the house, she looked out the kitchen window. His car was still outside. She stomped onto the front porch and yelled angrily, "Paul, where are you?" Silence was the only reply.

Anger began to give way to concern. "Paul?" She walked around the house looking and calling in every direction. Paul still had not answered.

April started back toward the porch. If he was out walking the fence line, she would be able to reach him by phone. As she reached the porch steps, she realized she hadn't looked in the barn. She stomped in that direction. *He's was probably been in there all along, pretending not to hear me.* She slowed as she got nearer. Something was out of place. She saw what appeared to be Paul's boots lying beside the barn.

"Paul, what on earth are you doing? Answer me! Are you hurt? Paul?"

He was lying on his left side with his hands at his chest. He didn't move. "Paul? What's wrong, honey?" She asked nervously as she knelt beside him. She gently shook his shoulder, causing him to roll onto his back.

Suddenly, the quiet stillness of the morning was shattered with the sound of her screams.

• • •

A loud ringing disturbed Lizzie's dreams. She slapped her alarm clock, but the noise didn't stop.

"I'm sorry. It's my phone. Go back to sleep," Wade said sleepily.

"K," Lizzie mumbled while snuggling back under the covers.

Wade walked into the kitchen before answering his phone. He thought about making coffee, but that thought evaporated as he heard what the caller had to say.

"I'm not quite awake yet. Would you mind repeating that? Hold on a minute."

Wade padded back to the bedroom. Covering his phone, he asked, "Lizzie, do you have any paper and a pen I can use?"

"I'll get it," she answered sleepily. She sat up and rummaged in the drawer of her nightstand, finally producing a notepad and pen. She sat on the edge of the bed listening to Wade's side of the phone conversation.

"Go ahead. Who was it? When?" Wade asked while he made notes. "Alright, get the team together, and call Doctor Hughes. I'll meet you there. What? No, don't call her. Let her enjoy her time off."

Wade stared at Lizzie as he listened. "I have an idea that might work. I'll meet you there. Bring an extra deputy's badge and the paperwork with you."

"What's wrong, Wade?"

"There's been a death at Rayland."

"Who? What happened?"

"Before I tell you that, I need to ask you something. Please, hear me out before you say anything."

"Alright," Lizzie answered apprehensively.

"You know I've been looking for another female deputy without any luck. Maddie is usually part of the interview team when we need to question a woman. I've found that women generally respond better to another woman. I need a woman to help with the interviews, and she'd have to be deputized."

Wade paused for moment before asking, "I'm in a bind, or I wouldn't ask. Would you be willing to be an interim deputy?"

Lizzie stared at Wade for a full sixty seconds before answering. "I don't know the first thing about interviewing someone, especially in that sort of situation."

"You won't be doing interviews right away. Listen and take notes while another team member does the interviews. Your main objectives will be to give the women some comfort and to listen to them. Listen with your eyes as well as your ears. Pay attention to facial expressions, body language, and the tone of voice. Some questions will come to you as you talk with them. Others may come later as we review your notes."

Wade waited while Lizzie thought about what he had asked her to do.

"I can try," Lizzie finally answered. "But what if I mess things up or miss something important?"

"I ask myself those same questions all the time," he smiled at her reassuringly. "I won't throw you in the mix all by yourself. The main thing I want you to do today is provide comfort. I'll do the interview. Pay attention to anything she says or does. She may give us a clue without realizing it.

"Do you think the woman in this case is responsible?" Lizzie asked surprised.

"I don't know. I can't rule anyone or anything out at this point."

"Who died?"

"Paul Randolph. April found him lying beside the barn. He was stabbed."

"I'll be ready as fast as I can. She must be devastated."

"I knew you were the person for the job. We'll make it official before you talk to April."

"What do you mean?"

"I have to deputize you. Dodson is bringing the necessities to make it official."

"I'm officially going to be a deputy?"

"Yes, I don't want any case we have to be thrown out of court because I didn't do things by the book."

Wade and Lizzie arrived at the Randolph home as the investigative team unloaded their equipment. Deputy Craig Dodson hurried over to Wade's truck.

"Sheriff, I have the items you requested."

"Great. Lizzie has agreed to work with us in Maddie's absence. Let's get her sworn in so we can get started."

Lizzie signed all the necessary paperwork and took her oath of office. Wade handed her a brand new deputy sheriff's badge and went right to work.

"You didn't happen to think of bringing a uniform for our new deputy did you, Dodson?"

"I thought about it once but didn't know what size."

"You're ahead of me. I didn't think of it at all. We'll have to make do for now."

"Deputy Fletcher, go inside and talk with Mrs. Randolph. Don't worry about questioning her. Your purpose this morning is to provide comfort and to listen. If you happen to think of a question that would be pertinent to our case, feel free to ask. Otherwise wait for me."

"Yes, sir," Lizzie said and grinned in spite of herself.

Wade didn't seem to notice and walked away with Dodson to the crime scene.

Lizzie stepped up onto the porch and lightly tapped on the door. "April? It's Lizzie Fletcher. May I come in?"

"Yes, please."

Lizzie opened the door and went inside. April was sitting in a recliner with tears streaming down her face. A box of tissue rested on its side in her lap, and a pile of used tissue lay on the floor at her feet.

"Sit down, Lizzie. I'm so glad you're here. I don't know what I'm going to do. Who would do such a thing to Paul? I don't understand it."

Lizzie sat in the chair nearest to April and took her hand. "I don't know but the Sheriff will do everything he can to find out."

April didn't seem to hear. She was lost in her own thoughts and grief. "We had an argument last night. I went in the bedroom and slammed the door. I waited for Paul to come in and apologize like he always does, but he didn't come. I was so mean to him last night." April burst into a fresh shower of tears. After a few moments, she continued.

"I must have fallen asleep because, when I woke up this morning, he wasn't in bed. I looked all over the house. I kept calling his name. I looked outside. I looked everywhere. I was about to call his cell phone when I realized I hadn't looked in the barn. When I got out there, I saw a pair of boots beside the barn. I walked over to them...he was just lying there." Another barrage of tears and loud sobs followed.

Lizzie patted April's shoulder while she waited for the grieving woman to regain her composure. She privately hoped she could remember everything she was supposed to remember.

"What am I going to do? Why would someone hurt Paul?" April sobbed.

Lizzie glanced up and saw Wade coming toward the house. "April, Sheriff Adams is coming this way. I'm sure he needs to ask you some questions."

"Alright," April sniffed. "I'll do whatever it takes to catch whoever hurt Paul."

Lizzie opened the door for Wade. He stepped inside and removed his cowboy hat in one smooth motion. He walked over to April and said, "I'm so sorry, Mrs. Randolph. I hate to do this now, but I have to ask you a few questions."

"That's alright, Sheriff. Please, sit down. I'll be happy to answer anything I can."

Wade sat down, hesitating a moment before beginning. "Did you touch Mr. Randolph or anything else when you found him?"

April thought for a moment before answering. "I don't think so. I saw Paul and went to him. I thought he was sick, or had fainted. I called to him, but he didn't answer or move. So, I shook him to wake him. That's when I saw..." April covered her face with her hands and sobbed.

"You shook him to try to wake him. Where did you touch him?"

"On his shoulder."

"Was he on his back when you found him?"

"No, he was on his side. He rolled to his back when I shook him."

"Did you touch anything else?"

"No."

"You didn't touch the weapon?"

"I... I don't know. I don't think I did."

Wade hesitated before showing April the evidence bag he had brought in. "Do you recognize this?"

As she examined the contents of the sealed cellophane bag, tears rolled down her face.

"Is this what was sticking out of his chest?"

Wade nodded.

"It's a pair of antique sheep shears. Paul has a pair just like them." Her eyes grew wide. "Are they his? Do you think he killed himself?" April sobbed.

"We won't know for sure until the investigation is complete, but I don't think so. Why would Mr. Randolph have a pair of antique sheep shears?"

"He collected antique farm tools. They fascinated him. He was very knowledgeable about them."

"Where is the collection kept?"

"He built a special room for them in the loft of the barn. He spends...spent a lot of time there, building displays and cataloging those silly things."

"Do you mind if I have a look at that collection?"

"Not at all. Paul loves...loved to show it off," April assured him as she reached for a fresh tissue.

"Who else knows about the collection?"

April blew her nose loudly before answering, "Lots of people. Paul took anyone who showed the slightest interest out to see it."

"Did your husband have any enemies that you're aware of?"

"N...no," April sniffed.

"Where did your husband keep his hunting rifle?"

"It's always in the closet by the back door."

"Why would he have taken it out to the barn with him?"

"He did? April answered clearly surprised. "I don't know. He's been very jumpy lately. He may have felt safer with it close by, or he may have seen something out there."

"Where were you when he went out to the barn?"

April's eyes filled with fresh tears. "We had a big fight last night. I went to bed and went to sleep. He wasn't in bed when I woke up this morning."

"Do you have any idea why he was out by the barn?"

April shook her head as she sobbed.

Dodson tapped on the door. "Sheriff, Doctor Hughes would like a word."

"Thank you, Dodson. Mrs. Randolph, I may have more questions after I talk with Doctor Hughes and examine that tool collection. Miss Fletcher will stay here with you. If you can think of anything no matter how unimportant it may seem, don't hesitate to let us know."

April sobbed and nodded.

Doctor Hughes was supervising the removal of Paul's body when Wade approached.

"I found this clutched in the victim's hand," he said, handing Wade an evidence bag containing a piece of pink cloth.

Wade stared at the fabric while he listened to the doctor.

"It doesn't appear to be part of his clothing. It could be part of his wife's clothing."

"I'll ask, but I don't think it is," Wade answered gloomily.

"I'll take Mr. Randolph into town and get started on the autopsy unless you need me for anything else."

"Give me a call when you've finished."

"Certainly," Doctor Hughes replied as he climbed into the truck.

Dodson and Reed waited nearby.

"What have you found?" Wade asked.

"Not a lot. We've bagged the hunting rifle, but there is very little here that looks like it doesn't belong. There are boot prints that are most likely the victims. There are some shoe prints that could easily be Mrs. Randolph's," Dodson replied.

"Did you find anything in the barn, Reed?"

"It looks like the murder weapon came from the tools we found in a loft upstairs."

"I'd like to take a look at that," Wade replied.

The three men walked into the barn and climbed the ladder into the loft. Wade was amazed at what he saw. Each tool hung on a peg board with a label. The labels listed the name of the tool, its use, and the probable date of manufacture. Paul had traced around each tool so that there could be no doubt where a tool belonged.

"You still have your gloves on Dodson. See if these shears belong in that space on the wall."

Dodson removed the shears from the evidence bag and hung them on the peg board. It was a perfect fit.

"Did the killer remove the label?" Reed asked.

"If he did, it may be in here somewhere," Wade replied. "See if you can find it while I go talk to Mrs. Randolph again."

"Yes, sir," the men replied in unison.

Wade walked slowly back to the house, pondering the evidence bag he still held in his hand. He had a feeling that this was going to be a long drawn out investigation. Rather than tapping on the door, he called out.

"Mrs. Randolph, are you up to a few more questions?"

"Yes, please come in. What did you find?"

"The sheep shears are most likely from Mr. Randolph's collection."

"Killed with his own tool?" April asked as she wailed.

"It appears that way. Did your husband label all of the tools in his collection?"

"Yes. He also kept them all polished to prevent rusting."

"Can you think of any reason why the shears didn't have a label?"

"No, Paul was very particular about keeping them clean and labeled. He used gloves when he handled them. He insisted that anyone touching them wear gloves."

"Do you recognize this?" Wade asked, showing April the pink fabric.

Lizzie looked at it a moment before meeting Wade's eyes. He was worried.

"No, I've never seen anything like that."

"Could it be from some of your clothing or another item here?"

"Not from here. I detest the color pink, particularly this pastel shade. Where did you find it?"

"I'd rather not say at this point in the investigation."

"Do you think Paul was having an affair?" April asked clearly angry.

"It may have nothing to do with the case at all, Mrs. Randolph. It was in the area around the body, so we bagged it."

April was not satisfied. "My Paul was a saint. He would never cheat on me."

"I'm sure he was. Are the shoes you're wearing the ones you were wearing when you found your husband?"

April looked at her feet. "Yes, I didn't realize that I still had them on."

"I'll need to take those with me. We'll compare them to the shoe prints found beside his body. Are you wearing the same clothes you had on when you found your husband?"

April looked down at her clothes. "Yes."

"I'm sorry, but I'll need those, too. Miss Fletcher will help you change."

"Alright," April replied apprehensively and stood up.

Wade handed Lizzie a large evidence bag he had brought with him. "We need everything she has on."

"Yes, sir," Lizzie replied as she followed April to her room.

Lizzie carefully placed April's clothing and shoes in the bag. She helped April redress before escorting her back into the living room where the sheriff waited.

"We've done all we can here for now. We'll be leaving in a few minutes. Is there anyone we can call to stay with you or somewhere we can take you?" Wade asked.

"Lizzie called my sister a little while ago. She should be here any minute. Thank you."

"Please, don't hesitate to call my office if you think of anything or notice anything that you think will help us find who did this."

"I will. Thank you. Lizzie, I don't know what I would have done without you. Thank you for coming," April called as Lizzie and Wade closed the door on their way out.

"Wade, what is it?" Lizzie asked when she was sure April could not hear.

"I don't know, Lizzie. I'm probably going to have to investigate the Randolph's affairs to find a clue."

As the couple approached the truck, Dodson and Reed caught up with them.

"No sign of that label, sir," Reed said.

"We probably won't find any prints on the shears either," Wade told them. "We'll compare notes when we get back to the office."

Wade helped Lizzie into the truck. He slowly walked around to his side. He looked toward the barn before getting in. He was clearly troubled about something. She didn't disturb him. They rode into town, each lost in private thought.

# CHAPTER 6

Sheriff Wade Adams sat with his deputies at a conference table cataloging evidence and comparing notes.

"Lizzie, we generally video our case related conversations," Wade said pointing to the video camera in the corner. We keep the recordings for playback and transcription. Even though we may be personally acquainted with the victims or the people we are investigating, we refer to them as the victim, or formally as Mr. or Mrs. Randolph." Wade started the recording.

"This is Wilbarger County Sheriff Wade Adams. Today is Saturday, October 19, 2013. The body of Mr. Paul Randolph was found by his wife April Randolph near the barn at their home at approximately eight fifteen this morning." Wade gave the address of the property before continuing. "Deputy Craig Dodson, what did you learn from Mr. Preston?"

"Kent Preston was outside this morning about to start the day's plowing when he heard a scream. He said it sounded a lot like the cougar screams that they've been hearing nearby. He heard it again after he had climbed into the tractor seat. When he realized it was coming from the Randolph place, he drove over there to see what was going on. He found Mrs. Randolph kneeling beside the victim, screaming and crying. He escorted her into the house before calling us. He said he did what he could to try and comfort her, but he was really glad when Deputy Fletcher showed up."

"Why didn't he call his wife or his grandmother for help?"

"His wife wasn't home. She had gone to Wichita Falls this morning to do some shopping. He said he thought about calling her anyway but realized we probably didn't want a lot of folks in our way.

His grandmother doesn't drive."

"Thank you. Deputy Gordon Reed, what sort of evidence did you find?"

"There wasn't a lot of physical evidence at the scene. I photographed and measured the few footprints that we found. Most of them were very faint in the dust. The slight breeze we had probably disturbed most of them. The boot prints are most likely the victims. We'll know for sure after the measurements are compared. The shoe prints are probably Mrs. Randolph's, but we'll need to compare them to her shoes to be certain."

"Thank you. We know that the sheep shears are a part of Mr. Paul Randolph's personal antique tool collection," Wade said. "According to Mrs. Randolph, he used gloves when handling his collection and asked others to wear gloves as well. He kept each item labeled, polished, and hung in a specific place on his display. It isn't likely that we will find fingerprints on the shears."

"Wouldn't the killer's prints be on them?" Lizzie asked.

"It's possible but not likely. Mrs. Randolph said that her husband loved showing off his collection. The killer is probably someone who knew the collection was there and that gloves were always worn when handling it," Wade replied.

"It still concerns me that we didn't find the label that should have been on the shears," Reed said.

"It may have been torn off and left to blow in the wind," Dodson replied.

"Or the killer may have it," Wade added.

"Why do you say that?" Lizzie asked.

"If the killer was familiar enough with the Randolph's to know about the collection, he knew about the labels. It might have been kept for a souvenir."

Lizzie shuddered.

"What did you learn from Mrs. Randolph, Deputy Lizzie Fletcher?"

Lizzie tried to sound as professional and matter of fact as the rest of the sheriff's team. "Mrs. Randolph repeated herself a lot. It was as if she were reliving an argument they had and finding him this morning."

"What did she say?"

"They had an argument last night. She went to bed and waited for Mr. Randolph to come in to apologize He didn't come in right away. She fell asleep. He wasn't there when she woke up this morning. She started calling for him but got no answer. When she didn't find him in the house, she went outside to look for him. She saw his boots as she approached the barn and found Mr. Randolph."

"Is there anything else?"

"After being questioned by you, Sheriff, she seemed to be concerned that Mr. Randolph might have committed suicide."

"I noticed that, too."

"She seemed at times to be grief stricken. At other times, she appeared to be in perfect control."

"She appeared to be perfectly coherent when I talked with her," Wade added. "Mrs. Randolph made two statements during our interview that concern me. First, she seemed to hesitate when asked if Mr. Randolph had any enemies. Second, when shown the piece of pink cloth found in the victim's hand, she assumed that we thought Mr. Randolph was having an affair. She immediately tried to convince me that he was not."

The sheriff and his deputies sat in silence for a moment before Wade continued. "Does anyone have anything else to add?"

After receiving negative responses, Wade continued. "We'll begin our investigation based on what we have until Doctor Hughes completes his autopsy. Dodson, I'd like for you to check into backgrounds of both of the Randolph's. Dig up everything you can. Reed, check the murder weapon for finger prints. Check his hunting rifle for prints, too. Maybe, we'll get lucky. Verify that those shoe prints belong to the victim and Mrs. Randolph."

"Yes, sir," both men replied.

"Deputy Fletcher and I will interview the neighbors after she is fitted for a uniform. Let's keep the scrap of pink cloth our little secret for the time being. It may be nothing, but I have a feeling it's important."

"Yes, sir," the deputies answered as Wade stopped the recording.

"It's eleven-thirty," Wade said. "Everyone, get some lunch before you get started. If you find anything significant, call me right away. Otherwise, we'll meet back here this evening."

There were no deputy sheriff uniforms that would fit Lizzie's petite frame in the stock room. Wade drove her to be measured for one at the dress shop before getting lunch. They sat, enjoying their burgers, and quietly discussed the case.

"Lizzie, do you remember the names of everyone that was at the Preston's party last week?"

"I think so. I had met most of them before except for the new couple."

"Make a list of all those people. We'll double check the list with the Preston's when we interview them."

"Do you think someone at the party had something to do with this?"

"Anything is possible. I want to cross-reference the party goers with the list of neighbors."

"Does that piece of pink cloth have something to do with it?"

"Think back to Mrs. Preston's ghost story. What color was the dress Ruby was wearing?"

Lizzie paused for a moment, trying to remember the ghost story they had heard. Wade watched her facial expression change from one of puzzlement to realization.

"Oh! It was pink!"

"Yes, it was. We are the only two people who have made that connection. Dodson and Reed haven't heard the ghost story. The only person outside of our team that knows about that particular piece of evidence is April Randolph. She immediately attributed it to someone else by suggesting her husband was having an affair."

"Couldn't it be a coincidence?"

"It's possible. I think the killer was someone who knew Paul Randolph well. That leads me to family, a friend, or a neighbor. That piece of cloth points me to the party and the ghost story."

"That makes sense to me." Lizzie thought for a moment before asking, "If the label could have blown away, couldn't the fabric have been blown there?"

"Yes, but why would it have been clutched in Paul's hand?"

Lizzie thought for a moment. Suddenly, she realized what concerned Wade. "I can see why it bothers you so much. It's hard to explain. It doesn't fit."

Wade smiled at her. "You're starting to think like a cop now."

They finished their lunch and walked to Wade's truck. "Lizzie, we aren't going to mention that piece of fabric while we're interviewing the neighbors and party guests. I'd like you to look around the homes as inconspicuously as possible. Look for anything that will match it."

"Alright. Do you want me to observe everyone while you interview them?"

"Yes. Make note of anything you think is particularly important."

"Where do we start?"

"Let's start with the Prestons. I want to make sure that list you made is complete."

# CHAPTER 7

Wade and Lizzie arrived at the Preston home to find Grandma Gail standing on the front porch. She greeted them as they got out of the truck.

"Well, if it isn't the local sheriff and his pretty lady. How are ya'll doing today? Isn't it a fine afternoon?"

"Yes, ma'am," Wade answered.

"I'm guessing this isn't a social call. It's such a shame about that poor boy."

"Yes, ma'am it is. I have a few questions to ask. Are Mr. and Mrs. Preston home?"

"They're inside. I was about to go inside myself. Ya'll come on in."

Wade and Lizzie followed Mrs. Preston inside.

"Kent, look who's here."

Kent Preston hurried to greet the sheriff and his deputy. "I expected I'd be seeing you pretty soon. Please sit down."

"Can I get you some iced tea?" Dara offered.

"No, ma'am. Thank you," Wade replied. "We need to ask all of you some questions." Noticing the confusion on their faces as they glanced at Lizzie, he added, "Lizzie is acting as interim deputy in Maddie's absence. She has officially been sworn in as my deputy. She'll be taking notes for me."

"Well, that makes sense," Grandma Gail replied.

"If you don't mind, I'd like for you to look at this list," he said nodding at Lizzie. Lizzie handed the list she had made to Dara.

"Is that an accurate list of those who were at the party last week?"

Dara looked at the list before saying, "Yes, it is. The last name of the couple across the road is Dylan."

"Dylan? I knew it started with a D but couldn't remember anything else," Lizzie replied.

"Do you think the party had something to do with Paul's death?" Kent asked.

"I don't know yet. It's too early in the investigation to speculate about anything." Wade paused before adding, "I plan to visit with as many of Mr. Randolph's friends and neighbors as possible. They might know something that will point us in the right direction."

"We'll do all we can to help," Dara answered.

"Thank you. If you don't mind, I'd like to talk with each of you individually. Is there someplace we can talk so that our conversations won't be overheard?"

"You can use our office," Kent said. "But I don't think there is anything I can tell you that Dara or Grandma shouldn't hear."

"I understand your concern. I've found that when interviewing people in groups, one person's answers tend to influence those of others in the room. I need to know what you saw or heard individually."

"Alright," Kent said obviously relieved "The office is this way. Would you like to start with me?"

"Yes," Wade said as he followed Kent to the office.

Lizzie followed the two men and made a mental note of everything she could see. Kent and Wade were taking their seats when she closed the office door.

Wade began the interview, "How well did you know Paul?"

"We've been neighbors for several years. We'd socialize once or twice a month."

"What can you tell me about his collection?"

"Paul was very proud of that farm tool collection. He loved to show it off. He was like a completely different person when he had visitors to his loft," Kent said smiling at the memory.

"What do you mean a different person?"

"I don't know how well you knew Paul, but he was kind of a...," Kent paused, looking at Lizzie. Choosing his words carefully, he continued. "He was kind of a wimpy guy. Some folks would say whipped. But when he was in that loft talking about that collection, he was smart. He was articulate and confident."

"Did you ever handle his collection?"

"No way! Paul was very particular about that collection. He had a look but don't touch policy. I remember once that he wanted me to have a closer look at one of the pieces. He put on a pair of gloves before he touched it. He asked me to put on a pair of gloves, too."

"How did Paul and April Randolph get along?"

Kent sighed before answering. "I felt sorry for Paul most of the time. April can be a very nice person. She'd help anyone in need. She's a good neighbor for the most part. Unfortunately, she bullied Paul. It didn't matter what he did; it would be wrong as far as she was concerned."

"Did they fight very often?"

"I don't think you would call them fights. She'd chew him out for something every time we saw them. Paul would just hang his head. I've never seen Paul stand up to her."

"Did Mr. Randolph have any enemies that you're aware of?"

Kent thought for a moment before answering. "I don't know that you would call them enemies. People liked to bully Paul because they could. I can't think of anyone who would want him dead."

"Paul seemed to be particularly afraid of Carl Ellis the night of the party. Is there any reason that he should be?"

"Carl Ellis is a cruel man. Anyone with any sense stays away from him."

"What is his issue with you?"

"He wants this place. I've told him repeatedly that we aren't interested in selling. It's been in our family for generations."

"Did Mr. Randolph know something about Carl that could have put him in danger?"

Kent sighed again. "This is probably just neighborhood gossip. No one knows it for a fact."

"Go on."

"Folks have been hearing screams from the direction of the Ellis place for years."

"I see. That explains why Paul and Nick were looking in that direction when they heard the scream the night of the party. Were the screams similar to the cougar scream?"

"Yes, but there's a difference. I can't explain it."

"Can you think of any reason why anyone might have wanted revenge or might have been threatened by Paul?"

Lizzie noticed a slight change in Kent's facial expression.

"No, not all."

"That's all I have for now. Please, let me know if you think of anything that might be important to the case. It doesn't matter how insignificant it might seem."

"Certainly. Who would you like to see next?"

"I'd like to visit with your wife, now. Please, don't discuss our interview with anyone."

Kent nodded as he left the room. Dara tapped lightly on the door before going in. It seemed to Lizzie that her friend was rather nervous.

Wade smiled at her reassuringly. "Mrs. Preston, I appreciate your help. I'm looking for any information that might point us in the right direction."

"I'll do what I can."

Wade asked Dara the same questions he had asked her husband. Her answers were similar to those given by Kent.

"Mr. Randolph seemed to be particularly afraid of Carl Ellis the night of the party. Is there any reason that he should be?"

Dara paused for a moment before answering. She seemed reluctant to answer. "What I'm about to tell you must to be kept a secret."

"Oh?" Wade answered clearly surprised by her comment.

"It would be extremely dangerous for someone if word should get around."

"What you tell me will be held in strictest confidence."

Dara hesitated a bit longer. "Paul and April have been helping Brandy Ellis."

"What do you mean?"

"Brandy has been doing odd jobs and selling eggs for some extra money."

"Why would she need extra money?"

"Carl controls every penny they have. He won't let Brandy buy anything that he doesn't approve first. She's trying to save up enough money to buy a special Christmas gift for their daughter. If Carl finds out, it won't be good for Brandy."

"I see. Who else has been helping her?"

"I'm not sure. She does a little secretarial work for me. Paul had her help with his collection once. She's done some sewing for April. I suspect that Pearl at the store buys eggs from her."

"How can it be kept a secret with so many people involved?"

"We don't talk about it. Brandy told me about the work she had been doing for Paul and April."

"What about the eggs?"

"I've just noticed an unusual supply of fresh eggs there lately. I don't know for certain that they came from Brandy."

"Would Brandy have told Carl about coming here?"

"I know that he saw her leaving here one afternoon. She didn't come back for several days."

"Did she tell Carl about working for you?"

Dara's eyes grew wide with fear. "That would have been disastrous for Brandy." Dara shuddered at the thought. "She said she told him that I had stopped her on the road and asked if she wanted a job."

"I see. Has Brandy told you anything about her life with Carl?"

"No. I know that she's afraid of him. Sometimes she has bruises when I see her."

"Will you do me a favor?" Wade asked.

"I'll try," Dara answered warily.

"Tell Mrs. Ellis that I am just a phone call away should she need anything," Wade said, handing his card to Dara. "Our communications will be confidential."

"I certainly will. I'll keep your card here if you don't mind."

"I understand. Other than Carl Ellis, can you think of any reason why anyone might have wanted revenge or might have been threatened by Mr. Randolph?"

"Not that I'm aware of."

"I don't have any more questions for you at the moment. Please, let me know if you think of anything that might be important to the case. Keep me posted on the situation with Mrs. Ellis."

"I will. Would you like me to send Grandma Gail in?"

"I need to confer with my deputy for a few minutes. I'll call her momentarily."

Dara smiled at Lizzie and left the room, gently closing the door behind her.

"Lizzie, how are you doing? Do you need a break?"

"No, I'm fine. Why do you ask?"

"I thought I heard you sniffling a moment ago," Wade said as he reached for her hand.

Lizzie blushed. "I was a little. It broke my heart to hear about Brandy's situation. Isn't there something that can be done?"

"Until she files a complaint, I can't do anything, officially."

"It's all so sad. It's obvious that Brandy isn't the only one afraid of Carl."

"That's true. When you're ready to continue, ask Mrs. Preston to come in, please?"

"And observe while in the process?"

"Exactly," Wade said smiling at her proudly.

Gail Preston was a short, plump woman with a bun of gray hair atop her head. Her brown eyes were shining with excitement as she entered the office behind Lizzie. According to Kent, she was in her mid-eighties but looked and behaved much younger.

"Please, sit down Mrs. Preston."

"Only if you'll call me Grandma Gail," she said wagging a finger at Wade.

Wade grinned. "Please, sit down Grandma Gail."

"I've never been part of a murder investigation before. I know I shouldn't, but I find it to be quite exciting," she admitted trying not to smile.

"This shouldn't take long Mrs…I mean Grandma Gail."

"Ask me anything you want. I'll tell you what I know."

"How well did you know Paul and April Randolph?"

"I've met them here a few times."

"Did you ever see his collection?"

"No, I didn't have the pleasure. I've heard about it from my grandson."

"Do you know if the Randolph's ever argued?"

"It was clear to me that she wore the pants in the family, but I never heard them argue."

"Do you know if Mr. Randolph had any enemies?"

"I barely knew him. I have no idea."

"Was there any truth to the ghost story you told at the party last week?"

Grandma Gail stared at Wade open-mouthed for a moment. "Well, I didn't see that one coming," she finally answered. "That story was going around when I was a young woman. There is usually some truth to be found in old stories."

"So, as far as you know, it was just a ghost story without any fact?"

"Well now, I didn't say that. There was a family here at one time by the name of Lawrence whose house burned down."

"When was that?"

"It was during the depression. Does my little story have something to do with Paul's death?" she asked obviously worried.

"I doubt it, but I have to cover all angles to find any possible clue."

"I hope it doesn't. I'd feel awful if my story was responsible."

"Grandma Gail," Wade said, placing his hand over hers. "Telling your story was not the reason for Mr. Randolph's murder. Someone already had it in mind."

Grandma Gail wiped a tear from her eye and nodded. "Thank you, Sheriff. You're a kind man." Glancing at Lizzie, she said, "Don't let this one get away, young lady."

Lizzie smiled at her and winked, "Yes, ma'am."

Grandma Gail chuckled and asked, "Do you have any more questions for me?"

"Yes, ma'am. I understand this farm has been in the Preston family for generations."

"Yes, it has."

"Why would Carl Ellis be so determined to buy it?"

Gail Preston sighed. "I don't know what has gotten into him about this place. He's been bullying Kent and Dara for months. He's talking to the wrong people. They couldn't sell it to him even if they wanted to."

"Who should he be talking to?"

"To me! I own this place. It will belong to Kent and Dara when I die, but for now it's still mine. I'd appreciate it if you'd keep that under your hat, though. I'd rather not deal with Carl Ellis if I can avoid it. He reminds me of someone from my past. It was a bad experience that I'd rather not relive."

"No one will hear it from us," Wade stood and held the door open for her. "Thank you, Grandma Gail." He motioned to Lizzie to follow. They joined Kent and Dara in the living room.

"Thank you all for your time. I may have more questions later in the investigation."

"We'll be happy to answer any questions you have," Kent replied.

"Thank you. I must ask you not to discuss your interviews with anyone. I'll probably be asking similar questions of others. I prefer that their answers aren't rehearsed."

"We understand," Dara answered.

"I have one more question before we leave you in peace. Could I possibly get a list of all of your neighbors in this area?"

"I'll make one for you," Dara answered.

"The ones I'm most interested in are those you live nearby but who weren't at the party and anyone who spent time with the Randolph's."

Dara jotted down a few names before handing the list to Wade.

"I'm not sure if any of our neighbors spent a lot of time with Paul and April other than those who were here. April could be more specific."

"Thank you. If there is anything you think of or remember, don't hesitate to call."

The Preston family assured the sheriff and his deputy that they would call if anything came to mind. They waved goodbye from the front porch as Wade and Lizzie drove away.

# CHAPTER 8

"I think we should see the Dylans while we're this close to them. Since they're new to the area, they may not have much to tell us," Wade told Lizzie.

"Do you want to talk about the interviews with the Prestons or wait until we get back to town?"

"Let's wait so that we can get it on the recording."

"Yes, sir."

Wade looked at Lizzie from the corner of his eye and grinned. "I like the sound of that."

"The sound of what?" Lizzie teased.

"You, calling me sir."

"Well don't get used to it. As soon as Maddie is back on the job, it's all over."

Wade was laughing when he stopped the truck in the Dylan's drive. Lizzie followed as he went to the door and knocked.

"Yes?"

Mrs. Dylan was tall and slender. Her brown hair hung past her shoulders in waves. Her gray eyes never focused on the faces of her guests. She looked past them or at the floor. Lizzie thought she seemed to be very sad. She spoke slowly and softly as if she were in a perpetual dream.

"Mrs. Dylan, I'm Sheriff Wade Adams, and this is my deputy Lizzie Fletcher. May we ask you a few questions?"

"Yes, of course. Please, come in. We met last week didn't we?"

"Yes, we did at the Preston's house."

"That's right. I didn't realize that Miss Fletcher was your deputy."

"She wasn't at the time. She has been officially sworn in and will be taking notes during our interview. She's my interim deputy while Maddie Clifton is on maternity leave."

"I'm sorry. I'm still trying to get names and faces straight. We haven't lived here very long. Is this about poor Mr. Randolph?"

"Yes, ma'am."

"Please, sit down. Would you like some lemonade or a coke?"

"No, thank you," Wade replied as they sat on the sofa. "Is your husband home? I'd like to speak with him also."

"He went into town for a few things. He should be home soon."

"If you don't mind, I'll ask you a few questions while we wait."

"I don't mind at all."

"I'm sorry, but I can't recall your first name," Wade said apologetically. The truth was that he wasn't sure which name was hers and which was her husbands.

"It's Morgan."

"How long have you lived here?"

"Since the beginning of August. As you can see, we're still unpacking."

"Where did you live previously?"

"We've lived in several little towns in the Texas panhandle. We came here from Claude."

"What brings you to this area?"

"Alex took a job with the Vernon school district."

"Why did you choose to live here rather than in town?"

"We prefer to live in the country. Alex enjoys having a little land to tinker with."

"What does he do for the school district?"

"He's the band director at the middle school."

"Are you employed?"

"Not yet. I've applied at several places but haven't heard anything yet."

"What sort of work are you interested in?"

"I have a degree in criminal justice, but I'll take what I can get."

"Have you applied at my office?"

"No."

"Please, do. We are in need of another female deputy."

"Thank you. I will," she said smiling slightly.

"How well did you know Paul and April Randolph?"

"Not very well. We've met two or three times I think."

"Have you ever been at their home?"

"Yes, there was a dinner party at their house last month. They were kind enough to invite us."

"Did Mr. Randolph happen to mention his collection?"

"He did more than mention it. He gave us a grand tour. He seemed to be very proud of it."

"Was there anything that happened at dinner that night that stands out to you now?"

"No, it was a lot like the party last week but without the ghost story."

"That was quite a story wasn't it?" Wade asked.

"Yes, it was. Mrs. Preston has a way with words."

"I know that you haven't lived here very long, but I must ask. Do you know of any reason that someone would want Paul Randolph dead?"

"No, I don't."

Alex Dylan bounced into the room from the kitchen. He was slightly taller than his wife. His belly was beginning to hang over his belt. A curl of his red hair fell across his freckled forehead. His brown eyes held surprise and curiosity at the sight of visitors.

"Hello, Sheriff. Miss Fletcher."

"Alex dear, Sheriff Adams and Deputy Fletcher have some questions for us concerning Mr. Randolph."

Wade extended his hand, "I'm visiting with all of the Randolph's neighbors."

"Yes, of course. We barely knew Paul, but anything we can do to help."

Wade briefly reviewed what had been discussed prior to Alex's arrival. Alex agreed with the answers given by his wife.

"Do you know of any reason that someone would want to kill Paul Randolph?"

"No."

"Well, that's all the questions I have for today." Wade stood silently for a moment before continuing. "As the investigation progresses, I may have a few more. I must ask that you not discuss our interview with anyone else. People tend to rehearse their answers, and I'd prefer they didn't."

"I hadn't thought of that. We won't mention it to anyone," Alex assured him.

"Thank you. Please, feel free to call if you think of anything that might be helpful in this case."

"We will. I'll walk you out," Alex said holding the door open.

Morgan touched Lizzie's arm as she started to leave. She hung back a moment while Wade and Alex Dylan walked outside.

"I'm sorry about the misunderstanding earlier, Miss Fletcher," she said.

"That's perfectly alright and understandable. There's no way you could have known. I was sworn in this morning. The sheriff is going to have to order a uniform for me. Maddie may be back on the job before it comes in."

"Does he really need another female deputy?"

"Yes, he does. He's been looking for someone for months. He hasn't been able to find anyone qualified. With Maddie on maternity leave, he's in a bind. You should apply."

"I may do that. I'll talk to Alex about it this evening."

Lizzie said goodbye and walked to the truck.

Wade helped her in before walking around to his side.

"I don't know about you, but I could use something to drink," he said after he closed his door. "Let's talk with the Carson's at the store next."

"I like the way you think, sir."

Wade chuckled and started the motor.

Sheriff Wade Adams and Deputy Fletcher stayed longer at the

store than anticipated. They had learned nothing new when they made their escape from the Carsons.

"They sure like to talk don't they?"

Lizzie laughed. "Yes, they do. Usually, you can learn all about this community by visiting with Mack and Pearl. I'm betting that, if they don't have any ideas about this murder yet, they will before you do."

"You're probably right. I'll check back with them from time to time for updates."

"Who are we going to see next?" Lizzie asked.

"Let me see that list." Wade took the list from Lizzie. He stared at it a moment before saying, "The Flynns don't live in this area, so we'll talk to them later. I want to talk with April Randolph again, but I'll wait until we see what Dodson and Reed have come up with. That leaves the Brinkmans, the Cliftons, and the Ellises."

"Can we see Drew and Maddie first? I'd love to see the baby."

Wade grinned at Lizzie. "I had a feeling you were going to say that. I'll call to let them know we're coming so that we don't wake up the baby."

Maddie Clifton was standing in the doorway, waiting when Wade and Lizzie drove up. Her short, curly, dark brown hair framed her face. Her brown eyes lit up as she smiled while opening the door for them.

"Hello, Maddie. How is motherhood agreeing with you?" Wade asked.

"It's exhausting, but I love it. Hi, Lizzie."

"Hi, Maddie. You look great! I would never have guessed you just had a baby."

Maddie laughed. "Thanks, Lizzie. I feel like I had a baby. As soon as Doctor Hughes gives me the okay, I'm going to start working out again. Come in and make yourselves comfortable. Brody is asleep right now. If you don't mind, you can start by interviewing me so that I can feed him when he wakes up."

Wade and Lizzie sat down on the sofa as Drew came into the room. His blue eyes held sadness as he ran his hands through his light brown hair.

"Wade. Lizzie," he said as he nodded hello. "It's a sad thing about Paul isn't it?"

"Yes, it is, Drew."

"We've heard a few rumors. Was it an accident or suicide?"

"It was murder."

"Murder?" Maddie asked, clearly stunned. "Who on earth would want to murder Paul Randolph?"

"We're interviewing all the neighbors and everyone that was at the party, trying to find out."

"I know how this works. I'll be outside when you're ready to interview me," Drew said as he hurriedly left the room.

"Are you sure it's murder?" Maddie asked again.

"No doubt about it."

"I can't believe it."

Wade asked Maddie the same questions he had asked the other friends and neighbors. She had nothing to add. The interview with Drew yielded the same results.

Maddie brought her young son out to meet her guests when he had finished eating. The chubby cheeked little boy had green eyes like his father and a full head of curly brown hair like his mother. Wade and Lizzie fussed over the child to his parents' delight. With a wide yawn, he went back to sleep. Wade and Lizzie started toward the door.

"Before you go, I need to ask you something," Maddie said. "Can you wait while I put Brody down?"

"We'll wait," Wade said as he and Lizzie returned to the sofa.

Maddie came back into the room with concern in her eyes. "I know it's not my place, and if I'm out of line, just say so. We've been friends as well as co-workers, and I think I need to point this out," she said to Wade.

Surprised, Wade said, "What do you want to talk about?"

"It's nothing against you, Lizzie; I think you and Wade are great together."

Now, Lizzie was surprised. She had no idea what had Maddie so concerned. "Go ahead, Maddie."

"I know you would never intentionally do anything to jeopardize the department or this investigation. That's why I feel like I have to say this." Maddie took a deep breath before continuing. "It could possibly cause some issues with Lizzie working for you while you're in a relationship with her."

Wade sat silently for a few minutes before answering. Maddie looked at him with worry while she waited for his comment.

"You're right, Maddie. I didn't think about that when I deputized Lizzie. I needed a woman who could talk to April. I was pressed for time and didn't think it through first."

Maddie sighed, visibly relieved.

"The problem is that I still need a woman who can talk with Mrs. Randolph and the female witnesses. No one else is available. Do you have any suggestions?"

"Everyone knows the two of you have been seeing each other for a while now. Maybe you should hold a press conference to explain the situation."

"Stop the concerns before they start?"

"Yes, and it might be wise not to be seen together too much other than on the job."

Wade sighed and looked at Lizzie. "What do you think?"

"I think Maddie's right. I don't want to jeopardize your case or your career."

Wade scratched his chin and sighed. "If this case is over quickly, I won't need Lizzie's help for long. If it drags on for a while, I'll need someone."

"I can cut my maternity leave short if need be," Maddie offered.

"I don't want you to do that. You need to take your time off. Let me think about this for a while. I'll let you know what I come up with. Thanks for bringing it to my attention."

Maddie smiled. "I'll support you whatever you decide."

"Thanks. We had better get to those other interviews. I'll talk to you tomorrow, Maddie."

Wade paused a moment before leaving." What did ya'll think about that ghost story last week?"

"To tell the truth, I didn't pay much attention to it. My labor pains had started just before dinner. I was a little preoccupied," Maddie answered.

Wade looked at Drew.

"I didn't hear much of the last half. I was watching Maddie. Was it a good story?"

"It was. I had never heard that one before. Take care of that boy. We'll be seeing you," Wade said as he opened the door.

Lizzie squeezed Maddie's hand as she said goodbye. She walked outside and got into the truck. Wade sighed as he got in and looked at Lizzie.

"Do you have any suggestions?"

"I have one, but you may not like it."

"You can tell me after we've finished the interviews. Let's go see the Brinkmans next." Wade started the truck and drove toward the Brinkman home.

Nick and Emily Brinkman lived near the county line. The farm they lived on was leased to one of their neighbors. They rented the house and enjoyed the quiet country living.

Emily was slightly overweight, with brown eyes and long blonde hair. She was weeding her flower beds when Wade and Lizzie arrived. She shaded her eyes with a gloved hand before putting her gardening tools down and rising to greet them.

"Mrs. Brinkman," Wade said. "Can you spare a few minutes? I'd like to ask you some questions."

"Yes. I'd invite you in, but the house is being painted. The smell is really strong. It's more pleasant out here," she said directing them to chairs on the covered porch.

Wade turned down the offer of a beverage and explained Lizzie's presence before he began.

"I'd like to talk with your husband, too. Is he home?"

"He was on duty today but should be home any minute."

Wade proceeded with his questions, receiving the same answers that the other neighbors had given. Nick arrived shortly after the interview with Emily was finished.

Nick was a tall, muscular man. His blonde hair was cut short, and his brown eyes were usually hidden by mirrored shades. He thought they made him look cool and intimidating. He was considered by many to be a very good looking man. That fact grieved his wife. The ladies liked her husband, and he liked the ladies.

Nick drove into his driveway. He realized that he would have to talk with the visitors before he could make an excuse to leave again. He waved to Wade and Lizzie as he got out of his car, but he barely acknowledged his wife.

"I assume this visit is about Paul. I still can't believe it."

"I need to ask you a few questions."

"Do you have any leads?"

"Not yet. I'm visiting with all the neighbors and everyone that was at the Preston's party."

"Why the party?"

"There was some evidence discovered that may indicate someone who attended that party."

"What kind of evidence?"

"I'd rather not say. It could just as easily be nothing at all."

"I hear you."

Wade repeated his questions. He heard practically the same answers he had heard all day. Wade and Lizzie said their goodbyes and started toward the truck. Wade stopped before getting inside. "What did ya'll think about Mrs. Preston's ghost story? Wasn't that something?"

"It certainly was. I couldn't sleep at all that night," Emily said with a giggle.

"It was pretty original. Usually, if you've heard one ghost story, you've heard them all," Nick added.

"I'd never heard it before," Wade said as he waved goodbye.

Wade and Lizzie drove silently to the Ellis farm. Wade wasn't looking forward to doing this interview. He was concerned it might cause problems for Mrs. Ellis if Carl was out. He dreaded dealing with Carl.

Wade drove into the driveway. He looked around a moment before getting out. He could see a pickup in the field nearby. Carl Ellis got into his vehicle and drove to meet the Sheriff and his deputy.

"What are you doing here, Sheriff?" Carl asked angrily as he got out of the truck.

"I've been visiting everyone is this area today, Mr. Ellis. I'd like to ask you a few questions.

"What if I don't want to answer any questions?" Carl stood with his fists on his hips looking menacingly at Wade.

"Well, I will have to assume that you have something to hide. I'd have to arrest you on suspicion of murder and ask my questions at the jail. It would be easier for both of us if you'd cooperate now. I'd also like to ask your wife some questions."

"Murder? Who was murdered?"

"Paul Randolph was found dead this morning beside his barn. April found him."

"That must have been the screaming that I heard this mornin'. I thought it was that damned cougar. It don't usually scream in the daylight though; I'll get Brandy out here."

"I'd rather ask you these questions separately. I don't want your wife's answers to be influenced by yours."

"She can't tell you nothin'. She's dumb as a post and hardly ever leaves the house."

"I'll need to speak with her anyway."

Carl reluctantly said, "What do you want to know?"

Wade asked the same questions. Carl's answers were the same as everyone else's but with added derogatory remarks and colorful language about Paul and his wife.

"I'd like to speak to your wife now if you'd send her out, please."

"Woman! Get your skinny butt outside. Sheriff wants to talk to you."

Brandy Ellis hurried out the door. "There's a sandwich on the table for you," she murmured as she looked at Wade in fear.

Mrs. Ellis was painfully thin. Her ragged dress hung on her frame like limp drapes on a window. She had dark circles under her pale blue eyes and deep worry lines on her forehead. Her dark hair, draped partially over her left cheek, was beginning to turn gray. She kept her eyes focused on the ground in front of her.

"Make it quick!" Carl said as he slammed the door.

"Mrs. Ellis, I'm Wilbarger County Sheriff Wade Adams. This is Deputy Lizzie Fletcher."

Brandy looked up, smiling weakly. "It's nice to meet you," she said quietly.

"We've been visiting your neighbors today. Paul Randolph was killed this morning."

Brandy focused on Wade's face for a moment. He could see the shock and sorrow on her face before she quickly returned her focus to his shoes.

"How awful! He was such a nice man. Mrs. Randolph must be devastated. What happened?"

"He was murdered beside his barn. I'd like to ask you a few questions."

A single tear slid down Brandy's nose, "I don't know anything that will help, but you may ask."

Her answers were a replay of all the answers Wade had heard that day. As he said his goodbyes, he noticed that Carl had been watching from a nearby window.

"That is a very nasty man," Lizzie said angrily as Wade climbed into the truck.

"Yes, he is. I have a feeling he knows more than he's telling."

"She may know more but is afraid to say anything," Lizzie added angrily.

"I'm sure we'll be talking to them again.

Wade's phone rang as he started his truck.

"Hello. Good, good. We're on our way," Wade said and hung up the phone.

"Doctor Hughes finished his autopsy. Dodson and Reed have come up with a few answers. We'll go back to the office to compare notes and then go somewhere for dinner. Can you help me with the rest of the interviews tomorrow?"

"I don't know of any reason I can't. Do you have time to take me by the inn?"

"We can make time. Why?"

"I'd like to check in with my folks and get my jeep."

"Why do you need your jeep? You can stay with me."

"Maddie is right. I'm concerned about compromising your investigation and your job. Is it ethical for you to sleep with one of your deputies?"

"It sounds pretty bad when you put it like that." Wade thought a moment before saying, "I can still drive you home."

"You may be really busy. I don't want you to have to drive me back out here tonight or come get me in the morning. I can drive into town or meet you somewhere between for the interviews."

"What do you suggest we do?"

"I don't really want to do this, but it might be best if we put our relationship on hold until this case is over or until you hire a new deputy; whichever comes first."

Wade sighed. He knew she was right, but he didn't want to put their relationship on hold. He changed the subject.

"If we're going back to the inn, we should stop and see the Flynns on the way. We'll only have follow up interviews to do tomorrow if needed. I'll let the office know we'll be a little later getting there."

Wade dialed his office. "We're going to do the last interview before we come back into town. Order some pizza to be delivered to the office. We'll start our meeting at six-thirty.

# CHAPTER 9

Brian and Kelly Flynn had no more information to share than anyone else Wade and Lizzie had spoken with that day. They were impressed with the ghost story but had little more to say about it.

Wade drove silently to the inn. Lizzie didn't know if he was worried about the case or her suggestion that they put their relationship on hold. She chose to remain silent as well.

Lizzie opened the door to the inn and stepped inside. Wade followed closely behind. For a moment, they thought they were alone.

"Well, where have you two been all day?" Granny asked. "Did you have a good time?"

"We had a sudden change of plans," Lizzie answered. "Paul Randolph was killed this morning."

"Oh no! What happened? Do James and Ellen know?"

Lizzie looked at Wade before answering, "I haven't told them. We've been pretty busy."

"I'll call them. We can have a little dinner, and you can tell us all about it."

"We came back to get my jeep before heading back to town. We won't have time for dinner."

"I would like to see your folks for a minute, Lizzie."

"Ok, why don't we drive to their house? Granny can ride with us. We'll get my jeep on the way back."

"Sounds like a plan to me," Granny joked. "Let me forward any phone calls to the house, and I'll be ready."

"Have you had many calls today," Lizzie asked.

"Three wanted to book events for days we already have booked. There was one for a luncheon in January. I didn't see anything on the calendar, so I booked it for the sixteenth."

"When are you going to have to be here for your guests and events, Lizzie?" Wade asked.

"We have a Halloween party booked for the thirty-first. We don't have anything else booked until the first week in December. After that, we have two or three holiday parties a week until New Year's Eve."

"I'm ready; let's go," Granny said.

Wade offered her his arm. She giggled as she allowed him to escort her to his truck. Granny talked during the quarter mile to James and Ellen's house. James was sitting on the porch when Wade helped the women out of the truck.

"Look who we have here. I wasn't expecting to see you two today," he said as he rose to shake Wade's hand and hug his daughter.

"I'd like to talk with you and Ellen if you have a minute."

"We have all kinds of minutes. Come on in. Ellen, look who's here."

Ellen rushed over to hug her daughter and Wade. "What brings you two here tonight? I thought you were going to be away all weekend."

"We had a sudden change of plans," Wade said. I'd like to talk with ya'll about something if you don't mind."

"Of course, we don't mind," Ellen exclaimed. "Have a seat. I'll find something for dinner."

"Mama, we can't stay for dinner. We have to go into town. Paul Randolph was killed this morning."

"Oh my word," Ellen sighed as she sat down.

"What happened to him, Wade?" James asked.

"He was murdered. April found him beside their barn this morning."

Lizzie's family sat in shocked silence.

"There's something else I need to talk to you about. As you know, I've been short a deputy for months. Since Maddie is on maternity leave, I desperately need a female deputy. This morning, I deputized

Lizzie."

Lizzie's family remained in shocked silence a moment longer before James spoke up.

"Why Lizzie? She doesn't know anything about police work."

"I chose Lizzie for several reasons. She was acquainted with the victim and his wife. I needed someone that April would feel comfortable talking with. She knows the area and most of the people we questioned today. I can trust her to keep things confidential, and she's pretty observant."

"I'm flattered, Wade. I thought you chose me because I happened to be there at the time."

"That, too." Grinning, Wade winked at her.

"Is it safe for Lizzie to be running around chasing a murderer?"

"Ellen, I would never put Lizzie in harm's way. She's been with me all day taking notes. If she continues to be my deputy, she will either be working at the office or with me taking notes."

"If she continues to be your deputy?" Granny queried.

"There are some concerns. The first concern is the inn. I don't want to keep Lizzie away from the inn, especially when it gets busy."

"We can cover the inn until December. We'll have to hire help even with Lizzie there that month," James assured him. "Will it take that long to close the case?"

"I have no idea how long it will take. We have no leads. I'm hoping my team will have some when we get back into town. It might be closed tomorrow, or it could take months, even years."

Ellen spoke up. "Would it be possible for Lizzie to work for you on an as needed basis until December?"

"That might be a solution to our other concern. It has been brought to our attention that our current relationship might jeopardize the case and my department. I was hoping you might have some suggestions."

"I assume there are rules about dating a coworker or a subordinate," Ellen said.

"Yes, there are," Wade replied.

The group sat in silence pondering possible solutions.

"I have an idea," Granny offered. "I don't like it, but I can't think of any other way."

"Let's hear it," Wade teased.

"The way I see it, you have only two choices. One is for Lizzie to quit or for you to fire her. Since you need her help, that isn't a good option. The other, and this is the part I don't like, is for you to stop seeing each other as long as Lizzie is your employee."

"I don't like that one either. Lizzie made the same suggestion earlier. I was hoping you would think of something we hadn't."

"Wade, do you mind if I put in my two cents?" James asked.

"Please do; that's why I wanted to talk with ya'll."

"You are an elected official of Wilbarger County. You have sworn an oath to protect and serve its citizens."

"Yes, sir."

"Do you truly need Lizzie's help as a deputy?"

"Yes, at least until I can hire and train another."

"Being in a relationship with her could potentially damage your case or your department."

"Yes, sir."

"What choice do you have?"

Wade sighed and looked sadly at Lizzie. "None, sir."

"We can still talk on the phone can't we?" Lizzie asked Wade.

"We'll need to be careful about any personal communication. We won't be able to be seen together in public when we're off duty."

"So we are no longer dating, and our relationship is on hold," Lizzie said teary-eyed.

"Unless I decide to fire you because I can't stand it anymore," Wade joked.

"Maybe, I'll quit for the same reason," Lizzie retorted.

"Wade, I hope this case wraps up soon. We're going to miss seeing you out here," Granny assured him.

"Yes, we're planning a nice Thanksgiving dinner. I really hope you can come," Ellen added.

"I'll miss all of you, too. I'll do my best to get this solved before Thanksgiving. We need to get into town. Hopefully, the case will be solved tonight."

"I'll be home later tonight," Lizzie said as she hugged her family goodbye.

Wade helped her into the truck and spoke with James before getting in himself.

James patted Wade on the shoulder while they shook hands.

"I promise I'll take care of Lizzie."

"I know you will."

The couple rode in silence to the inn. Wade turned off the truck engine before turning toward Lizzie. "I don't want to put our relationship on hold."

"I don't either, Wade. But we aren't breaking up are we?"

"It needs to appear that way to everyone. We can talk at work, but it has to be about business. It would probably be best if we're never alone at work."

"We can communicate after hours can't we?" Lizzie asked as a deep sadness began to envelop her heart.

"We can but not a lot. It would be bad if someone decided to check our phone records or emails."

"I don't want to do this either, but I want to be able to help you."

"I know. We'll discuss it with Dodson and Reed at the meeting. You'd better get your jeep. Wait about five minutes before you follow me."

"I will, but there's something I want to do first."

"What?"

Lizzie didn't say another word. She leaned over and kissed Wade as if she would never see him again.

• • •

Lizzie freshened up a bit and checked her mail before driving into town. She was heartbroken about their decision. She told herself it was only temporary, and at least she would get to see him while at work. She took her time but arrived at almost the same time as Wade. He grinned and waved at her before driving around the block until she was inside.

Reed seemed surprised to see Lizzie arriving alone. "Where's Sheriff Adams?"

"He isn't here yet? I haven't seen him since he dropped me at my house."

Lizzie secretly enjoyed the look on Reed's face. He directed her to the meeting room. Three large supreme pizzas had been placed on the conference room table. Lizzie suddenly realized she was starved. She had no idea what the protocol was when working through dinner. She decided to wait and follow the others lead.

She chose a chair as far away as possible from Wade's chair before sitting down. Dodson entered shortly after she was seated.

"Where's the sheriff?" he inquired.

"I haven't seen him since he dropped me at my house. I assumed he would be here already."

Dodson looked at her doubtfully but said nothing.

She smiled to herself when she heard Wade's voice in the outer room. *They can stop questioning me now.*

"Sheriff, Doctor Hughes is on his way. Dodson and Fletcher are already in the conference room," Reed informed Wade.

"Good, good. Let me know when Doctor Hughes arrives. I'll be in my office."

"Yes, sir," Reed answered clearly confused.

Wade checked his messages and made a few phone calls. He had been late on purpose. He needed time to deal with the effect of Lizzie's kiss before he saw her again. He smiled to himself at the memory before trying to push it from his mind. There was no way anyone would believe they were no longer seeing each other if he didn't.

He decided to review the case while he waited for Doctor Hughes. He was startled from his thoughts when Reed tapped on his door.

"Doctor Hughes is here, sir."

"Thank you. I guess we'd better join the others."

Wade followed Reed into the conference room. He silently thanked Lizzie for her choice of seats.

"Everyone, help yourselves to some pizza and a drink. We'll eat before we start the meeting."

"Lizzie, since you're new here, you should go first," Dodson said.

"Thank you," she answered and quickly filled her plate.

She returned to the same seat but avoided Wade's eyes. She couldn't get that kiss off her mind either.

Doctor Hughes seemed to be oblivious to the tension in the room. Reed and Dodson were both clearly confused about the behavior of their boss and the new deputy. They looked at each other and at Wade and Lizzie repeatedly but said nothing.

"If you've finished eating, I think we should get this meeting started so that we can all go home and get some rest," Wade said addressing the group. He waited for everyone to dispose of their trash before he started the recording.

"The first item we need to officially discuss is the obvious elephant in the room."

Reed and Dodson seemed apprehensive, but Doctor Hughes was confused.

"What elephant?" Doctor Hughes asked.

Doctor Gerard Hughes was a short stout man with a full head of brown hair. It seemed that he never aged. He didn't volunteer that information. He was one of six doctors in the city of Vernon. He was chosen to serve as county medical examiner primarily because he had the convenience of a large basement beneath his office.

"I'm so glad you asked," Wade joked in an effort to ease the tension. It's no secret that Miss Fletcher and I have been seeing each other romantically for some time now. What I want to tell you now is that said romance ended the moment we deputized Lizzie Fletcher."

"Deputy Fletcher, congratulations," Doctor Hughes said to Lizzie.

"Thank you, Doctor Hughes."

"Deputy Fletcher will be working with us on an as needed basis until we can hire another female deputy."

"Will the romance begin again at that time?" Doctor Hughes innocently asked.

Choosing to ignore the question, Wade continued. "Neither I nor Deputy Fletcher want to jeopardize this case or the integrity of this office. Therefore, we have ended our relationship."

"Sheriff, that's all well and good, but who outside of this office is going to believe that?"

"Dodson, that's a good point. I plan to release a statement to the newspaper as soon as possible to inform the public of our new hire and the circumstances of our relationship."

"Begging your pardon, sir, but will that be enough?" Reed asked.

"I don't know what else we can do. If you have any suggestions, I'm all ears."

Reed shook his head.

"If I may, I think it would be wise to deal with any problems as they occur," Doctor Hughes offered. "Provided that you are truly not seeing each other romantically anymore," he added looking at Lizzie.

Lizzie looked at Wade before answering. He nodded at her.

"Sheriff Adams and I have agreed to have no contact with each other outside the duties of this office."

"What will Deputy Fletcher's duties be?" Dodson asked.

"She'll be working here at the office and taking notes in the field. If need be, she will act as the female jailer. She will need some training. I'd appreciate it if you would handle that, Dodson."

"Yes, sir."

"Are the any other questions concerning our new deputy?"

"Yes, sir. I don't know when I'm to report for duty each day."

"Be here at eight Monday morning. We'll get all of your paperwork squared away and start your training," Dodson said.

"If there's nothing else, we'll get down to business," Wade

continued. "We're here to discuss our findings in the Paul Randolph case. Doctor Hughes, what did you learn from your autopsy?"

"Paul Randolph died at approximately two this morning. Cause of death was a puncture wound to the heart. I have no doubt that the pair of sheep shears found in his chest was the murder weapon. He was in relatively good health, except for the beginning signs of alcoholism."

"Was he drunk when he died?" Wade asked.

"No, his blood alcohol level was point zero four. There was no alcohol in his stomach."

"Thank you, Doctor Hughes. Deputy Gordon Reed, what have you learned?"

"The only fingerprints on the rifle were Paul Randolph's. His prints were also on the shears. It appears that he grabbed the weapon after being stabbed."

"No surprises there," Wade commented. "What did you learn about the shoe prints?"

"The boot prints are a match to the victim's boots. The shoe prints match the shoes that Mrs. Randolph was wearing when she found Mr. Randolph. There was no blood on Mrs. Randolph's clothing."

"Thank you, Reed. Deputy Craig Dodson, what have you been able to find out?"

"Mr. Randolph was part of a business deal that went bad. He had convinced a lot of people to invest. They all lost everything they had put into it."

"What sort of business deal?"

"It was a household appliance invention that was about to be patented. The money from Randolph and the other investors would have paid startup production costs. They expected a big return on their money. Before the patent was submitted, an identical product hit the stores, and everything fell apart. The man who claimed to be the inventor, Franklin Newton, took the startup money and left the country. I've found no record of Franklin Newton ever existing, and the product he was selling as a new invention wasn't his to sell."

"That sounds like a motive for murder. Do you have a list of investors?"

"Yes, sir. Most of the investors were his neighbors and his in-laws."

"Which neighbors?"

"Kent and Dara Preston, Nick and Emily Brinkman, Carl Ellis, Mack and Pearl Carson, Andrew and Maddie Clifton, Brian and Kelly Flynn, and the Gleason's, Mrs. Randolph's parents."

Wade frowned, "Most of those folks were at the Preston's dinner party last week."

"There's something else, sir. Mr. Randolph had a large life insurance policy. Mrs. Randolph is the beneficiary."

"How large?"

"A quarter-of-a-million-dollars!"

Wade raised his eyebrows and whistled.

"One more thing, I found nothing that indicates Mr. Randolph was having an affair as suggested by his wife. Mrs. Randolph, on the other hand, has been seen in the company of an unknown man at least twice in the last month."

"How did you find that out?"

"They ate at the steak house. My sister was their waitress," Dodson said.

Wade shook his head and grinned. "Find out who that man is."

"Yes, sir."

Wade paused, deep in thought for a moment. "Is there a clause in Randolph's life insurance policy about death by suicide?" he asked.

"The policy would be null and void in the event of suicide."

"That explains why Mrs. Randolph seemed so worried about her husband's death being a suicide, or wants us to believe she's worried about it."

Deputy Lizzie Fletcher, did Mrs. Randolph say what she and the victim argued about?"

"No, sir. She said they had a big fight and that she had been mean to him but no details."

"We'll need to visit with Mrs. Randolph again. Deputy Fletcher, please give us a run-down of the interviews conducted today."

Lizzie checked her notes and summarized the answers given by the people they had interviewed earlier that day. No one knew of any reason why Mr. Randolph would have been killed. They didn't know of any enemies that he might have had. No one who was at the Preston's dinner party seemed to be particularly affected by Mrs. Preston's ghost story.

"One person seems to have been bothered by that ghost story," Wade corrected. "Alex Dylan told me privately that his wife has been having nightmares and sleep walking since that night."

"Why didn't she mention anything about that?" Lizzie asked.

"Many people who sleepwalk are unaware of it. Others are frightened by it and don't want others to know," Doctor Hughes offered.

"It may or may not have anything to do with this case," Wade said. "Since most of the people we interviewed today lost money in the business deal with Mr. Randolph, either they truly hold no grudge against him or someone is lying," Wade continued. "We'll be talking with all of those folks again tomorrow. Deputy Fletcher, did you notice anything in any of the houses that would indicate where that little scrap of fabric might have come from?"

"The only place that I noticed any pink at all was when we visited the Ellis's. The curtains on one of the windows had a pink ruffle I'd have to compare the two to determine if it was the same shade of pink and type of fabric."

"Would you be able to tell pretty accurately?"

"I could tell you if it was close enough to have it tested."

Wade thought for a few moments before wrapping up the meeting, "It seems to me that we just went from having no suspects to having several. April Randolph and all the folks on that list of investors are now suspects. All have possible motives. Mrs. Randolph has the most motive. She also had the best opportunity based on what we know at this point in time. It's possible that she lied about what she was wearing when she found her husband's body. Let's get a search warrant. I want every stitch of clothing at the Randolph's home checked for blood."

"Deputy Fletcher will meet me at the store in Rayland at nine in the morning. We'll interview these folks again tomorrow. I want her to compare that curtain fabric with the fabric found at the scene. Dodson and Reed will be doing background checks on the people from that list of investors tomorrow. We'll meet back here tomorrow afternoon to compare notes again unless someone solves the case. Then, let me know immediately."

"Sheriff?"

"Yes, Deputy Fletcher?"

"I know that the Carson's will be at church services at nine in the morning. The others may be, too."

"Tomorrow is Sunday isn't it? Alright, let's get a good night's rest. We'll all get started on our assigned duties at one tomorrow afternoon. Does anyone have anything to add?"

"Is there anything that you would like for me to do, Sheriff? Doctor Hughes asked.

Wade looked at him apologetically. "I'm sorry, Doc. I should have given you the opportunity to leave after you gave us your report. I don't have anything for you to do tomorrow."

"That's perfectly alright. I found it all fascinating. Would you mind if I checked into those affair rumors? Sarah, my secretary, delights in knowing everything that is going on in our little town."

"That could be helpful. Thank you."

"If there is nothing else, we'll call it a night."

Wade stayed at the office until everyone else had gone. He hoped Lizzie would see the note he had left in her jeep. If not, he might get a chance to talk with her alone between interviews. He really hoped he could wrap this case up quickly. He didn't want to stay away from Lizzie any longer than necessary.

# CHAPTER 10

Lizzie arrived in Rayland first. She waited in her jeep thinking about what they had learned so far about Paul Randolph's death. She knew most of the people they had interviewed. She couldn't imagine that any of them would be capable of murder. *I've been wrong before.*

Wade parked beside her and nodded. She got out of the jeep and into his pickup.

"Who are we going to start with?" Lizzie asked.

"If the Carson's are home, let's start with them since we're already here."

"I believe they're home. I thought I saw Pearl looking out the window earlier."

"Good, I'd like to wrap this up quickly," Wade said as they walked the short distance from the store to the Carson's house.

Mack and Pearl Carson lived in a modest house that was located next door to their store. It was painted gray with white trim. An array of colorful fall flowers lined the walkway and the front porch. Mack opened the door before Wade and Lizzie stepped onto the walk.

"Mornin', Sheriff. Deputy. What brings you out here on this fine afternoon?"

"I have something that I need to talk with you and Mrs. Carson about," Wade told him.

Mack held the door open for them, "Pearl's in the kitchen doin' the dishes. She made a mighty fine pie. Would ya'll like a slice?"

"No, thank you."

"Suit yourself. Pearl!" he shouted toward the kitchen. "Lizzie Fletcher and the Sheriff are here."

Pearl hurried out of the kitchen, wiping her hands on a dish towel.

"Well, hello. Ya'll have a seat; make yourselves comfortable. Would you like some apple pie? It's homemade."

"I already offered them some. They don't want any."

"Now, how was I supposed to know that?"

Wade and Lizzie sat down patiently listening to the old couple's banter.

"If you'd stop talking once in a while, I could tell ya a few things," Mack said as he grinned, winking at Wade and Lizzie.

"Oh, hush," Pearl said smiling. "What brings ya'll over here today?"

"I have more questions," Wade said.

"Hopefully, we'll have answers," Mack replied.

Wade took that as his cue to begin. "Is it true that you were in a business deal with Paul Randolph?"

"Yep, sure is. It didn't turn out too well," Pearl said laughing.

Mack laughed with her shaking his head. "No, it didn't."

"Tell us about it," Wade said.

Mack began the story. "We were invited to a get together at the Randolph's house one weekend. We thought it was going to be a neighborhood pot luck deal."

"Well, it was," Pearl interrupted, "and it wasn't."

"Turned out to be more sales pitch than anything else," Mack continued. "He had some fella there that had some sort of kitchen gadget."

"One of them do-it-all-kind-of-things," Pearl added.

"Anyway, this fella was lookin' for investors to get his company started," said Mack.

"I didn't like the looks of that man right from the start," Pearl chimed in.

"He made his pitch and showed everybody his contraption," Mack said.

"Then he asked how much he could put everybody down for," Pearl said, rolling her eyes.

"Now, me and Pearl do alright, but we ain't got a lot of extra money floatin' around."

"No, we don't."

"Well, we talked about it for a bit."

"We decided we'd be real put out if it did well, and we didn't have a piece of it," Pearl said.

"I had a little cash in my pocket, so I handed it to the fella."

"Then, he had the gall to ask if we was going to put more in on a regular basis." Pearl was clearly insulted.

"I told him, 'Nope, that's all you're gettin' from us,' " Mack said with a chuckle.

"How much did you invest?" Wade asked.

"A hundred dollars."

"What was Mr. Randolph's part in the business deal?" Wade asked.

"He was sure it was goin' to be the best thing since sliced bread," Pearl said.

"Ya, he was talkin' it up big. He tried to convince everybody we'd be rich as soon as the patent went through," Mack sighed.

"It never did." Pearl added.

"A week later, we saw an ad on TV about a gadget just like it," Mack chuckled. "We were thinkin' it was the gadget we gave that fella money for."

"I saw Paul in the store a day or two later. I told him about the commercial for our gadget," Pearl said. "He turned pale as a ghost and said, 'We haven't made any commercials for it yet.' "

"The next thing we know, the fella is gone, and so is all the money. We were sure glad we hadn't put more into it," Mack said.

"Who else invested with Mr. Randolph and this man?"

Pearl named the same people that were on Wade's list.

"How did those people react to losing their money?" Wade asked.

"We don't know for sure," Pearl said. "I heard a few folks were real put out. They put down a lot of money that they couldn't afford to lose."

"Do you know who?"

Mack and Pearl looked at each other before Mack answered, "Carl Ellis and Paul's in-laws gave him a lot of grief over it."

"I see. How did you feel about losing your money?

"Oh, we figured it was like playing the lottery," Pearl told Wade.

"Yep, you buy a ticket hopin' to get rich but knowin' it ain't likely," Mack added.

Wade smiled at the couple. "I have a few more questions before we get out of your way. It was brought to our attention that Paul Randolph might have been having an affair. Have you seen or heard anything that might confirm that?"

Mack laughed long and loud. His round belly bounced in his mirth. Pearl frowned at him. With a huge sigh, he regained control and only giggled under his breath.

"I don't see why you think that's so funny. Paul was a nice fella. A lot of folks around here felt sorry for him," Pearl scolded.

Mack chuckled. "I'm sorry. I just don't see him runnin' around. He wasn't what most folks would call a ladies' man."

Pearl scowled at her husband. "I never seen nor heard anything about Paul runnin' around."

"What about Mrs. Randolph?" Wade asked Pearl.

Pearl hesitated before answering, "I don't know it for a fact, but I did hear that she's been goin' to Crowell now and again."

"To Crowell?" Wade asked confused.

"Like I said, I don't know it for a fact."

"I see. I'll check into that. Any idea who she might be seeing there?" Wade asked.

"I can't imagine."

"Any idea who killed Paul?" Mack asked.

"Not yet," Wade answered. "I do have to ask where you both were between midnight Friday night and eight fifteen yesterday morning."

"We was right here sound asleep," Pearl answered.

"You was sound asleep. I was wonderin' how on earth a body could snore so loud."

"Mack Carson, I don't snore."

Wade and Lizzie said goodbye to the Carson's as they walked toward Wade's truck.

"Didn't Doctor Hughes say Paul was killed around two?"

"Yes."

"Why did you ask where they were between midnight and eight fifteen?"

"If I don't give an exact time, the people we're questioning aren't sure what time they need an alibi for."

"I hadn't thought of that. Who are we going to see now?" Lizzie asked as they walked.

"I'd like to talk with Carl Ellis again. It will give you a chance to compare that fabric." He looked around before continuing the conversation, "I can't open the truck door for you since we're on official business."

"I understand. I wasn't expecting you to. I've never expected you to do that."

Wade smiled. "I know; that's why I like doing it."

Lizzie smiled as she climbed into the truck. When they were both inside, she said, "I got your note. What did you want to talk to me about?"

"Let's get down the road a little bit. I have a feeling Pearl can read lips," he said as he waved at the woman, peering out the window.

Lizzie laughed, "It wouldn't surprise me. In fact, I have a feeling she knows who April is meeting in Crowell but doesn't want to tell us."

"Me, too," Wade said as he backed his truck onto the pavement and started toward the Ellis farm. When he felt it was safe, he said, "I want to be able to communicate with you off the job. I had an idea last night that I want to run by you."

"What is it?"

"Is that emergency radio at the inn working?"

"Yes, I test it at least once a month."

"I have a small ham radio set at home. We could communicate that way if we are on the same frequency."

"What if someone else is on the same frequency?"

"That type of radio isn't used by a lot of people since cell phones are everywhere. I think we can find a frequency that isn't used much. If we use code names and limit our conversations to once or twice a week, we might be able to keep in touch without anyone raising an eyebrow."

"It's worth a try."

"We'll talk about it more if we have a chance later," Wade assured her as he stopped in front of the Ellis home. "That piece of cloth is in the glove compartment. Try to compare it to the curtains without being too obvious. If it's a close match, we'll get a search warrant.

Carl's pickup was nowhere to be seen. Wade knocked on the door while Lizzie waited behind him. Brandy opened the door cautiously. She peered through the opening. "Carl isn't here."

"I'd like to talk with both of you. May we come in?"

"I suppose so," she said uncertainly as she stepped aside.

"I have more questions for you both. Do you expect Carl back soon?"

"I'm not sure. He went to a meeting in town about the cougar that's been roaming around."

"I see. If you don't mind, I'll visit with you. Maybe, he'll be back before we've finished."

"I guess that will be okay."

"I understand that you and Mr. Ellis were part of a business deal with Paul Randolph."

"Carl was. I didn't have much to do with it."

"Why is that?"

"Carl handles all the business dealings."

"I see. Do you know how much he invested?"

"He said that he put all of his savings into it."

"How did he react to losing that money?"

Brandy's eyes grew wide with fear. "I don't think I've ever seen him that angry."

Wade paused a few minutes. He was about to ask if Brandy

thought Carl wanted revenge or if he was angry enough to kill. He doubted he would get a truthful answer. She was clearly terrified of the man. He chose to ask a different question when he heard a truck stop outside.

"It's been brought to our attention that Mr. Randolph may have been having an affair. Have you seen or heard anything that might confirm that?"

"No," Brandy answered as she looked toward the door.

"Where were you between midnight Friday night and eight fifteen Saturday morning?"

"Well, Carl had gone hunting. I waited up for a while, but I was asleep until the alarm went off at five."

"When did your husband get back?"

"I'm not sure. I think it was around two-thirty."

"What the hell is going on in here?" Carl said as he stormed through the door.

"I'm glad you're back, Mr. Ellis. I have a couple more questions to ask you," Wade said as he stood up.

"Mrs. Ellis, I was just admiring your curtains. Would you mind if I look at them more closely?" Lizzie asked Brandy.

Brandy stood and led Lizzie to the other room. Wade and Carl were alone.

"We've discovered a business deal that you're reported to have been involved in with Paul Randolph. Would you mind giving me the details?"

"Yes, I do mind giving you the details," Carl said mimicking the sheriff.

"Mr. Ellis, everyone involved in that deal is a possible suspect in this case. I was hoping I could eliminate you from the list. I can't do that without your cooperation."

Carl glared at Wade for several minutes. When he realized that Wade wasn't going to back down, he grudgingly asked, "What do you want to know?"

"Were you part of a business deal with Paul Randolph?"

"Yes."

"What happened to the deal?"

"Paul said that inventor took off with the money."

"Do you think that was the truth?"

"No, I don't."

"What do you think happened?"

"The other guy took off. Maybe he took all our money; maybe he didn't. I've been sayin' all along that Paul had it or knew where it is."

"Does anyone else think that way?"

"No! Bunch of idiots. They keep saying Paul lost his money and his in-laws' money, too."

"How much did you lose?"

"Five thousand dollars."

"That's quite a bit of money."

Carl was fuming. It seemed that he was trying to contain himself, but he was unable. "I told that little weasel that if I found out he had the money or knew how to get it, I'd beat him to a pulp. He started makin' promises I knew he wouldn't keep. He said he'd pay back every nickel if it took him the rest of his life."

"Did he pay anything?"

"He paid me a whopping fifty dollars. He swore he'd pay something every month until it was paid off."

"I see. We've been led to believe that Mr. Randolph might have been having an affair. Would you have any information to share about that?"

Carl sneered. "That little wimp? I still can't believe he found a woman willin' to marry him in the first place. No, I don't know anything about that."

"One more question. Where were you between the hours of midnight Friday night and eight fifteen Saturday morning?"

"I was out huntin' that cougar. I probably got back around two o'clock and went right to bed."

"That's all I have for now. I'd appreciate it if you'd stay in the county until this is all cleared up."

"Are you saying that I killed Paul?" Carl was furious.

"I'm saying that we're questioning everyone that was involved in that business deal. Losing money tends to make people angry. Sometimes angry enough to kill. You're obviously still angry. Is there anyone who can verify that you were out hunting during the time in question?

Carl stared angrily at the sheriff, "No."

Wade left Carl to ponder their conversation. He followed Lizzie to the truck. They didn't speak until they had driven off the Ellis property. Wade kept looking in his rear view mirror.

"What did you find out, Lizzie?"

The color is very close, but it's a completely different fabric. Those curtains are made of a light weight fabric. The scrap we have is heavier with a different weave."

"We'll stop chasing that angle unless something else comes up. It was a long shot anyway. We'll stop by the Brinkman's and the Preston's before we go to Maddie and Drew's place. That new couple, what was their name?"

"It's Dylan."

"Why can't I remember that name? Anyway, they weren't part of Paul's business deal. We won't need to see them. We'll talk to April Randolph again before we go visit the Flynn's. By then it should be about time to head back to town."

"Don't forget we have to get my jeep."

"We'll do that after we talk to Mrs. Randolph."

Nick Brinkman was getting out of his car as the sheriff's truck turned into the drive. He waited for his visitors to get out of the truck.

"Hello, Sheriff. More questions?"

"A few more. It shouldn't take long."

"Do you mind if we sit on the front porch again? The paint smell is still strong."

"That'll do. Is your wife home? I need to speak with her, too," Wade said.

"I'm here. I just made a fresh pitcher of tea. Would you like some?"

"Thank you, no. This shouldn't take long. We have more people to see."

"Well, have a seat and ask away," Nick said.

"I understand you were in a business deal with Paul Randolph that didn't go very well."

"Yes, we were."

"Tell me about it."

"Paul was so sure it was going to be a moneymaker. He was talking it up big. We all met at his house one night. The inventor was there demonstrating the product. Then, they started putting the squeeze on us."

"Did you invest?"

"We put in a thousand dollars," Nick said.

"No, we didn't," Emily interjected.

"We didn't? What do you mean?"

"April was upset because they weren't going to make their goal. They wanted each couple to put up five thousand dollars."

"You put in another four thousand dollars?" Nick asked in disbelief.

"No, I told her we didn't have any more to invest. She got angry and tore up your check."

"So, we didn't invest?"

"No, we didn't"

"That explains why that check hasn't gone through the bank yet," Nick said with a confused look on his face. "I don't think Paul knew that. He came to see me after that inventor disappeared. He swore he'd pay us back. He apologized over and over."

"Did you come to a repayment agreement?" Wade asked.

"No, I didn't want him to pay me back at all. It wasn't his fault that guy was a thief. He kept insisting, so I told him he could pay us back after he had payed everyone else back. He seemed to be satisfied with that."

"Do you know anything about Mr. Randolph having an affair?"

"Paul? No, I can't imagine Paul cheating on April," Nick answered.

"Not Paul. He wasn't that kind of man," Emily added.

"What about Mrs. Randolph?"

Emily watched her husband closely.

"April? No, I don't think she's seeing anybody on the side," Nick answered

Emily looked down for a moment before looking at Wade. "I haven't heard anything about her having an affair."

"Where were you between midnight Friday night and eight fifteen Saturday morning?"

"I was working. I took the Sheriff's shift so that he could take his wife on a weekend trip for their anniversary," Nick said.

"I was here all night. I fell asleep while reading," Emily told Wade.

"That's all the questions for now," Wade told them. "If you think of anything, please, give us a call."

"We will," Nick assured him.

# CHAPTER 11

Wade and Lizzie drove to the Preston's after leaving the Brinkman's. Wade was deep in thought during the short drive.

Dara Preston was standing in the yard with her hands on her hips when they drove up. She seemed to be talking to someone, but Lizzie saw no one else. They got out of the truck and walked to the house.

"How's that?" a voice said from above.

"How's that, Grandma?" Dara asked.

"Not yet," Grandma Preston answered from inside the house.

"What's going on?" Wade asked.

Dara jumped. "Oh Sheriff, you scared me. I didn't hear you drive up."

"I'm sorry. Is there a problem?"

"Only with our satellite dish. We're having reception issues. Kent climbed up there to see if the dish needed clearing. He found a bird nest in it."

"It's working!" Grandma shouted from inside.

"It's working, Kent," Dara said relaying the message.

Kent walked carefully toward the ladder that was leaning at the side of the house. He climbed down and hurried to greet his guests.

"Hello, Sheriff. Lizzie. What brings you out here again today?"

"More questions," Wade replied.

"We'll do our best to answer them."

They followed Kent and Dara inside. Grandma Preston was engrossed in finding something to watch now that the satellite was working. She sat in a recliner scanning through the channels with the remote.

"What can we do for you, Sheriff?" Kent asked.

"I understand you were involved in a business deal with Paul Randolph."

"Yes, we were."

"I also understand that it didn't turn out very well."

"You can say that again!" Dara snorted.

"How much money did you lose?"

"We lost five thousand dollars between us," Kent answered. "We put in twenty-five hundred each."

"Did Mr. Randolph promise to pay you back?"

"Yes, he did. We didn't expect him to do that. We knew it was a risky investment," Kent replied.

"Did he pay you anything?"

"No, we told him to take care of the other investors first. Especially, those who were really angry about the whole thing. We said we'd think about letting him pay us back after that."

"What was his reaction?"

"He was relieved. He didn't have that kind of money. If he did, he would have invested it rather than looking for others to invest."

"How much money was needed for the deal?"

"Fifty thousand dollars."

"Was that much raised?"

"I don't think so, but I'm not sure."

"It wasn't," Dara said. "April was complaining about it the day after the business meeting. They had been counting on each couple putting in at least five thousand."

"Who was angry with Mr. Randolph about losing the money?"

Dara sighed, "April was furious. I believe her parents were, too. I'm pretty sure they blamed Paul."

"Carl Ellis was on the rampage for weeks," Kent added. "Paul had gotten to the point that he was afraid to leave his house."

"There has been a suggestion that Mr. Randolph might have been having an affair. Would either of you have knowledge of that?"

"No, Paul loved April. He was afraid of her, but he loved her. He wasn't the kind of man to cheat on someone," Kent assured Wade.

"You're certain of that?"

"Yes."

"What about Mrs. Randolph?"

"I don't think she's seeing anyone else," Dara said. "She was often mean to him, but I believe she loved Paul."

"Where were you between midnight Friday night and eight fifteen Saturday morning?"

"I went to bed after the evening news at ten thirty. I slept until the alarm went off at seven. I had plowing that I intended to do the next morning," Kent answered.

"I worked until about one in my office before going to bed. I got up early and drove to Wichita Falls," Dara responded.

"I can vouch for both of them, Sheriff, if needed. I had insomnia. I was up until about two o'clock watching a movie."

"Are we suspects?" Dara asked.

"We're looking into everyone who lost money in that business deal."

Wade's cell phone rang as they said goodbye and walked toward the truck.

"Adams, alright meet us at Maddie's place," Wade said before he ended the call. "Dodson and Reed are going to meet us with the search warrant I asked for," he told Lizzie.

They left the Preston's home and went directly to the Clifton's house. They could hear the baby crying as they tapped on the door.

"I guess we don't have to worry about waking him up," Lizzie said.

Maddie opened the door, frustrated and near tears. "I'll be with you in minute."

Wade and Lizzie sat down at the little dining table. They watched helplessly as Maddie tried to comfort the crying infant. Drew hurried in with a fresh bottle of formula. The hungry little boy ate greedily.

"Whew, this kid has some lungs," Drew said as he sat at the table with the others.

"Dodson and Reed are going to meet us here. I hope that's

alright," Wade told them.

"That's no problem. Well, what did you two decide?" Maddie asked.

Wade told her of their decision. He quoted the already drafted press release to her. He added that Dodson and Reed were onboard.

"That's good. As long as you two can stay apart, it should be fine," she teased. "I know that isn't what brought you here today. You could have phoned that news in."

"No, it isn't. We have a list of people who were involved in a business deal with Paul Randolph. Your names are on the list."

"We invested a little bit. We didn't have much to spare with the baby coming," Drew said.

"How much did you lose?"

"We put in five hundred."

"How did you deal with that loss?"

"I had some money saved. I had planned to take Maddie on a nice vacation before we found out she was pregnant. I thought since I wasn't going to be using it as planned that I might as well invest it. The product was great. I could see doubling my money in a few months."

"I see. It wasn't a financial setback for you then?"

"No, in fact I only invested part of what I had saved. The rest went into a college fund for this little guy," Drew said caressing his young son's head.

"It has been suggested to us that Mr. Randolph might have been having an affair. It was also suggested that Mrs. Randolph might have been seeing someone. Would either of you have any information pertaining to that possibility?"

"No, I haven't heard anything like that. Have you, Drew?"

"No. Do you think they were?" Drew asked the sheriff.

"I don't know. It's a possible motive for Paul's murder."

Drew went to the door when he saw another vehicle in their driveway. "It's Dodson and Reed," he said. Should I invite them in?"

"Yes, I want them in to see our little Brody."

The deputies came inside. They praised the child as he ate to the delight of his parents before excusing themselves and returning to the car.

Maddie burped her now sleeping child. Drew took the baby from her and carried him to his bed.

"I did see April in town one day with a man I didn't know. They were having lunch at the steak house. I didn't think anything of it at the time," Maddie said.

"What did he look like?"

"He was clean cut, wore a suit, and had dark hair. He was sitting down, so I can't give you an idea of his height. He looked to be between one hundred eighty and two hundred pounds. I'd guess he was between thirty-five and forty years old."

"Thanks, Maddie. I'll compare that with other descriptions. I have to ask one more thing. Where were you between midnight Friday night and eight fifteen Saturday morning?"

"Right here, up with the baby every four hours," Maddie sighed.

"He was up every two hours. We took turns with him," Drew added.

After leaving the Clifton's, the sheriff and his deputies drove to April Randolph's home. A woman unknown to them answered the door.

"Hello, I'm Sheriff Adams. This is Deputy Fletcher, Deputy Dodson, and Deputy Reed. We'd like to speak with Mrs. Randolph."

"Please, come in. April is lying down. I'm her sister June."

June Powell was taller and thinner than her sister. She had the same dark hair, but her eyes were brown rather than green.

"Please, sit down. I'll see if April is awake."

"If you don't mind, I'd like to ask you a few questions first."

"Certainly," she sat down and waited patiently.

"Do you know of anyone who might have wanted Mr. Randolph dead?" Wade went right to the point.

"Paul was such a sweet man. I can't imagine who would have killed him."

"What sort of relationship did Mr. Randolph have with your parents?"

June sighed, "I would say it was rocky at best. Especially, with Dad. He has always felt that no one is good enough for his little girls. He made life miserable for Paul."

"Why would he do that?"

"I suppose he was hoping to run Paul off like he did my husband."

"What did your father do in your situation?"

A tear slid down the woman's cheek. "Forgive me," she said as she wiped her face. "I only recently found out that my father paid Walt a large sum of money to leave me. We've been divorced for two years. It wouldn't surprise me to find that he offered to pay Paul. The difference is that Paul loved April."

"Would your father have resorted to murder?"

"Dad may be a lot of things, but he's not a murderer."

"We've been led to believe that Mr. Randolph may have been having an affair. Would you have any knowledge of that?"

"No."

"Is it possible that your sister was having an affair?"

"I suppose anything is possible, but I don't believe April would have cheated on Paul. She was mean and nasty to him, but she loved him."

"How do you know?"

"Because I know my sister."

"I don't have any more questions for you at the moment. I'd like to talk with Mrs. Randolph now if you don't mind."

"I'll get her."

June left the room. A few moments later April entered the room alone.

"Do you have any news, Sheriff?"

"Not yet, ma'am, but I do have more questions. We also have a search warrant."

Dodson handed the search warrant to her. She read it before

returning it to the deputy.

"Search all you want. I'll answer your questions, anything to help find out who did this to my Paul."

Dodson and Reed searched the property while Wade conducted his interview.

"I understand that Mr. Randolph was involved in a business deal with some of your neighbors," Wade said.

"Oh, that was a total catastrophe," April said shaking her head. "Some of them didn't invest very much. I was upset at the time, but I'm so glad now that they didn't. Most of those who did were very nice about the whole thing."

"Most of them?"

"Yes."

"Were some of the investors angry?"

Carl Ellis was livid. He stormed over here one night and demanded his money back. Paul tried to explain to him that we didn't have the money, but Carl wouldn't hear it. He told Paul he wanted it all back, or he would take it out of his hide. Of course, all Paul could do was promise to pay it back over time."

"Was anyone else angry?"

April answered reluctantly, "Yes, my parents weren't happy either. Paul promised to pay them back over time, too."

"Did he make any payments that you are aware of?"

"I know he made a payment of one thousand dollars to my parents last month. Other than that, I couldn't say."

"How much did your parents lose in the deal?"

"Five thousand dollars."

"How much did you and Mr. Randolph lose?"

"We didn't have any money to invest. He was to get a percentage of the profits for helping to bring investors in."

"Did the others know that at the time?"

"I don't think so."

"Do you think it's possible that one of them found out?"

"I don't see how. My parents were the only ones who knew about it other than Paul and myself. I'm quite sure they didn't tell anyone."

"What are your parents' names'?"

"Monroe and Lorene Gleason."

"How can I get in touch with them?"

"They've been out of the country for the past two weeks. They are on a tour of Europe. They aren't due back until next week."

"They won't come back in this circumstance?"

"I'm sure they would, but I don't know how to get in touch with them. They get in touch with me."

"When did you last hear from them?"

"Thursday. I don't expect them to call again until later in the week."

"Is your sister in contact with them?"

"No," April said sadly, "June hasn't spoken with them for several months."

"Do you believe that Mr. Randolph might have been having an affair?"

"Of course not! Why would you say such a thing?"

"You're the person who suggested it to us."

"I did?"

"Yes, ma'am. I can have Deputy Fletcher read back her notes if you'd like."

"I don't remember saying anything like that."

Wade nodded at Lizzie. She flipped through her notebook. Finding the entry, she read, "Sheriff Adams asked if Mrs. Randolph recognized a small piece of pink fabric. She said she did not. It was not part of her belongings. Mrs. Randolph then asked if the sheriff thought Mr. Randolph was having an affair."

"Well, I guess I did," April said quietly. "I was a mess yesterday, Sheriff. I don't why I would say something like that. I'm certain Paul was faithful to me."

"More so than you were to him?"

"What do you mean?"

"Have you been having an affair, Mrs. Randolph?"

"I most certainly have not!"

"Who is the man you have been seen with at the steak house on at least two occasions?"

April was speechless for a moment. "If you must know, he's my father's attorney. We have lunch together when he comes to town."

"What is his name?"

"Carter Nolan."

"When did you last see him?

"Two weeks ago."

"Was the meeting for business or pleasure?"

April covered her face with her hands. "It was business. He had divorce papers for me to sign." She dropped her hands to her lap, "But I didn't sign them. I didn't want a divorce."

"Did Paul?"

"No, it was Dad. He wanted me to divorce Paul."

"You mentioned that you had an argument with your husband the night before he died. What was that argument about?"

April sighed, "Paul had been drinking heavily since that business deal fell apart. I confronted him about it weeks ago. He promised he would stop. I smelled liquor on his breath that night. I was angry that he hadn't stopped as he promised. We argued about it for some time. I said some mean, hateful things. He told me he was a grown man, and if he wanted a drink, he would have one. Paul had never spoken to me that way before. I went into the bedroom and slammed the door. He always followed me to apologize after a fight. He didn't this time."

"What time did you have the argument?"

"The evening news was on when he came in from the barn. So, I'd say between ten and ten thirty. We probably argued for at least an hour. The Tonight Show was on when I turned the television off."

"You didn't see him again that night?"

"No, I didn't. I went to sleep. I don't know if he came into the bedroom or not."

"What time did you wake up?"

"It was seven thirty."

"Were you aware that your husband had a life insurance policy naming you as beneficiary?"

"Yes, I knew."

"Do you know how much it was for?"

"Yes, two hundred fifty thousand dollars," April answered, seeming to realize that it made her a prime suspect in her husband's death. "I didn't kill my husband, Sheriff."

"Look at it from my point of view. You had an argument with your husband shortly before his death. You found his body this morning. You had access to the murder weapon. The shoeprints we found near the body match the shoes you were wearing. You are the beneficiary of a large life insurance policy. Don't leave the county until this is resolved, Mrs. Randolph."

Wade and Lizzie left April sitting open-mouthed in her chair.

After taking Lizzie to her jeep, Wade led the way to the Flynn's house. They had invested only one hundred dollars. It did hurt them financially, but they had since recovered. Paul had invited several people from the state hospital to the business meeting. Brian was the only one who had attended. They knew nothing about either of the Randolph's having affairs and were sleeping during the times in question.

The meeting with Dodson and Reed revealed nothing that would point the team in the direction of the killer. Their search of the Randolph property had been fruitless. Carl Ellis and April Randolph were at the top of the list of suspects, but the little evidence they had was circumstantial at best.

Wade couldn't rule out the others on the list. The remaining investors didn't have verifiable alibis He felt that the Brinkman's had been holding something back, but he had no way of knowing if it was related to Paul's death. Carter Nolan was indeed the Gleason family attorney. Wade talked with him and learned that April had told the truth about their meetings.

Lizzie completed her training and helped around the sheriff's office for a week. Wade told her that he didn't want to keep her from the inn. He was to call her if he needed her help.

Lizzie had hoped that Paul's murderer would be caught by now. Her heart ached for Wade. The possibility that she might not see him again for a very long time depressed her. Lizzie tried to stay busy, but her thoughts kept returning to Wade and the mystery they had been trying to solve together.

# CHAPTER 12

Lizzie kept busy for the next few days, preparing for the upcoming Halloween party. The Wagner clan had booked the party. They were expecting at least thirty people for the event. Lizzie wanted the first Halloween Party at the inn to be perfect.

The Fletchers had been buying assorted Halloween items online throughout the year. They hoped that Halloween parties would become an annual event. James particularly liked the radio controlled items.

This party was to be a costume party with lots of food and a haunted hayride. James and Ellen would be the judges for the costume contest. Dan and Lizzie were in charge of haunting the hayride. Granny was to act as hostess and greet the guests when they arrived.

The walkway to the front door of the Paradise Creek Inn was lined with solar-lighted pumpkin heads. Bales of hay on the front porch made a seat for the grim reaper as he waited for the guests to arrive. A garland of fall leaves lined the porch railing. A wreath made of fall flowers on the front door framed a blinking sign with the words "Enter If You Dare."

The entry was decorated with assorted spider webs and creepy crawly creatures. Granny, dressed as a witch, made a show of picking up a realistic looking rat or toad and dropping it into the smoking cauldron beside her as the guests arrived. She asked them all to write their names on a card and then cackled as she dropped the cards into the cauldron as well.

"Excellent, excellent. Wait until you see what happens when this spell is complete," she said in her best witch voice.

Ellen, dressed as a ghostly maid, led the guests to the large dining area. The large room was decorated with beautifully carved pumpkins, fall flowers, and assorted skeletons. The hors d'oeuvres and drinks had been prepared with the Halloween theme in mind.

The patio was decorated with hay bales, carved pumpkins, and solar lanterns. Two scarecrows stood propped against a light post. Floating in the swimming pool were severed legs, arms, and the occasional severed head.

At the end of the patio stood a trailer with hay bales arranged so that anyone participating in the haunted hayride would be able to see everything. James was dressed as Frankenstein's monster. He would be acting as the driver for the haunted hayride.

Dan and Lizzie were dressed in black. Lizzie was a cat when mingling with the guests, while Dan was Darth Vader. Their costumes were ideal for the quick changes they had planned during the haunted hayride.

Eli and Jan Wagner were the first to arrive. They had chosen Mr. and Mrs. Potato Head costumes to accommodate Jan's growing baby belly.

"Lizzie, this place looks amazing!" Jan exclaimed.

"I'm glad you like it. I love those costumes," Lizzie replied.

"I had to have something large enough to go over Junior."

"Junior? Is it a boy?" Ellen asked.

"We don't know. The baby refuses to be in the right position during the sonograms. Until he or she decides to cooperate, this is Junior," Jan said as she patted her baby bump.

Mike and Faith Foreman arrived dressed as Batman and Robin. Eli shook Mike's hand and hugged his sister.

Faith hurried over to hug Lizzie. She looked into Lizzie's eyes and hugged her again.

"Hi, Faith. I don't mind the hugs, but what's up?" Lizzie teased.

"I saw the announcement in the paper about your new job. Is it really over between you and Wade?"

"Yes, it is. At least for now. He needs my help with this case until he can hire another female deputy, or Maddie comes back. We can't work together and be involved. It could jeopardize the case, the department, and his career."

"What if it takes months or even years for the case to be solved?"

"We know that's a possibility. We discussed every alternative that came to mind. We agreed this was our only option."

"Lizzie, Wade is a very attractive man. You know as well as I do that every single woman in town is going to be very happy that he's available."

"I know. I'd rather not think about it. I'm just taking things one day at a time," Lizzie answered sadly.

Dan tapped Lizzie on the shoulder. "I hate to interrupt you, but it's time."

Faith hugged Lizzie again. "We'll talk later."

The guests were led to the patio as Dan and Lizzie changed costumes. Lizzie could hear her dad giving instructions as she got into place.

"Ladies and gentlemen, please take your seats on the trailer," he said trying his best to sound like his character. "Please keep your hands and feet within the confines of the trailer during this ride. I know not what we may encounter. It would be a shame if some of you were to be taken from us."

Everyone laughed nervously as they found their places. James took his place on the tractor seat. He looked to see that everyone was seated before saying, "I'm accustomed to screams on this journey. If you want me to stop for any reason, you must yell, 'Frankenstein! Please, stop!' However, I strongly advise against stopping," he said and started the tractor.

As the hayride left the lighted area around the house, guests could see a skeleton in ragged clothing beneath a tree. Clearly visible was a name tag that said "Martin."

"That one has your name on it!" One of the guests exclaimed.

Lizzie took that as her cue. She now wore a werewolf costume, and she posed as if she were howling at the moon. James pressed the remote control, turning on a dim spotlight and the sound of a wolf howling. The guests screamed as she ran toward them when the ride began to move away.

Inside a storage shed at the edge of the trees, Dan waited in a fanged clown costume with an axe. The trailer was directly in front of the door when he burst through. He laughed wickedly, swinging the ax through the air as they drove past. He laughed at the screams as he moved to his next position.

An eerie mist rose from the pond. Giant spiders crawled around the water's edge and snakes slithered into the water as the group drove past. Some of the guests shuddered as a low moan seemed to come through the mist.

A cemetery lay to the north of the pond. In the midst of the burial markers, a coffin waited beside an open grave. The guests began to recognize the names on the tombstones. They were the names of those on the trailer.

The lid of the coffin opened slowly at first. Ghostly fingers were visible as they slowly wrapped themselves around the edge. Screams erupted from the hay ride as the lid was flung open. A ghostly corpse slowly climbed out.

"Look out!" someone shouted.

Lizzie began following the trailer and smiled inwardly at the screams. She let the trailer move out of sight before running to her next station.

The hay ride wove around the property toward the east pasture. Animatronic creatures and ghostly sounds greeted them on all sides. James could tell that some of the guests believed the worst was over, while others expected something at every turn. He took the remote control from his pocket as he neared Dan's next station.

The whinny of a horse and the pounding of hooves could be heard. It was getting closer. The guests looked all around but could see nothing. Suddenly, one of the guests screamed.

"Look, over there!"

A horse with glowing eyes was nearing the trailer. James used the spot light on his tractor to illuminate its rider. There sat a man. His head was not on his shoulders but under his left arm. The eyes on the head began to glow as the rider laughed eerily. Suddenly, the rider threw the head toward the trailer. It landed on the opposite side and burst into flames when James pressed the remote control.

Dan had trained his horse well. He gave the command for her to rear and whinny as the hayride moved away. He laughed at the screams coming from the guests and rode quickly to the next station where he would join Lizzie.

As the hayride approached Paradise Creek, Dan and Lizzie waited out of sight in the creek bed dressed as zombies. When the strategically placed zombie parts began to move, they began to crawl up the bank.

"Nothing to worry about. They're fake," one of the guests said.

The two live zombies took that as their cue to move faster and toward the trailer. Screams pierced their ears as they grabbed for the edge of the trailer.

"Those aren't fake!"

James chuckled to himself as he drove back toward the house. He hoped Lizzie and Dan were having as much fun as he was.

Dan and Lizzie rode Dan's horse to their last station. Lizzie slid off and rushed to open the barn door. Dan rode the horse into the barn while Lizzie quickly changed her costume. She pushed the barn door closed as Dan came out in his costume.

They hurried to the patio and stood in their appointed places. Granny had exchanged her witch costume for that of the grim reaper. She waited in the shadows under a tree. Ellen waited on the patio to welcome their guests back.

James drove the tractor back to its original position and killed the engine. "Ladies and gentlemen, I hope we didn't lose anyone. You'll find refreshments inside."

Ellen said in her most ghostly voice, "This way, please."

The guests climbed down from the trailer. They stopped suddenly as someone screamed. The grim reaper had appeared, carrying the name cards of the guests. The reapers sickle slashed left and right but made no contact. As the guests ran toward the patio, the reaper threw the name cards into the air before it disappeared into the shadows.

Everyone was laughing as they made their way into the house. They hadn't noticed that the two scarecrows had joined them. The scarecrows each chose a guest and lightly tapped them on the shoulder. The guests screamed at the sight of the now living scarecrows as the remainder of the room erupted in nervous laughter.

While the guests enjoyed refreshments, Dan and Lizzie took the opportunity to return to their original costumes. James and Ellen chose the winners of the costume contest.

There were a variety of costumes. There were mummies, vampires, ghosts, zombies, and a couple dressed as a peanut butter and jelly sandwich. The winners wore homemade Little Red Riding Hood and the Big Bad Wolf costumes.

When they said goodnight to their guests, the inn keepers relaxed, discussing the hayride. They decided that the party and the hayride were a success but that a few changes would be made for the next one.

"I don't know about anyone else, but I'm beat," Lizzie said. "Let's clean this up tomorrow."

"No argument from me," Dan replied.

"We'll be over in the morning," Ellen said.

Lizzie said goodnight to Dan and her family before she locked the door. She was getting ready for bed when she heard the emergency radio squawk in the office.

"This is Mesquite calling Sagebrush, over."

Lizzie hurried to the office. "This is Sagebrush. Go ahead, Mesquite," Lizzie answered smiling.

# CHAPTER 13

Nick Brinkman was on swing shift this month. He alternated shifts with the sheriff and another deputy each month. This three in the afternoon to eleven in the evening shift was the one he liked best. He usually found this part of his job to be the most enjoyable. He enjoyed tormenting any inmate that might be occupying one of the cells while he was working. He often called upon various women to keep him company when the jail was empty.

His heart wasn't really into either of those recreational activities tonight. He was worried. He had felt this way since Paul Randolph's death. He knew that Wade Adams was an excellent investigator. It concerned him that the Wilbarger County Sheriff's office seemed no closer to solving the case than they were the day the body was discovered a month ago.

Nick shuddered at the thought of Paul being killed with one of his own farm implements before his thoughts turned to Emily. He wondered how she would have reacted had he been the one murdered. He hadn't exactly been a model husband. Far from it.

He promised himself that he would change. Tonight. Right now. He would make it up to her. He would be the husband that she deserved. Picking up the phone, he called his wife.

Emily Brinkman looked at the Caller ID before answering the phone. "Why is Nick calling? He never calls me while he's on duty," she wondered aloud. "Hello," Emily answered warily.

"Hi, Em. It's me. How's it going?"

"Fine. What's wrong?"

"Nothing. I just wanted to check in and make sure you're okay."

"I'm fine. I've been looking out the window at the full moon. Have you noticed?"

"Ya, I saw it on my break. It's pretty isn't it?"

"Beautiful."

"I looked at the duty roster tonight. I'm off Thanksgiving Day."

"That's good," she replied. "What do you want to do for Thanksgiving?"

"I thought you might want to have a traditional holiday for a change."

"Thanksgiving is next week."

"We can spend it with your folks if you want."

"That would be nice."

"Em, will you do me a favor?"

"What?"

"Don't leave the house tonight. Keep the doors and windows locked."

"What's wrong, Nick?"

"Nothing really."

"Nick?"

He hesitated before answering. "I've been thinking about Paul's death. I realized that I couldn't live with myself if anything were to happen to you."

"I think that's probably the nicest thing you've ever said to me."

"I know we've hit a rough patch lately, and I know it's my fault. I'd like to try to work it out."

"I'd like that."

"We'll make plans when I get home. I'll see you soon."

"Bye."

Nick sighed as he hung up the phone. He was still worried. He couldn't get over the feeling that he had missed something important. Something he should have seen or known. He sat deep in thought until the office phone rang. He answered quickly, and his mind was back on the job.

"Foard County Sheriff's office. Brinkman speaking."

"Is this Nick Brinkman?"

"Yes, ma'am. What can I do for you?'

"This is Irene Cutter. I hate to bother you, but I'm concerned about something."

"What is it, Mrs. Cutter?'

"There's something lying in the ditch across the road from my house. It's probably nothing, but it looks suspicious to me. I'm not able to go out and check for myself. I was wondering if you would stop by here on your way home to see what it is."

"I'd be happy to. I'm on duty here for another two hours, but I'll stop by on my way home."

"Thank you, Nick."

Nick smiled as he hung up the phone. Irene Cutter was one of his neighbors who lived west of Rayland. She had lived there alone since her husband passed away ten years before. She was as feisty and independent as any woman Nick had ever known. She never would have called him had she been able to walk out to investigate herself. Unfortunately, she was confined to her house with a broken leg.

When his shift was over, Nick drove to the home of Mrs. Cutter. She directed him to the object in the ditch. From her front porch, he could see something in the moonlight. It appeared that something or someone lay in the ditch a short distance down the road. She was convinced it was a dead body.

Nick assured her that he had everything under control. As a precaution, he went to the trunk and took out the shotgun that was kept there. He could have easily walked the short distance but got into his car and drove toward the ditch stopping so that the headlights illuminated the area. He got out of the car and walked slowly toward the object.

As Nick got closer, he realized that it was a carpet. He thought that it had probably been intended for the dump but for some reason wound up in this ditch. It was positioned so that from Irene's porch it appeared to be a body.

He laid the shotgun on the passenger seat and drove back to the house. Irene had been watching from her front door, balancing on her good leg with the help of crutches. While they stood in the doorway talking, they were startled by the eerie scream that they had heard so often. Irene quickly said goodnight and closed her door. Nick went back to his car and called in his report before driving home.

As Nick crossed the county line on the way to his house, he noticed something in the moonlight. Someone was running through the trees near the river bank. He really wanted to go home, but someone might be in trouble. It wasn't safe to be out at night with that cougar around.

He reluctantly drove over to investigate. As he got out of the car, he lost sight of the runner in the trees. He walked in the direction he had last seen the person. He called out but got no response. He decided that it was probably someone hunting but listened a few minutes longer. As he walked back toward his car, he noticed something on the radio antenna. He pulled it from the wire and walked around to the driver's side for a closer look. He sat in the driver's seat to examine his find.

He turned at the unmistakable sound of a shotgun being cocked.

• • •

Sheriff Wade Adams woke to the sound of his phone ringing. He looked at the clock before answering. He knew it was going to be bad news. No one ever called at six in the morning with good news.

"Adams," he answered groggily. "Who? Where?" Wade sighed. "Wake up the team. Tell them to meet us at the office. Have Fletcher meet us at Maddie's place. Let's keep this within our department until we find out what we're dealing with."

Wade hung up and rubbed his temples. He had been afraid someone else would die before he could solve Paul's murder. He didn't know if the two deaths were connected, but he still felt responsible.

He dressed quickly and drove to his office. Deputy Brandon Lodge had been working the night shift and had taken the call. He had a fresh pot of coffee brewing and all the information the team would need waiting for them.

"Morning, Lodge. Who called in the report?"

"Carl Ellis. He said he found the victim this morning immediately before he called us."

"Does the victim's wife know yet?"

"I don't know, sir."

"Well, Baker should be in soon. You can go home when he arrives."

"I'd like to go out with the team on this one if you don't mind, sir."

Wade grinned at his deputy. "Are you getting tired of office work?"

"Yes, sir."

"Alright, if Baker isn't here by the time we leave, you can meet us out there. When is your turn on the graveyard shift over?"

"At the end of the month, sir."

Wade looked up as Doctor Hughes bustled into the office.

"Good morning, Doc."

"Good morning, Sheriff. What are we going to find this morning?"

"Nick Brinkman was found dead in his car this morning," Wade informed him.

"I don't believe I've ever met Mr. Brinkman."

Baker came in followed by the rest of the deputies who would make up the days investigative team.

"Baker, you'll be running the office today. If the rest of you will join me in the conference room, Lodge will give us a quick briefing on this case."

The team replied, "Yes, sir," in unison as they went to their assigned places.

Dressed in her new uniform, Lizzie waited near the Clifton's home. She didn't know what had happened other than someone had been found dead early this morning. She had been given no information other than to wait at Maddie's until the team arrived.

She was relieved when Wade stopped his truck and motioned for her to get in. As she buckled her seat beat, he told her what he knew.

"Does Emily know yet?" Lizzie asked.

"I don't know. Your job will be the same as it was before. Provide comfort and pay attention."

"Yes, sir. Are we going there now?"

"Not yet. I want to look at the scene. I'll find out if Emily has been informed. If she hasn't, someone will go with you to her house. Telling someone that a loved one is dead is a very unpleasant job. I want someone with more experience to tell her."

When the sheriff and his team arrived, Carl got into his pickup and led them to Nick's body. Carl turned his vehicle around so that it was facing away from Nick's car before getting out.

"Lizzie, I'd like you to hang back and take notes. Keep anyone away who isn't part of our team. If you need help, give a shout."

"Yes, sir," Lizzie answered. She didn't particularly want to see what had happened to Nick anyway.

They both got out of the truck, and Wade approached Carl.

"Mr. Ellis, I understand you found the body."

"I did."

"About what time was that?"

"I'd say it was around five thirty this mornin'."

"How did you happen to find him?"

"I usually get up at five every mornin'. I looked out the window while I was waitin' for my breakfast. It was light enough that I could see a car parked on my land. I went out to run whoever it was off. That's when I found him."

"Did you touch him or anything else?"

"Na. When I got close enough to see the driver's door was open, I figured something wasn't right. I knew right off he was dead when I saw him."

"What did you do then?"

"I drove back to the house to call you. I've been waitin' there since then."

"Do you happen to know if Mrs. Brinkman has been informed?"

"Not as far as I know. I haven't told anybody else. I didn't even tell my woman what had happened."

"You don't think she might have overheard your phone conversation?"

"I took the phone outside. She was getting our daughter up for school anyway."

"What did you see when you got to the car?"

"Nick was kind of laid over in the seat. There was blood all over him and the inside of the car. I could see his hand hanging down. I knew he was a goner."

"I'd like for you to wait here until we've finished. I may have more questions for you."

"I wasn't plannin' on leavin' anyway," Carl answered with a sneer. "I don't like folks on my land."

"Yes, you've said that before." Wade looked as if he wanted to say a lot more but chose to walk away instead.

Carl sat on the tailgate of his truck to watch every move the sheriff's team made.

"What do you think, Doc?" Wade asked as the doctor moved away from the body.

"I'd say he's been dead several hours. He was killed by a gunshot wound to the chest, most likely a shotgun. I've done all that I can do here. He can be loaded into the truck now."

The deputies helped move Nick Brinkman's body from his car to the medical examiner's truck. As Doctor Hughes drove away, the team began to examine the car thoroughly. They dusted for prints, took blood samples, and searched the car for any evidence that might be useful in finding Nick's murderer.

Wade was bagging the shotgun when he heard Dodson say, "Uh oh!"

"What did you find, Dodson?"

Dodson put his discovery in an evidence bag. He looked at the sheriff. "You're not going to like this, sir," he said as he handed the bag to his boss.

Wade took the bag. Inside the plastic evidence bag was a scrap of pink fabric. He looked at his deputy. "You're right. I don't like this." Wade sighed. "Let's keep this to ourselves for the time being," he told the team. "Does anyone else have anything we need to discuss before we have the car towed into town?"

"The soil is fairly deep here. I found some footprints that led away from the car but stopped at the edge of the trees. It looked like someone walked from the car to the edge of the trees and back. There were three sets of footprints on the driver's side of the car. There were also two sets near the front passenger side. I found some of the third set of shoe prints down the passenger side and behind the car."

"I'm sure some of those belong to Mr. Ellis," Wade said as he walked toward Carl. "Mr. Ellis, are you wearing the boots you were wearing when you found the body?"

"Ya, why?" He asked as he stood.

"We're going to need those boots for a while," Wade said as he motioned for someone to bring an evidence bag.

"What do you need my boots for?" Carl asked angrily.

"We've found three sets of shoe prints around that car. We need to compare your boots to them so that we can determine which are yours."

"I don't want to give you my boots. They're the only pair of work boots I have."

"That's fine; you can come with us to the office and wait while we compare them. It could take several hours though," Wade said looking Carl Ellis in the eye.

Carl stared back at him for a few minutes seemingly weighing his options. Finally, he sat on the tailgate and removed his boots.

"I can't wait several hours. I've got work to do. Here take 'em, but I want 'em back as soon as you're done with 'em," he said as he tossed the boots at the sheriff."

"I'll personally get them back to you as soon as we've finished with them," Wade promised. "We'll be leaving as soon as the tow truck arrives. When we do, we'll be going to see Mrs. Brinkman. I'd appreciate it if you didn't tell anyone about this until we have broken the news to her."

"I wasn't plannin' to tell anybody anyhow," Carl answered. "Can I go now?"

"Yes, but I may need to visit with you again as things progress."

Carl mumbled about being shoeless as he carefully picked his way toward the cab of his truck. He glared at the sheriff before he drove away.

"Deputy Fletcher, let's go see Mrs. Brinkman," Wade said as he started toward the truck.

"Yes, sir," Lizzie said and followed.

After they were seated in the truck, Wade looked at Lizzie. "Do you think you can handle this?" he asked.

"I don't know, but I'll do my best," she answered.

"I know you will," he said as he started the truck.

# CHAPTER 14

Emily Brinkman was about to leave for work when the Wilbarger County Sheriff and his deputy arrived. She assumed they had more questions about Paul Randolph's death. She met them at the door.

"Good morning. What can I do for you today, Sheriff?"

"Good morning, Mrs. Brinkman. May we come in?"

"Yes," she said warily. Something in the sheriff's manner alarmed her.

"Thank you, ma'am," Wade said as he took off his cowboy hat and stepped inside.

"Is this about Paul Randolph?"

"No, ma'am," Wade said. He glanced at Lizzie as she stood beside him.

"Something's wrong isn't it," Emily said.

"Yes, ma'am. I think it would be best if you sat down."

"What happened?" Emily asked as she sank into a nearby chair.

"I'm so sorry to have to tell you this," Wade said with compassion in his eyes. "Your husband was found dead this morning."

"Nick is dead?"

"Yes, ma'am. We're so sorry for your loss."

Emily didn't cry. Instead she stared into the distance. "Nick is dead?" she asked again.

"Is there someone we can call to come stay with you?"

Emily stared at Wade a moment before answering. "My parents I guess."

"What are your parents' names?"

"Ashby. Tom and Rose Ashby."

"Deputy Fletcher will call them now." Wade nodded at Lizzie. She went out to the truck to make the call.

"I know this is not a great time, but I need to ask you some questions."

"I…I understand," Emily answered as if she were in a trance.

"When did you last see your husband?"

"Yesterday, before he left for work. He was working swing shift this month."

"Did you speak with him after that?"

"Yes, he called just before nine o'clock last night. Why did he call? He never calls when he's working?" Emily said to herself as much as to the sheriff.

"What did he say?"

"He told me to make sure all the doors and windows were locked and to stay inside."

"Why?"

"He said he was worried. He had been ever since Paul died. He said he couldn't stand it if something happened to me."

"Did he say anything else?'

"We talked about how beautiful the full moon looked. He said he knew we had been going through a bad time. He wanted to try to work things out. We were going to make plans for Thanksgiving together when he came home."

"When should he have gotten home?"

"He got off work at eleven. He should have been home between eleven twenty and eleven thirty."

"Weren't you concerned when he didn't come home?"

For the first time since she had heard about her husband, Emily looked directly at the sheriff.

"Nick seldom came home when he was supposed to. Sometimes he didn't come home at all."

"I see."

"Emily, your parents are on their way," Lizzie said as she walked back into the house. "Is there anyone else you would like for me to call?"

"No, thank you," Emily answered still looking at Wade. "I would like to know how my husband died."

"We won't know for sure until the autopsy is completed, but it is most likely he was killed with a shotgun blast to the chest."

"Who was he with?"

"Excuse me?" Wade asked surprised.

"Where did you find him?"

"He was found in his car on the edge of Carl Ellis's land?"

"Sheriff," she paused a moment before asking, "Was he found alone?"

"Yes, ma'am." Wade was suspicious now. "Who would he have been with?"

"It could have been any woman who crossed his path."

"Do you know of anyone specific?"

"No, only rumors and suspicions."

"Who do you suspect?"

"There was a rumor circulating before Paul died that April had been going to Crowell quite often. Other than that, I don't have any names, just different perfumes on Nick's clothes when I did the laundry."

Wade sighed. He knew this could lead to a large list of suspects, including Emily. Lizzie couldn't help feeling sorry for Emily and sat down near her. She reached for her hand and gently squeezed it as the first tear rolled down Emily's cheek.

"Deputy, there's someone else you can call. Please, call the Farm Bureau office and tell them I won't be in."

"I'll be happy to. Do you have any tissues here? I'll bring them for you."

"Yes, in the cabinet in the bathroom down the hall."

Lizzie found a box of tissues and handed them to Emily before stepping outside to make the requested phone call. She could hear Wade's next question as the phone rang.

"I have to ask this," Wade said apologetically. Did your husband have any enemies?"

"There could be any number of husbands who might want him dead. I don't know of anyone in particular. Of course, anyone he might have arrested could be responsible."

"Is there anyone who had an issue with your husband, other than husbands or people he arrested?"

Emily thought for a moment before answering. "He had an argument with someone. I don't know who it was or what it was about. Nick came home with a bloody nose and a black eye. When I asked about it, he told me that it was a misunderstanding with one of our neighbors."

"How long ago?"

"It was during the summer. Other than that, I can't tell you for sure."

"Were you here alone last night?"

"Yes, I waited for Nick until midnight and then went to bed. I was about to leave for work when you arrived."

"Is there anything you can think of that might help us with this case?"

"No, but I'll let you know if I do think of something," Emily assured him. "I'm sure you've gathered that Nick wasn't a model husband."

"Have you filed for divorce?"

"No, I kept hoping we could work things out."

Lizzie came back inside. "You're office said to take all the time you need. They would like for you to call them if there is anything they can do," she told Emily.

"Thank you. I can't think of anything anyone can do right now. I guess I'm still having trouble believing it. I keep expecting Nick to call or come through the door."

"We'll stay with you until your parents arrive," Wade told her. "Deputy Fletcher will wait here with you while I check in with my office."

"Thank you. I appreciate your kindness more than you know."

Wade walked out to the truck leaving the two women alone. He noticed that Lizzie had left the room. She returned with a glass of water for Emily. She left again and returned giving something to Emily that he couldn't see.

"I suppose you think it strange that I'm not crying very much," Emily said to Lizzie.

"Not at all. News like this takes a while to process."

"I've cried so many tears over that man that I didn't think I had any left. I guess I was wrong," she said as she dabbed at the tears threatening to spill from her eyes.

Lizzie sat with Emily as they waited for her parents to arrive. Emily didn't say anything more. She sat quietly sighing and shaking her head.

Wade spoke with Mr. and Mrs. Ashby for a few minutes when they arrived. Lizzie was sure he was interviewing them before they got inside so that Emily wouldn't have to hear it. As soon as Wade had finished, they rushed to their daughter's side. Lizzie quietly went outside and got into Wade's truck.

"Did you find out anything else?" Wade asked as he started the engine.

"She didn't have a lot to say after you left. She did have some pink in her wardrobe, but it wasn't the right shade or type of fabric."

"So that's why you were running around getting things for her."

Lizzie looked at him in surprise. "Wasn't I supposed to?"

"That was good work, Deputy Fletcher. I thought you were trying to comfort her. It didn't cross my mind you were looking for pink."

"I saw that scrap of fabric at the scene. Does that mean the two deaths are related?"

"I believe they are. We'll know for sure after those two pieces of fabric have been tested and compared."

"What are we going to do now?"

"I need to see the sheriff in Crowell. It's professional courtesy to inform him about Nick. He might be able to answer a few questions. He also might want to be part of the investigation."

Wade drove to Lizzie's jeep in silence. He was trying to decide what should be done first. Lizzie didn't interrupt his thoughts.

Stopping beside the jeep, he looked at his watch. "It's nine o'clock. Most of the people we need to interview have probably gone to work by now. Go back to the office. I'll call Dodson with instructions. He'll let you know what needs to be done. I'll call the office when I leave Crowell. We'll decide what we need to do next when I get back."

"Yes, sir." Lizzie said as she got out of his truck.

"Lizzie," Wade said smiling down at her. "That really was good work back there."

"Thank you, Wade," she said smiling back as she closed the door to his truck.

Wade drove to Crowell, dreading his upcoming meeting with Scott Duncan. He knew this would be almost as hard as informing Nick's wife about his death. He had called ahead to inform the Foard County Sheriff that he was coming and that he had something important to talk with him about.

Sheriff Duncan was waiting outside his office when Wade arrived.

"Howdy, Wade. How are you this morning?"

"Morning, Scott. I've been better. I think we should talk inside."

"Come on in, then. Coffee?" Duncan asked as he walked toward the coffee pot.

"Yes, please," Wade said, trying to delay telling the sheriff about his deputy.

Sheriff Scott Duncan was a big man. He was six feet five inches tall and strong as an ox. He played linebacker for his college football team. He had been drafted to play for the Dallas Cowboys, but an injury during practice ended his football career before it started. His dark hair was usually hidden by a cap. His dark eyes, facial features, and complexion indicated that he was of Native American descent. He had worked in law enforcement in bigger cities, but he preferred the small town life.

"Have a seat," Duncan said, indicating a chair in front of his desk. He gave Wade his coffee before moving around to his chair behind the desk. He took a few sips of his own coffee while he studied Wade.

"You look like a man with something serious on his mind. What can I do for you?"

Wade sighed and rubbed his forehead before he answered.

"There's no easy way to say this, so I'll just tell you straight. Nick Brinkman has been killed."

"What? How?" Duncan asked in disbelief as he leaned toward Wade.

"He was found with a gunshot wound to the chest early this morning."

Sheriff Duncan stared at his colleague for several minutes. Wade was becoming uncomfortable waiting for the inevitable questions.

"Do you have any suspects?" Duncan asked quietly after he had recovered from the initial shock.

"No one specific, but there could be dozens."

"What do you know?"

"He spoke with his wife around nine o'clock last night. He told her he would see her soon. He never made it home. He was found by a neighbor this morning at approximately five thirty. He was parked near the river. The battery of his car was dead with the headlight switch on. The driver's side door was open. Nick was positioned with his right foot inside and his left foot outside. He was probably sitting in the driver's seat when he was killed. A shotgun was found beside the car. We don't know for sure yet, but it is probably the murder weapon. I suspect it was his gun."

"Which county was he found in?"

"In Wilbarger, just over the county line."

Sheriff Duncan got up and walked around the office for several minutes. He rubbed his head as he walked. Wade sat silently allowing Duncan to process the information.

"I want to be kept informed," Duncan said as he finally took his seat again.

"Of course, but I thought you would want to work the case together."

"I do, but with Nick gone, I'm down to one deputy. I don't have the manpower. I'll do what I can from here, but it's going to have to be your baby."

"In that case, I have some questions that I hope you can answer."

"Ask away. If I can't answer now, I'll find out."

"Do you know when Nick left here last night?"

Duncan turned to the computer on the desk, tapped the keys, and opened a file.

"He clocked out at eleven. Looks like my other deputy clocked in just before Nick left," Duncan said as he tapped a few more keys, opening another file. "He took a call from Mrs. Irene Cutter at nine ten. She reported seeing something in the ditch across from her house that she wanted him to look into. Nick called in at eleven thirty. He reported that, in the moonlight from Mrs. Cutter's porch, something lay in the ditch that looked like a body. He went over to have a look. It turned out to be a roll of carpet. He said he was going home and signed off."

"Do you know Mrs. Cutter's address?"

"She lives on farm to market road ninety-eight between Margaret and Rayland. She usually called Nick if she wanted to talk to somebody here," he said as he wrote the address down and handed it to Wade.

"Did she call here very often?"

"No, she's a pretty independent gal. She only called if she couldn't deal with something herself."

Wade hesitated before asking, "Do you think there was anything going on between Nick and Mrs. Cutter?"

Duncan sighed, "I've been hearing those rumors, too. No, Mrs. Cutter is too old to catch Nick's eye. I doubt she'd be interested in him anyway."

"How old would you say she is?"

"I'd guess anywhere between seventy and a hundred."

"That leads us to other women. Do you know of any in particular?"

"You think somebody's husband caught up with him don't you?"

"I'm investigating all possibilities. There wasn't a lot of evidence at the scene."

"I've never seen him with a woman other than his wife. I've heard lots of rumors though. I even sat outside here one night, waiting to see if one of those rumors was true."

"Was it?"

"Not that night."

"What was the rumor?"

"It's been going around these parts for months that he would have female visitors while on swing shift. The story goes that ladies would come in and spend an hour or so. They'd be home before anyone got concerned."

"You did more checking didn't you?"

"You know me too well. I pulled the phone records for this office. There was nothing there that would indicate he was making or receiving phone calls other than for official business. I couldn't justify checking his personal phone records based on a rumor."

"I'll have one of my people check those."

"I thought you would."

"Is there anyone that you are aware of who had a grudge against Nick?"

"Other than the possible husbands you mean? I'll get a list of everybody Nick arrested to your office by the end of the day. How far back do you want me to go?"

"Let's start with the last two years. Will it be much trouble to go back farther if needed?"

"No, we don't have that many arrests here. The ones we do are generally repeat offenders. I don't know of anyone else who might have had something against Nick."

"Do you recall seeing or hearing about April Randolph being in town?"

"April Randolph? Is she part of this?"

"I don't know. It's been suggested that she has been meeting someone here in Crowell periodically."

"You think she might be one of Nick's friends. Aren't they neighbors?"

"Yes, they are. The two couples socialized often."

"I'll see what I can find out. I have a feeling there's something you aren't telling me."

"We found evidence at the scene that might link Nick's death to Paul Randolph's murder."

"All the more reason to find out if April and Nick were getting cozy. What sort of evidence?"

"I'd rather not say until the forensic tests are done. Only my office knows about it for the time being. I'd like to keep it quiet for now. We found something at both scenes that shouldn't have been there."

Sheriff Scott Duncan raised his eyebrows and whistled. He looked at Wade a few minutes before asking, "Are you thinking serial killer?"

"I'm not ruling it out."

"I'll be damned! Let me know when those tests are done. I'll do some checking around here. I'll let you know if I find anything."

Wade stood and shook hands with his colleague. He called his office before driving away.

"Sheriff's office," Lizzie answered.

"This is Adams. I've finished with Sheriff Duncan. He'll be faxing some information to us before the end of the day. I'm going to interview a woman that Nick Brinkman reportedly visited on official business last night. I need someone to pull the victim's personal cell phone records for the past six months. Call his wife to get the number."

"Yes, sir."

"I should be back in the office before noon. Have you heard anything from Doctor Hughes yet?"

"Not yet."

"Let me know if you hear from him before I get back."

"Yes, sir."

Wade thought about Lizzie on the way to see Mrs. Cutter. He missed her more than he had anticipated. He thought they would manage to talk by radio once or twice a week. So far that hadn't worked out as planned.

It had been a month since Paul's death. Unless something was discovered in the investigation of Nick's death, he knew it could drag on indefinitely.

Maddie would be back on the job eventually. She had saved her vacation time so that she could spend more than the traditional six weeks with her new son. She wasn't due back until mid-December. There had been no new applicants for the deputy position. He'd have to keep Lizzie on the team until something changed.

# CHAPTER 15

Lizzie had been busy since she returned to the sheriff's office. Dodson had assigned her the task of finding out where each of the Brinkman's friends and neighbors worked. The sheriff planned to interview those people again that afternoon. She searched through the background checks they already had to see if there was something there that would give them a clue in Nick Brinkman's death. She began the process of getting Nick's cell phone records.

Lizzie had doubted that Wade really needed her help during the investigation into Paul Randolph's death. Now that she saw what went on at the sheriff's office during an investigation, she knew that they could use all the help they could get.

Baker answered one line of the ringing phone. Lizzie answered another.

"Sheriff's office."

"Is Sheriff Adams available?" A woman asked sweetly.

"No, ma'am. He's out of the office. May I take a message?"

"Do you expect him back today?" The woman asked.

"Yes, ma'am, but it could be several hours," Lizzie replied. *This woman sounds familiar.*

"Would it be alright if I stopped by? I have a package for him."

"Yes, ma'am. You can leave it at the front desk. We'll make sure he gets it."

"Thank you," the woman said and hung up.

Lizzie stared at the phone for a moment, trying to remember where she had heard that voice before. She was brought back to the present by the sound of the fax machine. She hurried over to retrieve the information sent by Sheriff Duncan and took the fax to Dodson.

"I was hoping that would come in before Sheriff Adams gets back," Dodson said. "What are you working on now?"

"I've been through the background checks and requested Nick's cell phone records. I have work places and phone numbers for everyone who is employed," Lizzie answered. "I've been answering the phones while waiting for the phone records."

"Good. Do background checks on all of the people on this fax. See if you can find employment information for them as well. I'd like to have as much information as possible when the Sheriff gets back."

Nick had arrested a dozen people over the last two years, nine of those repeatedly. They were charged with possession of a controlled substance or alcohol related offenses. Of the remaining three, two were arrested for vandalism of government property, and one for domestic violence.

Lizzie started the background checks. She had been concentrating on her task when she heard someone come in. She glanced up and noticed that Baker had gone to talk with a woman standing at the front counter. Lizzie knew right away why the woman she spoke to on the phone earlier had sounded so familiar. It was Megan Ford.

Megan stood only feet away from her. Rather than deal with Megan, Lizzie chose to hide behind the computer screen she was using.

Megan smiled sweetly at Deputy Calvin Baker. She was a blue eyed blonde with an hour glass figure that turned every man's head. She had two goals in life. She dreamed of becoming rich and famous with as little effort as possible. She also wanted to marry a rich man. She had yet to accomplish either goal. She had been married to Dan Hayes, the Fletcher's right hand man. That ended when Dan realized she had never loved him and was obsessed with Drake Wagner and Lizzie Fletcher.

She caused enough trouble that the Fletcher and Wagner families filed restraining orders against her. Those orders were now expired. Lizzie had not seen or heard anything about Megan in months. She had heard that Megan had moved to another state. Either that information was wrong, or Megan was back.

The phone rang on Lizzie's desk. She answered it quickly.

"Sheriff's office."

"Hello, Deputy Fletcher. This is Gerard Hughes."

"Hello, Doctor Hughes."

"Is Sheriff Adams available?"

"No, sir. He hasn't returned to the office yet."

"Please, tell him that I've completed the autopsy on Mr. Brinkman."

"I will. I know he's anxious to hear the results."

Lizzie chatted with the doctor a few moments longer before ending their conversation. Baker walked past her, carrying a box beautifully wrapped with pastel blue paper and a royal blue ribbon. Lizzie watched with curiosity as he put the box on Wade's desk. She could see that a card was attached. Baker had a mischievous grin on his face when he passed by Lizzie again.

"What are you up to?" Lizzie asked.

"Nothing," he said innocently. "You can quit hiding now. She's gone."

"Has she been coming in a lot?"

"She's been here three or four times in the past month. She always has a package for the sheriff."

"Are they always wrapped like that?"

"She uses different colors but always fancy."

"What's in the packages?"

"So far we've had cakes and cookies. We had donuts one morning. We'll find out what it is after he opens it. He'll put it in the break room right away."

Baker was still grinning as he walked away. Lizzie longed to know more, but she didn't ask. She could only describe what she was feeling as both curiosity and jealousy. She didn't know what Megan was up to, but she was pretty sure she wouldn't like it.

• • •

Wade parked in Irene Cutter's drive. He looked over his shoulder to see the roll of carpet in the ditch. He could understand why she was concerned. At first glance, it did look like a body. He was sure it was more convincing in the dark. He got out of the truck, walked to the front porch, and gently knocked on the door.

"Come in. It's open," a voice said from inside.

Wade took off his hat before opening the door. He let his eyes adjust to the light before saying anything. "Mrs. Cutter?"

"Yes, who are you?"

Mrs. Cutter was sitting in a recliner with her left leg encased in a cast that extended from mid-thigh to her toes. He guessed her to be at least seventy years old but was inclined to agree with Sheriff Duncan that she could be much older.

"I'm Sheriff Wade Adams. I'd like to ask you a few questions."

"You're in the wrong county aren't you?"

Wade smiled, "Yes ma'am."

"Well, have a seat. I'm sorry I couldn't answer the door properly. I'd offer you a glass of tea, but I don't have any made. It takes me a while to get up and down with this contraption," she said tapping her cast.

"I understand, ma'am. I don't want any tea, but I'd be happy to make some for you if you'll point me in the right direction."

She looked him in the eye for a moment before saying, "That would be very nice. While you're making tea, you can decide how you're going to say what you came to say."

She directed Wade to a pitcher and a jar of instant tea. He made the tea according to the directions on the jar. He filled a glass with ice and poured the tea over it. She took the glass from him and took one sip before placing it on the table beside her.

"Thank you. I was thirsty but not thirsty enough to get up. I'll have to sip it slow so I don't have to get up too often. Did you decide how to get started?"

Wade smiled at her. "You're a very shrewd woman, Mrs. Cutter."

"The name's Irene. Mrs. Cutter was my mother-in-law. What's on your mind?"

"I understand Nick Brinkman stopped by here last night."

"Yes, he did. I called him to come by and check on that roll of carpet out there in the ditch."

"What time did he get here?"

"It was eleven fifteen. He said he'd come by on his way home from work. I started trying to get out of this chair at eleven."

"What time did he leave?"

"He wasn't here long. It was probably eleven thirty. What's this about?"

"Deputy Brinkman was found dead in his car this morning. He never made it home."

"Was it a car accident?"

"No, ma'am. He was murdered."

The old woman shook her head as a tear slid down her cheek. "I can't believe it. He was so good to me. He always came by if I called about anything. He said I reminded him of his grandma. Sometimes he'd just stop by to see if I was doing okay."

"I'm sorry for your loss."

"Thank you. What about his little wife? How is she doing?"

"About like you'd expect."

"Poor woman. I know what it's like to lose a husband. It's probably worse to lose one like that."

Something occurred to Wade as he waited for Irene to collect her thoughts.

"Is there anything else I can tell you?" she asked.

"Do you know of anyone who might have a grudge against Nick?"

"No, I don't, but he did come by here one day with signs of a healing shiner on his left eye. I didn't ask about it. I thought it was probably job related."

"It may have been. His wife mentioned it to me this morning." Wade hesitated before asking, "Irene, how did you happen to notice that carpet out there. Did you see it before dark?"

"No, I was sitting right here watching my television program. I heard a commotion outside. It sounded like someone had an accident. Tires screeched and doors slammed. By the time I got out of this chair to see what was going on, the only thing out there was that roll of carpet. I wouldn't have called Nick if it hadn't looked like a body lying there. If I could get around better, I might have seen who dumped it. I could have at least investigated it myself instead of wasting his time."

"I'm sure he didn't mind stopping by," Wade assured her.

"Thank you for that. As it turns out, I'm glad I called him. I wouldn't have gotten to see him again otherwise," she said sadly.

"How long will you be in that cast?"

"I have an appointment with the doctor next week. I'm hoping I can at least get something a bit daintier," she said grinning. "I'll be happy if I get one that's easier to get around in."

"I understand that. Thank you for your time. I may need to come back later. We might find something that only you would know."

"You can come back anytime you like," the old woman said smiling at him.

"Is there anything else I can do for you while I'm here?"

"No, I'm fine. You go on and find out who killed my friend Nick."

"Yes, ma'am. I'll do my best."

Wade said goodbye and walked outside. He took out his phone as he went over to the ditch. He photographed the roll of carpet before looking around. The tires of Nick's car left impressions in the dry grass and weeds where Nick had driven into the ditch. He imagined Nick shining his headlights on the carpet before getting out of the car to investigate.

He noticed skid marks on the pavement. Nick probably didn't see those since he didn't report them. Based on the impression in the grass, his car was positioned so that he couldn't see them. It looked as if someone stomped the brakes and slid a few feet before stopping. He photographed everything he saw that might give him a clue before going back to his truck.

Wade walked past his truck and back to Mrs. Cutter's door. She told him to come in before he could knock.

"I'm sorry to bother you again, but did Nick have his shotgun with him last night?" Wade asked.

"Yes, he did. He took it out of his trunk before going across the road."

"Did he put it back in the trunk?"

Irene stared into space trying to recall what had happened the night before. Finally, she said, "No, he left it in the front seat."

"Thank you. I'll be in touch," he said. He climbed into his truck and backed it toward the carpet. When it was close enough, he got out of the truck and lowered the tailgate. After struggling for several minutes, he managed to load the carpet into the back. He was gasping for breath when he climbed into the driver's seat. His phone rang as he closed his door.

"Adams."

"Sheriff? Are you okay?

"Yep, what's up," he said, trying to catch his breath

"Doctor Hughes has finished the autopsy," Baker told him.

"I'm on my way back. What else have you found out?"

"Dodson and Reed have been going over the evidence from the scene. Fletcher's been gathering a lot of information."

"Good. I should be there in twenty minutes. We'll meet with everyone in the conference room with what we have at eleven thirty."

"Yes, sir," Baker said. "Oh, you have another package in your office."

Wade groaned as he hung up.

The sheriff went directly to his office. He picked up the package that was waiting on his desk. He removed the card before he called Baker.

"Take this to the break room, please. I'm going to put a stop to this."

"Don't you want to open it first," Baker teased.

The sheriff glared at his deputy.

"Yes, sir. I'll open it in the break room," Baker said trying not to grin.

"Close the door on your way out, please," Wade instructed.

Baker closed the door. He took the package and its contents to the break room. He returned with a pastry in each hand.

Wade dialed the number on the card and waited.

"Miss Ford, this is Sheriff Adams."

"Hello, Wade. Did you get the package that I left for you today?"

"Yes, ma'am. That's why I'm calling."

"I hope you like my little care packages. I think I'll bring something different next time. Change things up a little. How about fruit? Fruit is so much healthier."

Before Megan could say anything else, he rushed to say, "Miss Ford, on behalf of my department, we'd like to thank you for your kindness over the past few weeks. My team has enjoyed the food items a great deal. However, it has become a distraction that we can't afford. I must ask that you discontinue the packages."

"Is there anything else I can bring? I love helping our local sheriff in any way I can."

"No, thank you. I'd prefer anyone who doesn't have official business with this department to stay away. We're shorthanded and extremely busy with cases. I hope you understand."

"Certainly, but.....

"Thank you for understanding, Miss Ford. I'm needed on another line. Goodbye."

Megan threw her phone across the room. "Us? My team? I thought I made it clear those were for you, not your whole department!" She screamed as she sat down on the sofa in her tiny apartment. She crossed her legs and wagged her foot in agitation. "I'll just have to find another way to get your attention, Wade Adams," she said aloud. She smiled as she said to the empty room, "I know you opened the card. You did call me after all."

Wade sat at his desk jotting down notes for the upcoming meeting with his team. He heard the phone ring outside and hoped everyone remembered the he was out if Megan Ford called. The phone on his desk rang. He answered apprehensively.

"Sheriff Adams."

"Wade, this is Scott. April Randolph has been coming to Crowell fairly regularly."

"She has?"

"Yes, she's been making deposits at the bank two or three times a month. The most recent one was last week. I'll need a warrant to find out more."

"Did she do anything other than go to the bank?"

"I'm still checking on that. Did you get my fax?"

"Let me check. Hang on a minute," Wade said as he put the phone on his desk. He opened his office door and called to Lizzie.

"Fletcher, did we get a fax from the Foard County Sheriff?"

"Yes, sir. I'm gathering information on the people listed now."

"Thank you," he said as he closed his door. Picking up the phone, he said, "We did. One of my people is working on it."

"Good, good. What did you find out from Mrs. Cutter?"

"Nick stopped by there on his way home. Just as he reported, there was a roll of carpet in the ditch. It was positioned in a way that on first glance I thought it was a body."

"Do I need to have someone haul it to the dump?"

"No, I brought it in with me. I'm going to have my team check it thoroughly."

"Why?"

"It may have nothing to do with the case, but it doesn't fit."

"Hmm. Nick goes to investigate an object in the ditch directly across the road from a woman that he visits periodically. He ends up dead later that very night. You're right. Better check it."

"I'm meeting with my team in a few minutes. I'll let you know what they've come up with if anything."

"Thanks. I'll keep checking into things here."

Wade hung up and gathered his notes. He stopped by Baker's desk before going to the conference room.

"Baker, send an email to everyone who is working today to join us for the meeting. I plan to announce some changes. Make signs for every outer door to inform the public that we will see only those people who are here for official business. After the meeting, send an email to everyone about the new policies."

"Yes, sir."

"What was in the package this time?" Wade asked.

"Cinnamon rolls, the really gooey kind with icing on top."

"Well, enjoy them. They're the last we're getting."

"I already did, sir," Baker said as he wiped a drop of icing from his desk.

"Good morning, again," Doctor Hughes greeted them as he came into the office.

"Good morning, Doc," Wade said. "Did you find any surprises when doing your autopsy?"

"No, but I do have a question. I've noticed that everyone here wears a nametag on their uniform. Did Mr. Brinkman wear one on his?"

"Yes, he did," Wade answered warily. "Why?"

"I didn't find one. I went through his clothing thoroughly but found no name tag."

"Did you happen to bring his clothes with you?"

"Yes, I did." Doctor Hughes handed a plastic bag to the sheriff. "I thought you'd want to examine them."

"Baker, take these to the lab, please. We'll be in the conference room," Wade told him.

Wade waited patiently for everyone to arrive in the conference room. As soon as everyone was gathered, he closed the door.

"Please, find a seat. I have a short announcement to make to the entire staff. I'll dismiss those who are not required to be here for the meeting afterward. He waited a moment before continuing, "As of now, no one is to be in this building unless they are here for official business. We have two murder cases that we need to concentrate on. We don't have time for distractions. Once we've cleared these cases, I'll relax the no visitors rule. Does anyone have any questions?"

Wade waited for questions. When there were none, he added, "I have talked with Megan Ford and requested that she stop delivering packages to this office. I don't think it will surprise anyone if she attempts to bring another. However, we won't be accepting any packages other than those for official business. No one, and I mean no one, is to accept a package from anyone unless it is related to official business. Deputy Baker is drafting an email addressing both of these issues so that everyone working here is informed. He is also creating signs to be posted on the doors to inform visitors. I will be drafting a notice for the newspaper. Are there any questions?"

"Does that mean we won't have goodies in the break room anymore?"

"You may bring things to leave in the break room if you'd like, but there will be no more from Miss Ford or anyone else outside this office. You may order food to be delivered if you let the deputy at the front desk know. If we don't have notification from someone in this building, it won't be accepted. If there are no more questions, only those who are here for the briefing need stay."

When all but the investigative team had left the room, Wade started the recording.

"Today is Monday, November 18, 2013.This is Sheriff Wade Adams. The body of Foard County Sheriff's Deputy Nick Brinkman was found by his neighbor Carl Ellis at approximately five thirty this morning on his property," Wade gave the address of the Ellis property. "Deputy Brinkman was last seen on official business at eleven fifteen last night. He called in the report to his office at eleven thirty. That gives us an approximate time of death between eleven thirty last night and five thirty this morning. Doctor Gerard Hughes, what did you learn from the autopsy?"

"Mr. Brinkman received a gunshot wound to the chest and neck.

The right carotid artery was penetrated. Both lungs and his heart sustained damage. There was significant damage to his other organs. He bled to death within a matter of minutes. I'd estimate his time of death to be midnight."

"Thank you, Doc. You're free to go."

"I'd love to stay, but I have living patients to see. Good luck," Doctor Hughes called as he left the room.

"Deputy Craig Dodson, do you have anything to share?" Wade asked.

"Yes, sir. Deputy Lizzie Fletcher has collected work information for all of the neighbors and information for those who were arrested by Deputy Brinkman. We've gone through the background checks again and have found nothing new."

"Deputy Reed?"

"The blood samples taken from the car match the victim. There were no prints on the car other than the victims. There were no prints on the shotgun."

"Not even the victims?"

"No, sir. The shoe prints from the car to the trees and back to the car match the victim's shoes. The prints from the truck tracks to the front door of the car match Mr. Ellis. There were two sets of footprints on the passenger side of the car. One set matched the victim. The other set is unidentified at this time. There were some of the same unidentified prints that went around the back of the car to the driver's side and into the trees."

"Did you check them against the shoes we have from April Randolph?"

"Yes, sir. The style is the same, but the size is different."

"Those most likely belong to our shooter," Wade said. "I learned from Sheriff Duncan that he had been hearing rumors that our victim was entertaining female guests while on duty at the jail. He was unable to verify those rumors. Did someone check the victim's cell phone records?"

"Yes, sir," Lizzie said. There are four phone numbers that were called frequently other than his wife and his office. I have the names and addresses of them listed here," she said, handing the file to Wade.

Wade looked at the file before saying, "All women. Irene Cutter isn't one of the victim's alleged jail visitors. I visited with her today. She's one of the victim's neighbors. He saw her on official business last night. She's a shrewd elderly woman who was probably the last person to see him alive other than our shooter."

Wade shared the information he had gathered with his team. "I want that carpet analyzed and the information to me as soon as possible. Doctor Hughes informed me that the victim's name tag was not among his clothing. Did anyone find it in or around his car?'

"No, sir," Reed answered.

"We have two deaths. Our victims, both men, resided in the Rayland area. We know that they knew each other and often socialized. The first victim was killed with his own farm implement. The second victim was killed with a shotgun that was likely in the victim's possession. At both crime scenes, a scrap of pink cloth was found. There are items missing from the scenes that should have been there."

"Do you think we have a serial killer, sir?" Reed asked.

"We have someone who wanted both men dead. I believe it was the same person based on the evidence we have. I pray that the killer has finished killing. I'm afraid he, she, or they have not. Baker, contact Sheriff Duncan in Crowell. Find out if the shotgun we found was assigned to him by that office. If it isn't, find out if it was registered to our victim. Then, dig into the histories of both victims. Find out if there is any other link between them."

"Yes, sir."

"Dodson and Reed, interview the folks on our list who are working in town. Find out if anyone knows who our victim had an argument with a few months ago. If you don't catch all of them at work, let me know. We might be able to catch them at home. Fletcher will go with me to interview the people in Rayland and Crowell."

Dodson nodded. Reed said, "Yes, sir."

"Fletcher, before we start those interviews, I'd like you to take this fabric to the dress shop. Find out everything you can about it. Find out if anyone has purchased something like that from her recently. Don't tell her that it's part of our investigation. If you have time, check with other places that sell fabric. Then, come back here. I'd like to get started by two o'clock."

"Yes, sir."

Wade turned off the recording. "Grab some lunch and relax before you get started. It's probably going to be a long day. We'll meet back here after the interviews are finished. Call me if you find anything important."

# CHAPTER 16

Lizzie took one of the pieces of cloth to the dress shop. She waited patiently for the owner to finish with a customer.

"Hi, Lizzie. What can I do for you?

"Hi, Melinda. I have some questions about a piece of fabric," Lizzie took the sample from her pocket. "I found this in some of Granny's things. I thought it would be great for recovering some of the throw pillows at the inn. Do you have anything like this?"

"Let me see," Melinda took the fabric and rubbed it between her fingers. "It's medium weight linen. I have some pink, but I don't think it's the right color. Wait here; I'll bring out what I have."

"Thank you," Lizzie said.

Five minutes later, Melinda had three bolts of pink fabric in her arms. She laid them on the counter and took the sample from Lizzie again.

"This one is the wrong weight," she said as she set the top bolt aside. "This is the wrong shade of pink but the right weight. This last one is wrong on both counts. I'm sorry, Lizzie."

"Have you had anything similar?"

"No, these are the only pink linens I've had in stock. I can order something for you, but it may not be exactly right either."

"Could I have a little sample of the second one? I'll compare it with the room décor to see if it will work as well as the piece I brought in."

Melinda cut off a long narrow piece of the linen for Lizzie. "Here you go."

"Thank you, I'll let you know what I decide sometime next week. What do I owe you?"

"Not a thing. Just promise you'll buy the fabric here when you decide."

"I will. Thanks, Melinda."

Lizzie left the dress shop and went to her favorite burger place for lunch. While eating, she googled places to buy fabric in Vernon. There was only one store other than the dress shop that sold fabric. She finished her lunch and drove to the craft store.

She went in and stood by the counter. After waiting a few minutes, she rang the bell near an old fashioned cash register. An elderly woman emerged from the back of the store. "I'm sorry dear. I didn't hear you come in. What can I do for you?"

"I'm trying to match this piece of fabric. I wondered if you happen to have any."

The woman took the sample and stared at it. "Let me get over here in the better light," she said as she turned on a reading lamp. "No, I don't have anything this color. It doesn't look like anything I've had in here. I don't have a lot of fabric in stock. I haven't had any pink for a couple of months. I could order some, but it might not be the right shade."

"I'll keep looking. Thank you for your time."

"Would another color work just as well?"

"No, ma'am. I'm trying to match colors that I already have. Thank you for your help."

Lizzie left the store and drove back to the sheriff's office.

Wade was in his office when she went inside. She tapped on the door before she noticed that he was on the phone. He motioned for her to come in. She sat down to wait.

"Thanks, Scott. We'll stop by your office first when we get there," Wade said and hung up the phone.

"What did you find?"

"I went to the dress shop. She had some pink cloth but didn't recognize our sample. I brought back a piece of one that is probably the same type of fabric but not the right shade of pink. Melinda says its medium weight linen," Lizzie said handing both pieces to the sheriff.

"I'd say they're the same type," he said as he compared the two.

"She had three types of material that she compared with our sample. The other two were the wrong weight or color. After lunch, I went to that little craft store on Main Street. She said she hasn't had any pink for months. She didn't recognize the sample either."

"It was a long shot. It could have been purchased anywhere," Wade said. "At least, we know something about it now."

"I told Melinda that I was going to compare her sample to the room I wanted to update. Looking at that in the sunlight, I noticed something. Is it possible that our sample is the same material but has faded?"

"We'll send it to the lab. They'll find out," Wade said. "Has anyone shown you how to get evidence ready to send to the lab?"

"No."

"Follow me." Wade led Lizzie to the outer office and stopped at Baker's desk.

"Baker, walk Fletcher through the procedures to send these two samples to the lab. I want them to do a comparison."

"Yes, sir."

"Fletcher, when you've finished here, we'll do those interviews in Crowell and Rayland."

"Yes, sir," Lizzie answered as she followed Baker.

When the samples were safely on their way to the lab, Lizzie tapped lightly on the sheriff's office door.

"Come in."

"The samples have been sent to the lab," Lizzie told him.

"Good. Call Baker in here please."

Lizzie found Baker and returned to Wade's office. The two deputies stood in front of the desk, waiting for the sheriff to begin.

"Do you feel like getting out of the office for a while today, Baker?" Wade asked.

"Yes, sir," Baker said with a grin.

Wade grinned back at his deputy. "I thought you might. Have

Lodge take over for you here. You're going with us today. I've been making a plan of attack for the day so to speak. Since we will be coming back here before anyone goes home, you'll both be riding with me. Sheriff Duncan wants to be part of the Crowell interviews. We can split the list in half and get finished there much faster that way. Fletcher and I will be interviewing Nick's alleged girlfriends while Baker and Sheriff Duncan interview the people Nick arrested."

"Yes, sir," both deputies answered.

"In Rayland, you'll both be observing while taking notes. I don't know how many people we'll need to interview there, but we'll definitely talk with anyone that Dodson and Reed haven't interviewed. Any questions or suggestions?"

"No, sir," replied both deputies.

"We leave in ten minutes."

The two deputies left to gather what they needed for the afternoon and waited for the sheriff in the outer office. Wade passed through without a word. His deputies followed him to his truck. Lizzie climbed into the back seat as Wade and Baker got in the front.

Wade turned on the radio. They listened to country music during the half-hour drive to Crowell. No one spoke, but each took the opportunity to relax and think of anything other than the murders for a short while.

Wade parked the truck, and the three walked into the Foard County Sheriff's office. The two deputies were introduced to Sheriff Duncan before the group got to work.

"The two arrested for vandalism of government property are in college now. I checked on their whereabouts with their parents. Both were supposed to be at school. I'm waiting for verification from the campus police."

"That leaves ten from your list and three on ours." Wade asked, "How do you want to divide up those ten?"

"Well, I really just have five on my list. One was here in a jail cell this weekend. I released him this morning. Four have moved out of the county since their arrests. I've got local authorities checking on them. That leaves four of the alcohol and possession charges. You can choose one of those. I want the domestic violence interview. That will be four interviews for each team. Who have you got on your list?"

Wade gave Duncan the list of names.

"That's surprising; these women are all single. She's a single mom with three young kids," Duncan said pointing at one of the names. This one is divorced and has a daughter in junior high. The last one is a widow. She has a son is in the military."

"That shoots our idea of a jealous husband out of the water," Wade said.

"Well, it could be one of those women. You never know what a woman is capable of until you cross that invisible line."

Lizzie grinned at the expressions on the faces of the three men while Baker and Sheriff Adams nodded in agreement.

The group agreed to meet back at Sheriff Duncan's office when the interviews were completed. Both teams were back within two hours and discussed what they learned.

"We didn't learn a lot that will help," Sheriff Duncan began. The domestic assault says he was working last night. His employer verified it. The remaining three all check out, too."

"The one from your list checked out, but we can't rule out those three women. They found out about each other. They confronted Nick while he was on duty."

"That does it! I'm getting a video camera set up in here!" Duncan exclaimed "I would've loved to see that. When did it happen?"

Wade grinned at his colleague. "Saturday night. They all have alibis for the time of Nick's death, but we haven't verified them yet."

"Where were they?"

"They all claimed to be at the Watering Hole in Vernon. They were trying to decide if they should tell you and Mrs. Brinkman about Nick's activities. If you don't mind, I'll call to see if anyone can verify that."

"Be my guest. Can you imagine having four women and one of them your wife after your hide?" Sheriff Duncan shivered.

Wade sighed as he ended his phone conversation. "Trey, the bartender at the Watering Hole, says they were the only women there last night. They got there around eight o'clock. They didn't leave until closing at two this morning."

"I'd say we've narrowed your suspect list down considerably for Nick's death. Here's another bit of information for you. I've visited every establishment in town. If April Randolph was meeting anyone here, it was privately. No one has seen her other than the folks at the bank."

"Thank you, Scott," Wade stood and extended his hand. "I'll give you a call after my team meets tonight."

"If it's between eleven tonight and three tomorrow afternoon, call me at home. My deputy is working graveyard tonight and the day shift tomorrow. Come to think of it, send any qualified applicants for deputy my way. We can't work double shifts for long."

"I haven't found one for our department yet. Fletcher is an interim deputy working as needed until my deputy on maternity leave comes back."

"Fletcher, would you be interested in working here if I haven't found a deputy by then?"

"I appreciate the offer, but my family and I own the Paradise Creek Inn. We'll be extremely busy after Thanksgiving," Lizzie answered.

"I've heard good things about that place."

"That's good to know. Stop by anytime and have a look around. Or better yet book a weekend stay," Lizzie suggested.

Duncan laughed, "I might just do that."

The Wilbarger County Sheriff and his deputies got into the truck and drove toward Rayland. Wade contacted his office to find out if the other team of deputies had returned. Dodson answered the phone.

"Sheriff's office."

"Dodson, did you find out anything useful?"

"Nothing new. We talked with Drew Clifton, Alex Dylan, April Randolph, and Brian and Kelly Flynn. Mr. Clifton and Mrs. Randolph had already heard about Mr. Brinkman's death. Mr. Dylan and the Flynn's didn't know until we told them. Their alibis aren't verifiable. All of them were home asleep. No one knew of anyone who had a reason to kill our victim."

"Baker started gathering some information. Have you heard back about any of that?"

"Lodge is on top of it, sir."

"Alright, I'll call in before we start the last interview out here. You boys can decide what we're having for dinner."

"Yes, sir."

Wade made the turn off of Highway Seventy toward Rayland. He stopped at the Clifton home.

"We're going to interview everyone out here except Drew and Alex. I know April Randolph has already been interviewed, but I want to know what she has been doing in Crowell. I'm hoping Maddie has some information for us."

They got out of the truck and walked to the door. Maddie had been expecting them and watched from her front window. She opened the door before Wade could knock.

"I heard. Come on in. Hi, Baker."

"Hi, Maddie," Baker replied.

"Do you have any leads?" Maddie asked.

"Not really. Do you know of anyone who might have wanted Nick Brinkman dead?" Wade asked.

"No, I've been racking my brain since Drew called and told me the news. I can't come up with any reason for it. Does it have anything to do with Paul's death?"

"We haven't ruled that out. Emily Brinkman told us that Nick had gotten into an argument with one of his neighbors a few months ago. Nick had a bloody nose and a black eye but wouldn't tell her who it was. Do you have any idea who it might have been?

No, I didn't know anything about that. My first guess would be Carl Ellis."

"Is there any particular reason?"

"No, but Carl's bad attitude and quick temper makes him part of most of the disputes between our neighbors. I don't know of any reason why Nick would be arguing with Carl."

"Maddie, I'm going to tell you something that can't leave this room," Wade said.

"Okay," Maddie replied "My lips are sealed. What do you have?"

"There were items missing from both bodies that are unaccounted for. We found unexplainable evidence at both scenes." Wade removed an evidence bag from his pocket and handed it to Maddie. "Have you seen anything like this at any of your neighbor's homes?"

Maddie looked at the pink cloth. "I don't remember seeing anything like this at anyone's house. What does it mean?"

"We don't know yet. Do you know of any connection between Mr. Randolph and Nick other than living in this area?"

"They knew each other in high school. Most of us were acquainted when we were in school."

"Keep your eyes open. Let us know if you find out anything."

"You can count on it. Before you ask, Drew and I were here all night taking turns with the baby."

"Thanks, Maddie," Wade said as he put the evidence bag in his pocket and closed the door behind him.

"Let's visit the Preston's next. They both work from home and should be there," Wade suggested.

The sheriff knocked on the Preston's door.

"Oh, hello, Sheriff." What can we do for you?" Dara asked.

"I have some questions for both of you. Is your husband home?"

"Yes, he is. Kent, Wade Adams is here."

Kent entered the room, extending his hand to Wade and his deputies. "Have you found out something about Paul's death?"

"Nothing that we can share at this time, Wade answered. "I suppose you've heard that there has been another death."

"Another death? Who?" Dara asked as she sank into a nearby chair.

"Nick Brinkman was found dead this morning."

"Oh no, poor Emily."

"What happened?" Kent inquired.

"He was found this morning in his car."

"A car accident?"

"No, sir. He was murdered."

Kent sat down beside his wife, "I can't believe it."

"Do either of you know of anyone who would benefit from Mr. Brinkman's death?"

"No, this is terrible. What's going on, Sheriff?"

"Dara, we don't know yet."

"I can't imagine anyone would want Nick dead," Kent added.

Emily told us that Nick came home with a bloody nose and a black eye a few months ago. He told her that he had an argument with one of his neighbors. He wouldn't tell her who. Would either of you happen to know?"

Dara and Kent both said, "No, idea."

"Where were you between eleven last night and five thirty this morning?"

"We were both here. We watched the news and went to bed at ten thirty," Kent replied.

"We didn't get up until eight this morning," Dara added.

"Is your grandmother still staying with you?"

"No, she went home the day after Halloween."

"Please, let me know if you think of anything that might help us close this case."

Wade and his deputies turned to leave. Kent followed them to the truck.

"Do you think the same person killed both of them?" Kent asked.

"It's possible, but we don't know yet. It would be a good idea to take precautions just in case."

"Believe me. I plan on it." Kent went back inside as the sheriff and his deputies climbed into the truck.

They drove to the Dylan's house to find Morgan Dylan sitting on a bench in the front yard. Wade got out of the truck followed by the deputies.

"Hello, Mrs. Dylan. I'd like to ask you some questions if you don't mind."

"About poor Mr. Brinkman? Alex called me a moment ago. It's so terribly sad," she answered in her far away voice.

"Yes, ma'am. It is. Do you have any idea who might have wanted to kill Mr. Brinkman?"

"I'm sorry. I don't. I only met Mr. Brinkman one time."

"Mr. Brinkman reportedly had an argument with one of his neighbors. Would you happen to know anything about that?"

"No."

"Where were you last night between eleven and five thirty this morning?"

"Alex and I were here sleeping."

"Thank you, for your time, ma'am. Please, don't hesitate to call if you think of anything."

"We will, Sheriff."

When they had taken their places in the truck, Baker asked, "Is she alright?"

"I don't know." Wade sighed.

"She seems to be very sad," Lizzie said.

"Mrs. Dylan isn't much for conversation, but you're about to meet some of the most talkative people I've ever known," Wade told Baker as he started the truck.

# CHAPTER 17

Mack Carson was in his usual place in front of the store when the sheriff and his team arrived. He lowered the chair he had been balancing on two legs to the ground and walked over to greet them.

"Howdy, folks. What can I do for ya today?"

"Mr. Carson, this is Deputy Calvin Baker. We'd like to ask you and Mrs. Carson some questions."

Mack extended his hand to Baker. "Pearl's inside. Is this about Nick?"

"Yes, sir."

"I just can't get over it. Irene called us this morning and told us all about it," Mack said as he held the door open for them.

"I knew we'd be seeing you again soon," Pearl said. "Isn't it just awful? I can't imagine what poor Emily is goin' through right now."

"Yes, ma'am. I need to ask you both more questions," Wade replied. "This is Deputy Calvin Baker."

"Pleased to meet ya," Pearl said as she patted Baker on the back.

Neither of the Carson's knew of anyone who had a grudge against Nick or wanted him dead. Both were home asleep between eleven thirty and five thirty.

"Nick recently had a black eye. He told his wife it was a misunderstanding with one of his neighbors, but he wouldn't tell her who. Do either of you know who it might have been?"

Mack and Pearl looked at each other. They seemed to come to a silent agreement.

"We do," Mack replied.

"We promised Nick that we wouldn't say anythin' to anybody," Pearl added.

"I think he'd want us to tell you considerin' what's happened," Mack said.

"Nick was in here one day, picking up a few things that Emily needed," said Pearl

"Brandy Ellis was inside buying sandwich meat. Carl was outside at the gas pump," Mack added.

"Nick said hello to her, just bein' neighborly you know," Pearl chimed in.

"Carl saw Nick talkin' to Brandy and just about tore the screen door off gettin' inside."

"Nick said hello to him, but Carl didn't answer, just hauled off and punched Nick in the face." Pearl demonstrated the event with her fist.

"Well, Nick was lyin' on the floor. Carl was standin' over him. Nick said, 'What did you do that for, Carl?' " Mack told the Sheriff.

"Carl said, 'I've heard about you carryin' on with other women. You stay away from my woman,' " Pearl continued with her best impression of Carl. "He drug poor Brandy out to the pickup, and they left."

"Nick thought that it might make life harder for Brandy if other folks knew what happened."

"What about the rumor that Mrs. Randolph has been visiting Crowell?"Wade asked. "Was she visiting Nick?"

"I don't think so," Pearl laughed. "That's two different rumors tied together."

"Separate them for me," Wade said.

"Well, there's a rumor about Nick having girlfriends all over the country," Mack replied.

"There's one about April going to Crowell to meet with a lawyer," Pearl added. "I hadn't heard anything about April meeting Nick in Crowell."

"She wasn't." Wade informed the couple. "She has been going to Crowell, but we've found no evidence that she's been meeting anyone there."

"Well, it just goes to show that you can't believe everything you hear, Pearl."

"Mack Carson, you just hush."

"We'll be on our way now. We may be stopping by again if more questions come up," Wade told the couple.

Lizzie hung back as Wade and Baker went to the truck.

"Pearl, do you sell fabric?"

"I have a little in the back. I sell some now and again."

"Do you have any pink? I'm trying to find a match for some pillows at the inn."

"I did have some back in the summer but sold most of it. Let me see if I have any left," Pearl said as she disappeared into the storage room.

Lizzie looked out the window. Wade was looking at her questioningly. She held up her hand, signaling him that she would be only a minute.

Pearl came out of the storage room with a bolt of fabric. "There's not much left. If it matches, we can probably order some from the information on the end of the bolt."

Lizzie jotted down the information provided by Pearl. "Do you know who bought this? I don't want to use it if they're frequent customers at the inn."

"Let me think a minute," Pearl said as she frowned in thought. "It was so long ago that I can't remember. I don't think it was anyone from out here. It might have been somebody from town."

"Do you mind if I take this with me? I'll bring it back if it doesn't match."

"Sure, take it. That's not enough to make anything anyway."

"Thanks, Pearl. I'll let you know if I need to order some."

Lizzie took the fabric, waved goodbye, and joined the men in the truck.

"She had this pink fabric," she told Wade as they drove away.

"I wondered what you were up to. We'll get it to the lab to compare it with the others."

"I was looking around some while we were in there," Baker said. Is there anything they don't sell?"

"If people out here need it, the Carson's will sell it," Lizzie told him.

April Randolph was getting out of her car when the Sheriff and his team arrived.

"I've already talked with your deputies in town. Is there something else you wanted?"

"Mrs. Randolph, I won't take up much of your time. I have one question for you."Wade answered.

"Alright," April reluctantly replied.

"It's come to my attention that you've been making frequent trips to Crowell, specifically to the bank. I know that you've been making deposits into an account that didn't show up when we ran background checks after your husband's death. Who does the account belong to, and why are you making deposits into it?"

April suddenly paled. She looked around before saying, "I'd rather not answer out here. Let's talk inside."

Wade followed her inside while Lizzie and Baker stood outside the door.

"No one can know about this. Paul didn't even know it."

"What are you so afraid of Mrs. Randolph?"

"It would be very dangerous if Carl Ellis were to find out. "

"Go on."

"The account is Brandy's. Carl knows nothing about it."

"Why were you putting money into it?"

"She's been doing some work for us; secretly. Carl would take the money from her if he knew she had it. She's trying to save for something special. I deposited what she earned in the bank instead of paying her directly."

"What was she saving for?"

"She said it was for a Christmas present for their daughter."

"You don't believe that?"

"I did at first, but she must be working for others, too. She started bringing money to me to deposit for her along with what she earned from us. She has quite a bit saved."

"How long have you been making deposits for her?"

"Since the middle of May."

"How much money have you deposited for her?"

"A little over two thousand dollars."

"How old is their daughter?"

"I'm not sure. She's in school. First or second grade I think.

"That would be a noticeable Christmas gift for a young child."

April nodded.

Wade thought for a moment before saying, "One last question. Were you meeting anyone when you went to Crowell?"

"No, I'd just go to the bank. I know about the rumors. I sort of encouraged them to protect Brandy and myself. I'd get angry with Paul, but I loved him. I never considered cheating on him, and I didn't kill him."

"Then the rumor about you and Nick Brinkman meeting at the jail is false?"

April stared at the sheriff a moment before answering, "You're the second person to ask me that. I wasn't attracted to Nick even when we were in school. He was always the kind that couldn't be trusted. I'd never betray Paul or my friend Emily."

"Who else asked you about the rumor?"

Tears filled April's eyes, "It was Emily. She came by a few days after Paul died. She asked me if I had been meeting Nick at the jail. I told her the same thing I told you."

"Did she believe you?"

"I hope so, but I'm not sure. Wade, do you think Nick's death is connected to Paul's somehow?"

"There wasn't much evidence at either scene, Mrs. Randolph. I can't rule anything out right now."

"I suppose I'm still a suspect."

"Yes, but you aren't the only one."

"Who else do you suspect?"

"I'm not going to tell you that. Keep your eyes open and your doors and windows locked."

"And don't leave the county," April sighed.

"I think the occasional trip to the bank in Crowell would be permissible," he said smiling at her. "I'm sure I'll have more questions as the investigation progresses."

"I'll be here or at work," April assured him.

Wade walked back to his truck, followed closely by his deputies. He called the office before starting the engine.

"Sheriff's office," Lodge answered.

"This is Adams. We're about to conduct the last interview out here. Is there anything I need to know before going back to the office?"

"No, sir."

"What did Dodson and Reed decide on for dinner?"

"They ordered from that new barbeque place."

"That sounds good. We should be back within an hour."

Wade hung up the phone. "Baker, be ready. Carl Ellis is a nasty character. It'll probably take us both if we have to arrest him."

"Yes, sir. Are you planning on making an arrest?"

"I'm not planning on it, but he's unpredictable. We might have to haul him into town to get our questions answered."

Carl answered the knock on the door, "What are you doing out here again? Did you bring back my boots?"

"No, we haven't finished with them yet. I have more questions to ask."

"Didn't I answer your questions this morning?"

"Yes, you did. I have some new questions now."

"How am I supposed to get anything done around here?"

"It won't take long."

Well, get on with it. I've got work to do."

"I understand that you had an altercation with Nick Brinkman at the Carson's store a few months back. What was that about?"

Carl's face turned deep red. His eyes began to bulge. His big hands were fisted at his side. "He was making eyes at my woman."

"I understand he only said hello to her."

"I've heard about all his women. I knew he was hopin' to add mine to his harem. I let him know right then that I wasn't about to let that happen."

"Assaulting a peace officer is a serious offense. Why didn't he press charges?"

"I guess I didn't give him time. How should I know?"

"I'd like to speak with Mrs. Ellis now."

"She don't know anything about this."

"I'd like to speak with her anyway."

Carl grumbled and stared at Wade. Wade returned the stare. Finally, Carl went inside. Brandy walked outside alone.

"You wanted to see me, Sheriff?" she asked while looking at his shoes.

"Where were you and Mr. Ellis between the hours of eleven thirty last night and five thirty this morning?"

"We were both here asleep."

"Do you know of anyone who might have held a grudge against Mr. Brinkman?"

Brandy's eyes met Wade's before returning to the ground. "No," she answered.

"I understand there was an incident at the Carson's store a few months ago. What happened?"

"Mr. Brinkman said hello. Carl didn't like it."

"Is there anything else you think I should know?"

"No, I don't know anything that could help."

"Thank you, Mrs. Ellis. As the case progresses, I may have more questions. I don't have any more just now, but if you need to tell me anything, anything at all, my office is just a phone call away."

"I understand," Brandy nodded and went back inside.

Carl stepped out and said, "Hurry up with my boots. I need them to get my work done."

Wade only waved as he walked to his truck. Instead of driving back to town, he drove to the Brinkman home. He tapped lightly on the door while Lizzie and Baker stood behind him.

"Please, come in, Sheriff," Emily's father said. "Do you have any news?"

"I'm sorry, no. I have more questions for Mrs. Brinkman if she's available."

"I'm here," Emily called from the next room. "Sit down, please. I'll be out in a minute."

Wade and his deputies waited patiently for Mrs. Brinkman. They refused her mother's offer of something to drink. Her parents excused themselves as Emily entered the room.

"Do you have any news?"Emily asked.

"Only more questions. They could be painful questions," Wade warned her.

"Ask anything you need. I'll do my best to answer."

"You made a comment this morning that led me to believe that you're aware that your husband was involved with another woman. Do you know who he was seeing?"

Emily sighed. "Yes, I knew he was seeing someone, but I don't know who."

"But you suspected someone?"

"Yes, I did."

"Who did you suspect?"

"I heard a rumor that April Randolph had been making frequent trips to Crowell. I didn't want to believe it at first, but I smelled her perfume on his clothes one night."

"Did you confront your husband?"

"He always denied seeing anyone, so I confronted April instead. She denied it. I'd have believed her if it hadn't been for the perfume."

"Was Mrs. Randolph the only person you suspected?"

"I know there were others, but I don't know any names. I'd recognize their perfume."

"It's been my experience that several women could wear the same perfume," Wade suggested.

"I understand what you're saying, Sheriff. I know that I can't be sure based on perfume, but it does narrow down the possibilities."

"Is there any chance that one of them could have been Brandy Ellis?"

"Brandy? No, she's too afraid of her husband to even consider it."

"Do you know Mrs. Ellis well?"

Emily hesitated before answering. "She's been doing some house cleaning for me."

"Is it possible that she met Nick here?"

"No, I made sure she was here when Nick was on duty. I never told him that she was working for me. In fact, I never told anyone."

"Does Mr. Ellis know?"

"Brandy asked that it be kept a secret. She's saving for a Christmas surprise for their daughter."

"That's all I have at the moment. As the case progresses, I may have more questions for you.

"I'll be happy to help if I can."

The sheriff and his team said goodbye. They drove back to town silently contemplating what they had learned.

# CHAPTER 18

The sheriff's team had their dinner before sharing the information they had gathered. Wade started the recording after they had finished eating.

"We are here tonight sharing information pertaining to the case of Nick Brinkman. Deputy Brandon Lodge, what do you have?"

"The shotgun was not issued to the victim by the Foard County Sheriff's office. It's registered to the victim. Mr. Brinkman and Mr. Randolph were students at Vernon High School at the same time. They most likely knew each other, but it's unclear if they were friends at that time. Neither of the victims had a criminal record."

"What about the Brinkman's financial situation, Deputy Calvin Baker?"

"Mr. Brinkman had a life insurance policy for twenty-five thousand dollars. Mrs. Brinkman is the beneficiary," Baker answered. "They rent their house. Her car is financed, but his isn't. They have a small credit card debt."

"It's not a lot of money but might still be motive for murder," Wade added.

"Deputy Craig Dodson, do you have anything to add?"

"Deputy Gordon Reed and I interviewed the people connected to the case who were at work today. All were home asleep at the time of the murder. No one knew of any reason for Mr. Brinkman's death."

"Deputy Lizzie Fletcher, what have you found?"

"I took the fabric sample to two fabric stores. I found one possible match that has been sent to the lab for comparison. I found another at the store in Rayland that could be a match. It will be sent to the lab as well."

"Did anyone happen to check into those tire marks that were in front of Mrs. Cutter's house?"

"Yes, sir," Lodge answered. The tread pattern matches the Goodyear Wrangler Radial tires. Half the farmers in the area use those tires. I happened to notice that Mr. Ellis had that type of tire on his pickup, sir."

"So we can't rule out any of the neighbors or party guests as suspects," Wade said. "However, we do have three very strong suspects. April Randolph had an argument with her husband shortly before he died. She had access to the murder weapon, and she is the beneficiary of a large life insurance policy. The shoe prints found at the scene match the shoes she was wearing when we questioned her. Those could have been made when she found the victim."

"Shouldn't we arrest her for Paul Randolph's murder," Lodge asked.

"We could arrest Mrs. Randolph, but we have no proof that she committed the crime. We have no finger prints, no blood on her clothing, and no witnesses. I don't believe we would get a conviction based on what we have. Does anyone disagree with that?"

Everyone shook their heads. They knew it wasn't enough.

"Emily Brinkman is a strong suspect in her husband's death. He was having multiple affairs. She knew it. She knew when he would be home. There's a life insurance policy naming her as beneficiary. It's a small one, but it could still be enough to motivate someone to murder, considering the other circumstances. Still we have no evidence. No fingerprints and no witnesses. She didn't find her husband, so we have no reason to search for blood on her clothing without a warrant." Wade walked around the table before continuing. "Based on the evidence we've found, I'm convinced that the two murders are connected. But there's nothing to indicate that April Randolph or Emily Brinkman killed the other woman's husband."

"Could they have planned it that way?"Reed queried. "I know we don't have any evidence to support that line of thought, but could it be possible?"

"Anything is possible," Dodson added. "This reminds me of a book I read, *The ABC Murders*. A man wanted a particular person dead but didn't want to be suspected. He killed other people in different towns according to the alphabet to camouflage his crime. Maybe something like that is happening here."

"If so, who was the decoy and who was the real target? We can't rule out any possibility right now," Wade said.

"You said there were three strong suspects. Who is the third?" Lizzie asked.

"Carl Ellis," Wade answered. "He had disagreements with both of our victims. He threatened Mr. Randolph over the money he lost in the business deal. He knew where the murder weapon was kept. His alibi can't be verified. He punched Deputy Brinkman in a presumed misunderstanding about Mrs. Ellis. He found Brinkman's body. According to Mrs. Cutter, Brinkman's shotgun was in the front passenger seat when she last saw him. Ellis could have taken the gun from the seat and used it to kill Nick Brinkman. It's possible that he went home and waited until he felt enough time had passed to call us. His alibi can't be verified."

"Of the three, I'd put my money on Ellis," Lodge said.

"We don't have enough evidence to arrest any of them," Baker said.

"I'm afraid we won't unless someone else is killed. We may not even then," Wade said. "I'm certain that those strips of pink cloth are the key, but we can't seem to find out anything about them."

Each person at the meeting sat quietly going over the evidence in their minds. Finally, Wade broke the silence.

"Let's get search warrants for the Ellises and Mrs. Brinkman. We're searching for traces of our latest victim's blood. Let's also get warrants to compare truck tires to those we found and to compare carpets to our sample. We might be able to narrow our list of suspects that way."

"How does the incident at Mrs. Cutter's place connect to this case?" Baker asked.

"I mentioned in the Randolph case that I thought it was someone who knew him well. I think someone who knew Brinkman well is behind his death. Someone knew that he frequently visited Mrs. Cutter. They knew she would call him if she had a concern. According to Mrs. Cutter, there was a lot of noise outside. If the carpet bounced out of the truck or if it was intended to be dumped there, she wouldn't have heard anything unusual. It was as if someone wanted to get her attention. The carpet itself was positioned so that from her front porch it looked like a body lying in the ditch. I think someone set things up to make sure that Brinkman would stop there. It's possible that someone watched as he investigated that roll of carpet. It's possible that someone lured him toward the river. It's possible that someone lured Paul Randolph toward his barn."

Wade adjourned the meeting. He sent everyone home or back to the appointed tasks. He phoned Scott Duncan to tell him what had been learned. The Foard County Sheriff agreed with Wade's opinion that someone had set up Nick Brinkman. Wade worked in his office a while longer, trying to make the pieces fit.

Two hours later, he decided to call it a night, but he didn't go home. He needed to relax and take his mind off the case for a while. In the past, he would have gone to see Lizzie. He couldn't do that this time, so he went to the Watering Hole for a drink.

He found a table in a corner so that he could see one of the televisions. He would have a meal while he watched what was left of the Monday night football game. The New England Patriots were playing the Carolina Panthers. It was the end of the third quarter, and the Panthers had just scored a touchdown, putting them ahead by seven points.

The bar wasn't as crowded as it would have been for a Dallas Cowboys game, but there were a few people cheering for one team or the other. Wade enjoyed a beer and an appetizer as he settled in for the remainder of the game.

"Well, hello! May I join you?"

Wade glanced up to see who was talking. The woman sat down

without invitation. She ordered a drink and smiled at him.

"Miss Ford, I'd prefer to be alone and enjoy the game if you don't mind."

"I don't mind at all Wade. I just love football don't you?" Megan said as she helped herself to some of Wade's food.

Wade did his best to ignore her while he watched the game. Megan did everything in her power to distract him. When he finished his beer, he got up to leave. Megan took his arm as she followed him out the door. He felt he had no choice but to walk her to her car before he could make his getaway.

"I had such a good time tonight, Wade," she said obviously waiting for a goodnight kiss.

"Goodnight," Wade said.

He was about to walk away when Megan threw her arms around his neck. She pressed her breasts into his chest as she kissed him full on the mouth. Finally, disentangling himself, he pushed her away and quickly walked to his truck. Megan blew him a kiss as he drove out of the parking lot.

*I've got to tell Lizzie about this before anyone else tells her.* He started toward his house but noticed that he was being followed. He was so sure it was Megan that he went back to the office instead. He'd have to wait to contact Lizzie. He prayed that no one else would tell her before he could.

Lizzie was watching an old movie and relaxing when her phone rang. She considered letting it ring but answered when she realized it was her cousin, Jan.

"Hi, Jan. What's up?"

"Lizzie, are you sitting down?"

"Yes, why?"

"I just heard something that I can hardly believe. I thought you should know."

"Okay, tell me."

"Wade Adams is dating Megan Ford."

Lizzie was speechless. She listened as Jan told her the story.

"Amanda was at the Watering Hole with her boyfriend, watching the game tonight. She said Wade came in just before the fourth quarter. Megan came in a few minutes later. She sat down with him. They had a drink and then left together. She called me because she wanted to know if she should tell you or not."

It took all the courage Lizzie could muster to answer, "What does that have to do with me?"

"Lizzie, I know you two aren't together anymore, but I thought you'd want to know that Megan has her hooks into him."

"Jan, he's a grown man. He can see whoever he pleases. He knows Megan well enough to know he's in for trouble, but if that's what he wants, then, so be it."

"Are you telling me you're not upset? Not even a little?"

"Maybe a little but just because it's Megan."

"So, it's really over between the two of you?"

"Yes, it is," Lizzie answered, trying her best to sound normal.

"Does that mean you're going to be seeing someone else?"

"Not anytime soon. I prefer being alone right now."

"Okay, I just thought I'd let you know that Drake is supposed to be here during the holidays."

"That's nice. I'm sure you'll all have a great time together."

"I thought maybe you'd want to see him, too."

"I know what you're hinting at. It might be nice to see him to catch up, but that's all. He lives in Colorado, and I have this inn to run. I don't want to give it up. I'm sure he doesn't want to give up his life."

"You never know. That could change if the two of you still have that spark you used to have."

"I don't know. Maybe, but I doubt it. Visions of Megan appear every time I think about Drake."

"Ah ha. You do think about Drake."

"Only when people like you bring him up," Lizzie laughed. "Jan, I'm not interested in dating right now. I need some time."

"I know. It was just a thought. I love you, and I want you to be happy."

"I appreciate that. I love you, too. Goodnight, Jan."

"Goodnight."

Lizzie turned off the movie before going to the kitchen for a snack. She was about to change into her pajamas when she heard the emergency radio squawk to life. She padded into her office and sat down before answering the call.

"Go ahead, Mesquite. This is Sagebrush. This had better be good."

"I take it that you've already heard."

"Yes, but I'd love to hear your side of the story but remember no names."

Lizzie listened as Wade told her what had happened with Megan.

"Are you angry with me?" he asked.

"No, I knew she was up to something."

"I tried my best to get rid of her, but she had no intention of leaving."

"I know. This could work to our advantage though."

"I don't see how."

"There are still people who doubt that we've broken up. If word gets around that you're seeing that woman, it should put an end to those doubts."

"Some of those doubters are in our office. That's why we have to be careful when we're working."

"I know. I should tell you that my cousin is already pushing me to consider seeing my ex again."

"Now, I know how you must have felt when you heard about that woman."

"Trust me, Mesquite; I have no intention of dating my ex again."

"I trust you. I hope you know I have no intention of dating that woman, but you're right, it could work to our advantage."

"I miss you."

"I miss you, too. We should sign off before someone stumbles onto our frequency. Goodnight, Sagebrush."

"Goodnight, Mesquite."

# CHAPTER 19

It was determined during the week following Deputy Brinkman's death that none of the suspects could be eliminated. The searches had revealed nothing useful. All of the suspects had at least one vehicle with tires matching the tracks found near Mrs. Cutter's home. No one had any traces of carpet that matched their evidence. No one had the victim's blood on their clothing.

The Wilbarger County Sheriff's department followed every possible lead they had to no avail. The lab report on the fabric samples was still pending. All they could do was to wait for a break in the case.

"Fletcher, the sheriff wants to see you," Reed told her as he passed her desk.

Lizzie minimized the computer screen before going to Wade's office. She tapped on the open door.

"Did you want to see me?"

"Yes, come in," he said, indicating the chair in front of his desk. "When do you need to be back at the inn full time?"

"We have a baby shower scheduled for December seventh. I really need to be there the entire week before. After that, we have at least two parties a week until Christmas and a big New Year's Eve party."

"Could you possibly help out here through December first? We'll be closed Thanksgiving Day. Those who are staying in town will be on call. I have vacation requests from those who need to travel to be with family. We're going to be even more shorthanded than we already are."

"I can do that."

"Great, thank you. Are you comfortable running the office?"

"Yes, but I might need a few pointers from time to time."

"Someone will be here to help you if needed. I haven't got the schedule worked out yet."

"Is there something else?" Lizzie asked.

"Yes, Maddie is scheduled to come back December ninth. I don't expect that we'll need you after she returns," Wade said, trying not to look at her.

"I understand. I knew she would be back soon but wasn't sure when. That means my last day is the first of December?"

"Yes, unless we get into a bind. I'd like you to keep the badge and uniform at least until this case is over. We might need your help again."

"Yes, sir."

"Thank you, Fletcher."

Lizzie took that as her cue to leave. She walked back to her desk and tried to concentrate on her work. She was disappointed that she wouldn't see Wade on a daily basis anymore. *You knew this situation was only temporary. You'll just have to deal with it.*

The phone rang, interrupting her thoughts. Lizzie cringed when she heard the voice on the other end.

"May I speak to Wade, please?"

"Please, hold while I check to see if he is available."

Lizzie pressed the hold button before buzzing Wade's office.

"Yes?"

"Sheriff, are you accepting calls from Megan Ford?"

"No, tell her I'm in a meeting and take a message. Nothing has changed since my last directive. I'm always in a meeting or out, or something, when she calls."

"Yes, sir."

Lizzie returned to the incoming line and said, "I'm sorry, ma'am. Sheriff Adams is in a meeting. May I take a message?"

"Oh, darn! I really wanted to talk to him about last night. Please, have him call me."

"Who is this?" Lizzie couldn't resist pretending she had no idea who she was talking to.

"Lizzie Fletcher! You know very well who I am."

"I'm sorry, ma'am, but I don't," Lizzie said grinning.

"Megan Ford!" The caller screamed.

Lizzie held the receiver away and rubbed her ear before continuing, "I'm sorry; I didn't recognize your voice. Does he have your number?"

"He should; he calls me every day," Megan lied.

"I'll give him the message. Have a nice day," Lizzie said as she hung up.

Lizzie scribbled the message on a note pad. She took it to Wade's office and placed it on his desk without a word.

Baker was grinning at her when she returned to her desk.

"What?" she asked. "Do I have something on my face?"

"I know what you did," he teased.

"What did I do?" she asked innocently.

"You know what you did," he joked.

"Can't a girl have a little fun?" she replied grinning. "She's caused me a lot of trouble. I don't see any harm in aggravating her just a little."

"Uh huh. Did you really give the sheriff the message?"

"Yes, I did. You can ask him if you don't believe me," Lizzie replied with irritation in her voice.

"Hey, I'm just giving you a hard time. I believe you."

"Just to make sure," she said carrying the note pad to his desk. "You can see the impression in the paper below. You're a detective; detect."

Baker looked at the notepad and then at her in amazement. He was speechless until he realized she was smiling at him.

"Give me that pad," he said as he snatched it from her. He used a pencil and rubbed it lightly across the page. "You really did take the message. I'm sorry I ever doubted you."

"That's okay. Just don't do it again," Lizzie said as she playfully punched him on the shoulder.

Baker feigned a broken arm for a moment and grinned at her as they both returned to their work.

Lizzie secretly looked forward to going to work every day so that she could see Wade. They couldn't talk about anything other than business, but she enjoyed being there with him. They tried to talk at least once a week with their radios, but sometimes the jobs got in the way. Lizzie knew that they'd probably lose touch entirely when she left the department.

She hoped that the case would be over soon, but she knew in her heart that it wouldn't. Her only hope was that they could reconnect after Maddie returned to work.

The following week, Lizzie was working in the office alone. She had two lines on hold and was helping a person on the third line. She had no sooner hung up than another call came in.

"Sheriff's office, please hold."

"Wait, I've been on hold for ten minutes already."

"I'm sorry; I'm the only person in the office today. I'll be with you in just a moment," Lizzie said pressing the hold button.

"Thank you for holding. How may I help you?"

"Is the Sheriff's office going to be open tomorrow?"

"No, ma'am, but there will be officers on call."

"I wanted to bring Thanksgiving lunch over for those who are working. May I bring it over on Friday?"

"Thank you very much, ma'am. We appreciate the thought, but with our current case load, we aren't accepting visitors or packages at this time."

"Oh, that's a shame. Well, I'll call again after the holidays."

"Thank you, ma'am. Goodbye," Lizzie said as she disconnected that line and answered another. "Thank you for holding. How may I help you?"

"May I speak with Sheriff Adams, please?"

"Who may I say is calling?"

"This is Alex Dylan."

"I'll check to see if he is available. I'll have to put you on hold for a little longer."

"That's alright."

Lizzie buzzed Wade's office.

"Yes?"

"Are you available to speak with Alex Dylan?"

"Yes, which line?"

"Line two."

Lizzie waited until Wade had answered the line before returning to the remaining caller on hold.

"Thank you for holding. How may I help you?"

"I'd like to speak with Wade."

"I'm sorry, but he isn't available at the moment. May I take a message?"

"Lizzie, why is it that Wade is never available when you answer the phone?"

"Is this Megan?"

"You know it is. What kind of game are you playing?"

Lizzie wanted to say a lot to Megan. Instead she resisted the urge. "I'm not playing games. I'm just very busy, and so is the sheriff. I'd be happy to take a message for you."

"Is there someone else there I can speak, too?"

"No, we have a skeleton crew today. Everyone else is at lunch. Would you like to leave a message?"

"So, Wade's at lunch. Where did he go for lunch?"

Lizzie didn't correct her. "The sheriff doesn't share his lunch plans."

"I'll bet that just burns you up doesn't it," Megan said gleefully.

"Megan, I'm very busy. I'll be happy to take a message, otherwise, I need to answer the other line."

"No message. I know where he likes to go for lunch. I'll just find him there," Megan said as she broke the connection.

Lizzie rubbed her forehead and took a deep breath.

"I thought you had to answer another line."

Lizzie jumped and turned around. "You scared me, sir."

"Was that who I think it was?"

"Yes, she said she knows where you like to eat lunch and will find you there."

"She won't find me today. I'm going to a meeting with Alex Dylan. Go to lunch as soon as Baker gets back. Put two of those lines on hold, so you'll only have to answer one while you're here alone."

"I thought about that earlier, but I didn't know if it was a good idea."

"Emergency calls will get through faster that way rather than being on hold while you answer the other lines."

"Got it. One more thing, Miss Ford seems to think that I'm not forwarding her calls to you or giving you her messages. I expect she'll try to cause some trouble over it."

Wade grimaced. "I suppose I'll have to take a call from her at some point. If she calls again, put her through if I'm available. After that, just take messages again."

"Yes, sir."

"I don't know how long I'll be away. Call my cell if something comes up."

"Yes, sir."

Lizzie put two of the phone lines on hold as Wade left the building. She had a short reprieve before the remaining line rang again.

"Sheriff's office, how may I help you?"

"Lizzie, are you busy?"

"Hi, Mama. It's slowed down a bit now."

"Good, I don't want to keep you from your work."

"This is a nice break. What can I do for you?"

"Would you mind stopping by the store on your way home? I forgot to get some of the things I'll need for Thanksgiving dinner tomorrow."

"Sure, do you want me to bring them by tonight or in the morning?"

"Tonight, if you aren't too tired. You can stay and have dinner with us."

"That sounds good to me," Lizzie assured her mother. "What do you need?"

Lizzie jotted down a few items. "I'll see you later, then." She hung up, and the phone rang again.

"This is Sheriff Duncan. Is Sheriff Adams available?"

"No, sir. He's out of the office at the moment. Would you like me to have him call you?"

"It's nothing urgent. Have him call me when it's convenient."

"Yes, sir."

Lizzie placed the message from Sheriff Duncan on Wade's desk and bumped into Baker on her way out.

"I'm sorry, Fletcher. I didn't see you."

"That's okay. Since you're back, I'm going to lunch. The sheriff is meeting with Alex Dylan. We're to call him on his cell if needed. Sheriff Duncan would like for him to call when it's convenient."

"Alright, enjoy your lunch. Oh, by the way, I'd avoid the barbeque place if I were you."

"I wasn't planning on going there but why?"

"Your buddy Megan Ford is there."

"Thanks for the tip. I should go just to mess with her," Lizzie teased.

"No, really don't go." Baker was serious. "She's badmouthing you to anyone who will listen."

Lizzie hesitated and grinned. "It wouldn't be good to get into an altercation while in uniform would it?"

"No, it wouldn't," Baker grinned. "I did my best to defend you, but you know how she can be."

"Oh boy, do I. Thanks for standing up for me."

"Hey, what are friends for. You'd better get some lunch before I put you to work."

"Say no more," Lizzie said and hurried out the door.

Wade drove to a small restaurant at the edge of town. He sat down to wait for Alex Dylan. He couldn't help but wonder what the man wanted to see him about.

"Sheriff," Alex said as he approached the table. "Thanks for meeting with me on such short notice."

"I assume this has something to do with the one or both of the cases we're working on," Wade answered as he shook hands with Alex.

Alex sat down before answering, "Yes and no."

Their conversation was interrupted by a waitress, "May I take your order?"

They placed their orders. The waitress moved away before they spoke to each other again.

"I wanted to ask you privately. This has really upset my wife. She has nightmares every night and sleep walks most nights. I found her outside in front of the house one night last week. She was standing in the middle of the road."

"What do you want to know?"

"Do you have any idea who's behind this? Are you close to an arrest?"

"Not at this time."

"That's disappointing. Morgan wants to get a job, but I want her to stay home at least until she can rest at night. She's exhausted."

"Couldn't you have asked me this on the phone?"

"I could have, but I didn't want Morgan to hear. Today is an early release day at school. I decided to try to meet with you before going home."

"Why wouldn't you want your wife to hear?"

"I don't want to upset her anymore. We're leaving for a little get away as soon as I get home. I'd like it to be a pleasant trip."

The waitress again interrupted their conversation when she returned with their drinks.

"I still don't see why the secrecy is necessary."

"I guess I'm behaving strangely. I wanted to see you face to face so that I could see your reactions to my questions. I know it's silly, but I thought you might not be straight with me on the phone."

"I'm always as forthcoming as I can be, depending on the circumstances."

"I know you are, but let me explain. I've learned over the years, when dealing with people, that there is often more to the story than is being said. I watch people's faces and their expressions when they're talking. Often times, I can determine the truthfulness of the statement or if there is more to the story."

"I use the same tactic myself. Is there something else you wanted to ask?"

"Do you think there will be another murder?"

Wade sighed and looked down at his hands. He looked up again into the anxious eyes of his lunch companion.

The men waited to continue their conversation while the waitress placed their meal on the table.

"I can't answer that because I don't know," Wade answered truthfully.

"This is why I wanted to see you. I hear your words, and I believe you, but your face also tells me that you're afraid there will be."

"Yes, I believe there will be. I have no reason to think so but…."

"There's no way to know who might be next or when it might happen?"

"No, there isn't. I noticed you didn't mention where." Wade pointed out.

"I assume it will be near Rayland, but it could be anywhere couldn't it."

Wade nodded. The two men ate their meals in silence.

# CHAPTER 20

Lizzie slept in. She knew it would be her last leisurely morning for weeks to come. Everything was ready for Jan's baby shower that evening. Her family would be there to help with the twenty people they were expecting. Gifts from those who couldn't take part in the festivities had been arriving all week.

Looking at the clock, Lizzie decided it was time she got out of bed. She needed coffee. She padded into the kitchen, started the coffee, and looked outside. It was a cold, dreary morning. It matched her mood.

She missed her new friends at the sheriff's office and the excitement. Above all, she missed seeing Wade. They had not spoken since the day she left the office for the last time. Needless to say that was less than satisfactory since they could only discuss business. They had not been able to communicate with each other since then.

Other people had been communicating with her. If she got one more report about Megan and Wade, she might explode. The hardest part was pretending that she didn't care.

Lizzie decided to shower and try to erase the thoughts of Wade. She turned it on full blast and let the hot water run over her until it began to get cold. Reluctantly, she turned off the water and toweled dry. She could smell the coffee as she went to her room and got dressed.

After pouring herself a cup of the steaming liquid, she turned on the television to see what the weather had in store for the day. A strong cold front was due to come through the area some time after midnight. Small amounts of sleet and freezing rain were predicted to accompany the front.

Lizzie was startled by a tap on the back door. Dan Hayes waved at her through the glass. She motioned that he should come in. They had been friends since they were in high school. They had always gotten along well although he had been a year ahead of her. Lizzie was pleased when James hired him to help out at the inn and around the farm.

"Hi, Dan. I have a fresh pot of coffee. Do you want some?"

"Yes, please. I brought some firewood up close to the house. You might need it tonight."

"Thank you," Lizzie said, handing him his coffee.

"I'll bring up more before I leave."

"I thought you were taking the weekend off."

"I am, but I wanted to talk to you about something," he said sipping his coffee.

"What's on your mind?"

"I have a message for you from Sheriff Adams."

"From Wade?"

"I saw him in town yesterday. He said to tell you he's sorry that he hasn't been able to contact you. Please, don't believe what you've heard or will hear. It's all part of the plan."

"Okay."

"What does that mean?"

"Dan, will you promise you won't tell anyone?"

"You know me, Lizzie. You can tell me anything. It won't leave this room."

"I suppose you know that Wade and I had to stop seeing each other when I started working for him."

"I heard that, but I didn't believe it."

"The problem is no one else seemed to believe it either. Anyway, we haven't seen each other outside of work since this all started. We only discuss business when at work. We try to communicate by radio once or twice a week, but our jobs keep getting in the way."

"So, it's like you broke up but are still friends."

"Yes, that's what it feels like. We can't see each other again until the case is over."

"Why not?"

"It might jeopardize everything. If we start going out again, no one will believe we ever stopped."

"So, the plan is that you two stay friends, but you won't see each other while the case is active."

"Right."

"How long is that going to be?"

"We have no idea."

"What did he mean by 'don't believe what you've heard'?"

Lizzie sighed and reached for Dan's hand. "Megan is making a play for Wade."

"That poor man!"

"She was bringing him packages of baked goods to the office until he put a stop to that. She was calling at least twice a day that I know of when I was there. I know she managed to corner him at the Watering Hole one night. People are calling me all the time, reporting what they saw or heard about Megan and Wade."

"I used to get some of the same kinds of calls. I'm just happy she's out of my life. I don't know why people thought I cared about what she was doing."

"Wade and I may never be able to see each other again. Even if this case is solved someday, it might be too late for us. I wish people would just drop it."

"They will when something more interesting to talk about turns up."

"I hope something turns up soon."

"We could give them something else to talk about."

"What do you mean?"

"Do you know of any reason why we can't let people think that you and I are seeing each other?"

"Are you serious?"

"Lizzie, there are folks who already think we see each other occasionally. I've always set them straight. Why not let them think it?"

"It might stop the phone calls."

"It might. We'll never say we're together or be seen together other than while working. We just won't correct folks who say otherwise. What do you think?"

"It's worth a try, but what will Samantha say?"

"Samantha moved back to Kansas a couple of weeks ago."

"I'm sorry, Dan. I didn't know."

"It's okay. It was a mutual split. We decided that we really didn't like each other that much. I'd better get going. I'm supposed to help Dad today. I'll bring some more wood up before I leave."

Lizzie walked around the counter and hugged Dan, "Thank you."

Dan grinned and kissed her on the forehead, "I'll see you Monday."

Lizzie was dressed and putting the finishing touches on the party preparations when her family arrived.

"When did you bring all that wood up?" James asked as he hugged his daughter.

"Dan did that for me before he left. He thought we might need it when the cold front comes through."

"I knew I liked that boy," Granny said. He's always thinking ahead."

"He's made a really good hand for us. I don't know what we'd do without him," Ellen added. "Lizzie, the inn looks beautiful."

"Thanks, Mama. The other hostesses should be here soon."

"What do you need us to do?" Granny asked.

"Nothing at the moment. Why don't you have some punch and relax?"

"I don't mind if I do," Lois said with a grin.

The office phone began to ring. Lizzie answered it while her family helped themselves to punch. She walked back into the kitchen, shaking her head and grinning.

"What's wrong, Lizzie?"

"Eli is bringing Jan. He's afraid the roads will be bad by the time the shower is over. He doesn't want her to drive."

"At least, I won't be the only man at this hen party," James joked.

At six thirty the first guests arrived. Fifteen minutes later, Jan knocked on the door. Lizzie hurried to answer it.

"Lizzie, I hope you don't mind. I just couldn't tell him no. Eli didn't want to be the only man here. I hope its okay," Jan said in a rush.

"What are you talking…," Lizzie didn't finish her sentence. She knew the moment she saw Drake. He was six feet tall with dark hair and green eyes. He was as handsome and muscular as he had been when she first met him. They dated four years and had planned to marry. Megan Ford changed everything.

"Hi, Lizzie."

"Hi, Drake," Lizzie answered.

"If you two don't mind, I'd like to get inside with these gifts," joked Eli.

"I'm sorry. Come in. I'm just so surprised to see you," Lizzie moved aside as the Wagner's trooped inside.

The Wagner's arrived in two SUV's. Eli drove one vehicle with Jan, his mother Carol, and his sister-in-law Kirsten. Drake drove a second vehicle with his sister Faith, and his sister-in-law Dawn.

Barbara Pearson arrived shortly after the Wagner's. Lizzie always marveled at how much her Aunt Barbara and her mother looked alike as Ellen hugged her sister.

"Hello, sweetheart," Barbara said as she hugged Lizzie.

"Hi, Aunt Barbara."

"Where's my good looking son-in-law? I need his muscles."

"I'm right here."Eli hugged his mother-in-law and teased, "You've already used up all my muscles; use Drake's."

"I have something in the car, but I can't lift it. Would you get it for me, please?"

"Anything for you," Eli grinned and left the room. He came back a few minutes later. "How did you get it in there?"

"Well, I didn't. They loaded it for me at the store. It's been in there a week," Barbara said with a laugh.

"Drake, would you mind giving me a hand?"

The two men left the room again eventually returning with an obviously heavy box. They maneuvered it through the door and put it down to catch their breath.

"What on earth is this?"

"It's the crib Jan picked out. You'll have to put it together when you get it home," Barbara told her son-in-law and pinched his cheek.

James strolled over to the Wagner boys and whispered something that they seemed to agree with. The three men disappeared into the office.

The baby shower was winding down. The gifts had been opened, and everyone was enjoying refreshments when suddenly a strong wind made the windows rattle. Lizzie looked outside to see the branches of the trees being blown to the point of breaking. The clock on the kitchen wall said eight thirty. She went in search of her Dad. She found him and the Wagner brothers in her office watching a college football game and enjoying a beer.

"Daddy, have you seen any weather updates?"

"No, but I can switch it to a local channel during the commercial. What's wrong?"

"The wind is really strong outside. I was wondering if that cold front is early or if this is just strong wind."

"I'll find out and let you know."

"Thanks, Daddy. I don't want anyone to be in danger on the way home."

Lizzie went through her room on her way back to the party. She could hear the unmistakable sound of ice hitting her bedroom window. She looked outside to see sleet falling from the sky. She was about to go back to the office when the power went off. She felt her way to the pantry and located the flashlights. She carried three with her back to the party.

"Please, remain seated everyone until we can get some light in here," Lizzie said to her guests. "I have some flashlights and candles that we can use until the power comes back on."

"Let me have one of those Lizzie," James said. "I'll start the emergency generator."

"Did you find out anything about the weather?"

"No, the power went off before I could. Keep everyone in here until I get the generator running."

"Can I help, James," Drake asked.

"Grab a flashlight and follow me."

"What can I do?"Eli offered.

"I could use some help with the flashlights and candles," Lizzie told him.

"Lead the way."

Within minutes, the room had enough light that the party could resume. James and Drake had the emergency generator humming when they came back inside.

"How bad is it?"Lizzie asked.

"There's a thin layer of ice already forming out there. We didn't realize it until your dad slipped and fell. I think he's hurt worse than he'll admit," Drake told her.

"Daddy, are you hurt?"

James was protecting his left arm. "It's nothing serious. I banged up my shoulder a little. I'll be alright."

"Don't you think we'd better let a doctor decide that?" Ellen scolded.

"Not tonight," he said gravely.

"Then come over here in the light so that I can have a look at it," Ellen ordered.

James looked at Drake. Drake nodded and went into the office with Eli close behind. A few minutes later, they returned. Eli sat beside his wife while Drake walked to where James was seated. Ellen was busy making a sling for her husband.

"How's your shoulder?" he asked James.

"My nurse here doesn't think anything is broken or dislocated," James replied. "What did you find out?"

"This is just the front edge of the storm. The freezing rain and possible snow is supposed to continue well past midnight before it begins to taper off," Drake whispered.

"We'd better ask everyone to stay here until this is over. We'll have to do the best we can. It might be a little uncomfortable for our guests, but I'd rather they were safe."

James motioned for his family to join the conversation. They made a plan of action before telling their guests the situation.

"Ladies, may I have your attention, please," James said to the shower guests. "We have a dangerous situation here tonight. The cold front arrived early, bringing with it much more precipitation than expected. It's already dangerously slick outside. We believe it is much safer for everyone to remain here for the time being. We'll do everything we can to make you as comfortable as possible. Please, bear with us as we work toward that end. I suggest you phone your families to let them know the situation and that you're safe. Thank you for your cooperation."

"What can we do to help?" Carol Wagner offered.

"It will probably be best if we all camp out near that center wall and the fireplace. Feel free to move furniture in that direction. I could use some help bringing all the blankets down from the upstairs rooms," Lizzie replied. "We'll be turning off any unnecessary electrical appliances so that the generator won't have to work so hard. The heat will be turned down so we'll want the blankets to stay warm."

"I noticed some firewood stacked outside," Drake said. "Eli and I will bring that in."

"Thank you," James said. "Mom, Ellen, if you'll turn off anything that isn't necessary to keep us warm and safe, I'd appreciate it."

"What about the television?" Lois asked.

"If we're still getting a signal, leave it on. We might get another weather update before the satellite ices over."

After all the necessary arrangements had been made, everyone gathered near the fireplace. They continued the party in the light of flashlights and candles. Everyone was in good spirits, considering the circumstances.

"Jan, I don't think I've ever been to a baby shower quite like this one. I have to say it's the most fun I've had in years," Faith exclaimed.

"Why thank you. I'd like to take credit for it, but I don't think Mother Nature would be pleased."

As the night wore on, the guests snuggled under the blankets and drifted off to sleep. Most had made their beds on the floor as close to the fireplace as possible while others slept sitting on the sofas.

Drake and Lizzie sat side by side sharing a blanket. They talked in whispers so as not to wake the sleeping guests. Soon their conversation stopped as they too dozed off.

Lizzie's dreams were interrupted by the squawking of the emergency radio. She opened her eyes and realized that she had fallen asleep on Drake's shoulder. Trying not to wake him, she got up slowly. He began to move in response to the loss of her body heat. She quickly covered him with the blanket and tiptoed to the office.

"Paradise Creek Inn, do you read me? Come in."

"This is Paradise Creek Inn; go ahead." Lizzie answered.

"This is Sheriff Adams. Is everyone alright out there? I've tried calling your land line but haven't been able to get through."

"Yes, Sheriff, everyone is fine. The power is off, but the emergency generator is working. The phone lines are down, too."

"I've been getting calls from the worried family members of your guests. How many people do you have there?"

"Approximately twenty-six people including us. Everyone is sleeping. They've turned their cell phones off to conserve the batteries. "

"Have their families been contacted?"

"I believe so, but I'll give you a list just in case." Lizzie gave him the names of everyone at the inn.

"It's a good thing James has some men there to help out."

Lizzie thought Wade sounded like he didn't really think it was a good thing. "Yes, they've been a lot of help. Daddy injured his shoulder when he fell on the ice. He's one-armed at the moment."

"Is it serious? Do you need medical help?"

"We don't think so. He's using a sling until we can get into town."

"Travel may be hazardous for quite a while. We have reports of ice between two and three inches thick in the area. Power and phone lines are down all over the county. The highways are closed in all directions because of the icy conditions. How long can you hold out with that many people?"

"I'm not sure. The pantry and freezer are full. What is the weather forecast?"

"It's supposed to clear off in the morning but remain very cold. You could be there a while. Is your satellite working?"

"Not at the moment. The dish is covered with ice."

"Alright, keep this channel open. We'll do our best to keep you informed. Let us know if you need assistance."

"Thank you, Sheriff."

"It's a good thing that radio runs on batteries," James said.

Lizzie jumped and squeaked, "Oh Daddy, you scared me."

"I'm sorry, honey. I saw you come in here and followed you."

"How long do you think our supplies will last?"

"I don't know, but we'll use them sparingly. I don't know if we have enough gas for the generator. We may have to siphon from our cars."

"What if we put the food that's in the freezer outside? We could turn off the freezer so that the generator wouldn't have to work so hard."

"That's a good idea. We could do something similar with the food in the refrigerator. I'll go wake you mother and grandmother. We won't wake the guests unless we have to."

"I'll round up the coolers and boxes to put the food in."

"It was like old times out there tonight wasn't it?"

Lizzie looked at her father in confusion.

"You and Drake," he said looking into her eyes.

Lizzie only smiled at him and went in search of boxes.

# CHAPTER 21

Drake woke to the sounds coming from the kitchen. He stretched before he carefully made his way over to the Fletcher's. They were busy removing the contents of the freezer.

"What's wrong? Can I help?" he whispered.

James explained the situation, "We're trying to conserve gas for the generator. It's cold enough outside that we can put everything outside the door and unplug the freezer."

"I'll wake Eli, and we'll help."

"I'm already awake. I was about to get more firewood," Eli yawned.

"Let's try to get this stuff out and the firewood in as quickly as possible. I don't want to lose too much heat," James told them. "I'll check the fuel level on the generator while we're out there. It may need more gas."

"I'll do that James. I don't want you to fall on that arm again," Drake offered as he put on his coat.

"I'll be careful. It's all I can do with one arm. I need you boys to do the heavy lifting."

"That's all of it," Lizzie told them. "Daddy, I'll check the generator. You stay in here and protect your arm."

James started to argue but saw the look in his wife's eyes. "Alright, just be careful."

Ellen and Lois moved the boxes of frozen food to the door. Lizzie and the Wagner brothers, bundled up against the elements, worked together to get the boxes outside as quickly as possible. Drake and Eli moved firewood in while Lizzie checked the generator.

Lizzie struggled to walk against the wind as it blew pellets of ice horizontally into her face. She reached the generator only to discover that the fuel gauge was covered with ice. It was impossible to read. She needed something to clear it. There were tools in the shed that might do the job.

The wind was at her back as she made her way to the shed. She struggled to stay on her feet as she crossed the ice covered ground to the shed. Finally reaching the shed, she found the door frozen shut. She pulled with all her might and lost her footing. She fell onto her side, hitting her head on the ice. She lay there for a moment, trying to clear the cobwebs from her brain.

"Lizzie! Lizzie, are you all right?" Drake shouted in the distance.

"I'm okay. Just catching my breath!" she shouted back.

"Stay there! I'm coming!"

She saw a flashlight approaching as she carefully sat up. She gingerly touched her head and winced. She had what her grandmother liked to call a goose egg forming on the left side of her head.

"I'm here, Lizzie; don't move!" Drake shouted in order to be heard over the wind as he helped her to her feet.

"I'm okay; I just bumped my head!"

"Let's get you back inside! What are you doing over here? I thought you were checking the generator!"

"The fuel gauge is covered with ice! I was looking for something to clear it, but this door is frozen shut!"

"How long is it supposed to run?"

"Up to ten hours! It's been running at least four now! I doubt it has enough fuel to last all night."

"Where is the gas for it?"

"There's a five gallon can in here!" Lizzie pointed at the shed.

"Stay right there! I'm going to see if I can get the door open!"

"Need help?" Eli shouted as he carefully walked toward them.

"Help me get this door open!"

The two men struggled for several minutes. Finally, the ice cracked, and the door opened. They hurried inside closing the door behind them. It felt good to escape the wind and freezing rain for a moment. Drake scanned the little room with his flashlight. He located a gas can and lifted it easily. It was empty.

"Is there another gas can in here?" he asked Lizzie.

"There should be a couple of them in this corner over here," Lizzie said shining her flashlight in the right direction.

Eli lifted one of the cans. "This one is about half-full, and the other is full. "I'd say we have between seven and eight gallons of gas left."

"That should be good until morning. Let's take the cans with us to the house. I don't want to have to wrestle with this door again," Drake suggested. "Lizzie, can you handle the empty one?"

"Yes, I've found something that should clear the ice from the gauge, too."

Lizzie and the Wagner brothers steeled themselves for the blast of icy wind that they knew would be coming when they opened the shed door. They carefully made their way back to the generator. Drake shielded Eli from the wind as he cleared the gauge.

"How much gas does it hold, Lizzie? Eli shouted.

"Sixteen gallons!"

"It has less than half-a-tank! We'll have to shut the generator down while we fill it. It will probably take all of the gas we have left!"

"We can handle this, Lizzie!" Drake shouted. "Go back inside; we'll be in when we've finished here!"

Lizzie nodded and carefully walked back to the door where James and Ellen had been watching. They welcomed her inside.

"What took so long?" James whispered.

Lizzie pulled the hood back on her coat. Chunks of ice fell to the floor. "Everything is frozen over. They're going to shut the generator down so they can put the last of the gas in it now."

"What happened to your head?" Ellen asked.

"I'm fine, Mama; it's just a little bump."

"Go get out of those wet clothes. I'll look at it when they get the generator running again."

Lizzie quickly obeyed. She returned to find Jan coming in her direction.

"What's going on? Where's Eli?" Jan asked.

"We didn't mean to wake you." Lizzie told her cousin. "He's outside with Drake. They're putting more gas into the generator."

"You didn't wake me. Junior likes to dance on my bladder. I have to get up several times a night. Is the ladies room free?"

"Yes, take this flashlight with you."

As soon as the generator was working, Drake and Eli duck walked back to the house. Ice fell from their coats as they stripped them off.

"Do we have any more news about the weather?" Eli asked. "It's getting worse out there."

"I spoke with the sheriff's office on the radio while you were outside. This storm is supposed to blow through in a couple of hours," James told them. "When the storm hit, the wind blew an eighteen wheeler over on highway 287. People are stranded on the roads, doing their best to stay warm. State troopers and the fire department are shuttling people into town. The power is out in most of Vernon. The fire department, police station, and sheriff's office are running on emergency generators, too."

"It's a good thing we stayed put," Drake said. "I'd hate to be stuck on the road in this."

"Why don't you boys go into Lizzie's room and get those wet clothes off," Lois suggested. "James will bring you some blankets. I'll hang your clothes on the banister to dry."

"Yes, ma'am," the men replied.

Ellen tended to the bump on Lizzie's head. It wasn't as bad as she had feared. Lizzie had a slight headache but had no other symptoms to be concerned about.

Eli and Drake joined the Fletcher's as they watched the freezing rain change to light snow fall.

"I appreciate your help boys. I don't know what we would have done without you," James told them.

"If there's anything else we can do, just let us know," Eli offered.

"All we can do now is wait it out," James said. "Let's all try to get some rest."

Eli sat down next to Jan. The expectant parents snuggled together under the blankets. Lizzie found a vacant place on the sofa near the fire. Drake sat down beside her, wrapped in his own quilt.

"I'd offer to share my quilt with you, but I don't think your folks would approve, considering my lack of apparel," Drake whispered grinning.

"I'm sure they would understand, but I don't see how we could share without you flashing everyone in the room," Lizzie replied.

"Hmm, good point. I guess we'll just have to make the best of the current situation."

"I think that would be wise."

The pair talked quietly until they both fell asleep.

The following morning, Lizzie woke to bright light streaming in through the windows. The storm was over. The sun shone brilliantly on the snow and ice that covered the land.

Lizzie tried to get up without waking Drake who still slept soundly on the sofa beside her. She tiptoed into the kitchen and was about to make coffee when she remembered that they were running on emergency power. She was trying to decide how to feed her guests while using as little power as possible when her father woke up and joined her.

"Do you think we have enough gas to cook breakfast and stay warm?" she asked.

"Do we have enough donuts or pastries?" James asked.

"Yes, but I'm sure everyone will want coffee with it."

"The coffee maker uses less energy than the stove or the microwave. Go ahead and start the coffee. I'm going to check in with Wade's office to see what we're in for today."

"Wilbarger County Sheriff's office, come in."

"This is the Sheriff's office; go ahead."

"This is James at the Paradise Creek Inn. What's the latest on road conditions and the weather?"

"Good morning, James. This is Sheriff Adams. The roads are still closed, but the weather conditions are improving. How is everyone out there?"

"Everyone is safe and warm for the time being. We may have to siphon gas from our vehicles to keep the generator running, but otherwise all is well."

"We're supposed to have sunshine and clear skies all day. If that's the case, the roads may be passable by this afternoon. The power companies are already working to get power restored."

"That's good news. I'll check back with you again around noon," James said and signed off.

The smell of coffee brewing woke many of the guests. Lizzie had set out assorted breakfast cereals along with donuts and muffins for the guests to enjoy.

Drake and Eli brought in the remainder of the firewood after checking the fuel level of the generator. The energy saving precautions had helped, but they would need more gas soon.

"James, Eli and I have been talking," Drake began. "We'd like to drive toward town to see how far we can get. You're going to need more gas to keep the generator running."

"I just talked with the Sheriff's office. The roads are still closed. There are some full gas cans in the barn at my place. I need to break the ice on the water trough for the cows anyway. If we can get there safely, we can load up more firewood and get the gas cans."

"We'll do that for you. I don't want you to injure that arm again," Drake offered.

"I want to get out and see what's what," James replied. "Besides, I'm feeling a little cooped up. I need some fresh air. We can take my truck."

After they had eaten breakfast, the three men bundled up and climbed into the truck. They moved slowly and carefully toward the Fletcher home. When they arrived safely, James took his ax from behind the driver's seat. Carefully, he walked toward the water trough. He broke the ice away and scooped out the biggest chunks, allowing the cattle access to the water. The thirsty cows drank greedily before returning to the warmth of the barn.

Drake and Eli loaded the back of the truck with firewood and six full gas cans. They wouldn't siphon from the Fletcher's vehicles unless it became necessary.

James and the Wagner brothers went inside the house, gathering warm clothing, blankets, and quilts before making the quarter mile journey back to the inn.

While the three men had been away, the women had breakfasted and rearranged some things at the inn. They had set up tables for games and a reading area for those who chose not to play. They had all been in contact with their families and were trying to make the best of things until the roads were passable.

By noon, the sun's rays had begun to melt the snow and ice. James contacted the sheriff's office and learned that the highways were open but still dangerous. It was decided that now was the best time to travel. If they waited much longer, everything would refreeze before the guests could get home.

"Ladies, we have some news. The sheriff's office informs us that the roads are open but still hazardous. They advise extreme caution. The Wagner's have suggested that if you choose to leave that you travel together into Vernon. Drake will lead the caravan, and Eli will be last. They will be in contact with each other and with us as you travel so that we can alert the authorities if help is needed. You 're welcome to stay here if you don't feel safe traveling until the roads have improved."

"I've been away from my husband and kids too long. I need to get home," answered one of the guests.

The other guests agreed that it would be best to try to get to their homes. Everyone gathered their belongings and loaded into their vehicles. For safety reasons, the shower gifts would remain at the inn until the ice had melted away. No one wanted to risk injury while loading the gifts into the SUV's.

Drake took Lizzie's hand before getting into his car, "I'd like to see you again while I'm home. May I call you?"

"How long are you going to be here?"

"I'll leave the day after Christmas. I have to be back at work on the twenty-seventh."

"I can't promise anything. We're really busy with parties this month."

"I heard a yes in there somewhere. I'll let you know when we make it home." Drake kissed her hand before going to his car.

The Fletcher's stayed together at the inn. They busied themselves with the after party cleanup before settling by the fire with a meal of ham sandwiches and chips.

"Lizzie, it looked like things were heating up between you and Drake," Lois casually mentioned.

"Granny, I don't want to get involved with Drake again."

"It sure looks like he'd like to get involved with you," Ellen teased.

"I told you, honey," James said joining in the conversation. "Seemed like old times."

"I'm happy here with all of you and running this inn. If I were to get involved with Drake again, one of us would have to make a huge change. I have no intention of leaving here. I don't think Drake would give up his career and move back to Texas."

"How do you know? Did you ask him?" James asked.

"No, I didn't. The subject didn't come up," Lizzie answered irritably.

"If you really aren't interested, you're going to have to tell him plainly," Lois pointed out. "If you don't, he's going to hear yes in there somewhere all the way to the altar."

"I know, Granny. He caught me off guard. I'll tell him if he calls."

"Oh, he'll call. You can bet on that," Ellen said.

"His career might not be everything he hoped it would be. Would you be so reluctant if he were to volunteer to move back?" James asked.

"I don't know. We have all this history, so it's familiar in a way. It also feels like we're strangers trying to decide if we want to get to know each other better. It's almost like two men all wrapped into one.

Does that make any sense at all?"

"I think I understand," Ellen said as she brushed a strand of hair from Lizzie's face. "Only you can decide if you're ready to trust Drake again. Only you can decide if you're willing to take the chance of his breaking your heart again. We know you aren't over the break up with Wade."

"Take your time, honey," James told his daughter. We aren't trying to rush you. We just want you to be happy."

"It can be miserable being with the wrong man particularly if you are in love with another," Lois said. "Drake has been hoping to win you back practically since you broke up all those years ago. He's waited this long. He can wait a while longer."

Lizzie hugged her grandmother and her parents. "I love you all so much. Thanks for understanding about Drake and about Wade. I keep hoping that when this case is over, it won't be too late to start again with Wade."

"I've been hearing some rumors about Wade and Megan Ford. Are they dating?" Ellen asked.

"I've been hearing the same rumors. People are calling me all the time to tell me the latest. He knows what Megan is like. Until I hear it from Wade, I'm going to take the rumors with a grain of salt."

Hearing the pain in his daughter's voice, James said, "Lizzie, lets drive to the house. I need to break the ice for the cows again. You can help me refuel the generator and bring in some firewood when we get back. We won't have to go out again until morning."

Lizzie and James bundled up. They braved the cold to do their chores. It was cold but not as difficult as it had been the night before. No straight line winds or freezing rain to deal with this time.

"Thank you, Daddy," Lizzie said as they climbed into the truck.

"For what?"

"For giving me a reason to get out of the house. I hate being cooped up as much as you do."

"I needed your help since I've only got one good arm. I also wanted to ask you something without your mother and grandmother around to overhear."

"Okay, ask away."

"You wouldn't happen to know who might be using the handles Mesquite and Sagebrush on the radio would you?"

Lizzie stared at her father, speechless.

"I was having trouble sleeping one night. I decided to play with the emergency radio in the den for a while. I came across a man and woman talking. Their voices sounded real familiar. They were careful not to mention any names." James looked at his daughter. "They sounded like young lovers who weren't able to be together. I sure wish I knew who they were. I'd tell them that it might be wise to be more careful and random with their modes of communication."

"Have you heard them on the radio a lot?" Lizzie asked.

"Just one time, but it sounded to me like they used that form of communication often. It's none of my business, but if they want to keep things a secret, they can't risk their voices being recognized."

"That's true, Daddy. I wonder who they could be."

"If I hear them again sometime, I might butt in and tell them what I've told you."

"I haven't heard them, so I'd say they don't communicate that way very often."

"I hope things work out so that those two love birds can get together one of these days."

"Me, too, Daddy. Me, too."

# CHAPTER 22

Power was restored at the Paradise Creek Inn the following morning. The Fletcher's worked together to restore everything to its proper place. They would soon begin preparing for two Christmas parties scheduled for the week.

Lizzie's family had gone home when Drake and Eli came to the inn to collect the gifts from the baby shower. They loaded the heavy box containing the crib in the back of their father's truck.

"Jan asked me to invite you to have dinner with us at the steak house on Thursday night. There will be several of us there, and Drake needs a dinner partner," Eli told her.

"Hey, I can find my own dinner partner. Thank you very much," Drake teased. "How about it Lizzie? Will you have dinner with us?"

"I'm sorry; I can't. We have a Christmas party scheduled here that night."

"Maybe, we can get together before Drake goes back to Colorado."

"We're booked until Christmas. I don't know if I'll have a night off before then or not."

"I'll tell Jan to call you. The two of you can compare calendars to see if you can come up with a date."

"That would be great." Lizzie laughed.

"I hope we can get together, Lizzie. I'd really like to see you again before I have to go home."

"I hope so, too," replied Lizzie surprised that she actually meant it.

When the Wagner brothers had gone, Lizzie made a list of supplies she would need in preparation for the upcoming holiday parties. After typing a letter to be mailed, she quickly dressed and called her parents.

"Hello," answered Ellen.

"Hi, Mama. I'm about to go into town for supplies. Is there anything you need while I'm there?"

"Yes, there is. Come get your daddy. The two of you are going see Doctor Hughes. I want him to make sure your injuries aren't serious. I've already made the appointments. He's expecting you."

"Does Daddy know yet?"

"Yes, he does. I don't want to hear any argument from either of you."

"Yes, ma'am. I'll be right there."

Lizzie drove the short distance to her parents' house. Her father was standing on the porch grinning when she stopped her jeep in the drive.

"I guess we're going to see the doctor," he laughed as he got into Lizzie's jeep.

"It looks that way. Are we supposed to stop at his office first?"

"Those are the orders I got."

"Okay, we might as well get it over with."

"Don't tell your mama this, but I was planning to go see the doctor anyway. I can't work with my shoulder in this shape."

Lizzie laughed. "My lips are sealed."

They talked about the events coming up at the inn and discussed purchasing a Christmas tree on their way into town. Lizzie drove by the post office to drop off the mail before going to see Doctor Hughes. The doctor was talking with his secretary when they arrived.

"Well, a little bird told me you two were on your way."

"That little bird twisted our arms," James joked.

"It won't hurt to check to make sure you don't have any serious damage. James, I'll examine you first. Your injury is more obvious."

Lizzie browsed through the magazines in the waiting room while her dad was being examined. She glanced out the window and noticed Wade's truck parked outside. Two seconds later, he walked into the office.

"Hello, Lizzie. What are you doing here?"

"Daddy is having his shoulder looked at," she answered. Realizing she had been staring at him, she looked at the floor.

"All right, Lizzie. It's your turn," Doctor Hughes said as he came in from the other room.

Lizzie stood and looked at Wade. Seeing the concern in his eyes, she said, "I got a little bump on the head. Mama insisted that I have the doctor look at it."

"What can I do for you, Sheriff?" Doctor Hughes asked.

"It can wait until you've finished with Miss Fletcher."

Doctor Hughes examined Lizzie and pronounced her injury as being minor. Her father had a sprained shoulder. He was ordered to take it easy for a few more days and to return at the end of the week.

They returned to the inn when the shopping had been completed. They were looking forward to a nice quiet evening before the holiday parties began in earnest. Lizzie's family would be at the inn early the following morning to begin decorating. The entire inn was to be decked out in Christmas finery. It would be completed just in time for Lizzie to start the food preparations for Thursday's party. Friday morning meant cleanup and preparation for another party on Saturday night.

They would have a few days off and then parties on three consecutive nights. It would take a lot of planning and coordination to get everything done. Lizzie was both nervous and excited at the prospect of being so busy. The inn was becoming what she had always dreamed it would be.

• • •

Wade was a little out of sorts. He had been hearing rumors all day about Lizzie and Drake while stranded at the inn. He knew he could trust Lizzie, but he hated hearing about how Drake had been so nice to her. It made him sick to his stomach. He imagined that Lizzie must have felt the same way when hearing rumors about Megan.

There were still no leads in the murders of Paul Randolph and Nick Brinkman. The fabric samples that Lizzie collected didn't match the samples from the crime scenes. The lab report stated that, while the samples were similar, they were not a match. The crime scene samples were much older and came from the same source.

He went over the case notes again before quitting for the night. He went to a drive-in to pick up something for dinner before he drove home. He didn't want to risk being cornered by Megan again. He knew she was probably following him or waiting at his house. He could drive into the garage and close the door quickly. He might even stay out there in case she knocked on his front door. He decided against that idea when he realized that she preferred to have an audience.

He ate his meal alone at his kitchen table while he thought about Lizzie. He really wanted this case to be over so that he could see her again. When he had finished eating, he went to his radio. He tried several times to contact her before going to bed. *She's probably sleeping or getting ready for another event. I'll try again tomorrow.*

• • •

Lizzie heard Wade's call on the radio. She almost answered but knew it was a bad idea. She covered her head with her pillow and tried to ignore it. She wanted to talk to him so badly, but she didn't dare risk it.

She was so busy for the next few days that she didn't have time to think about communicating with Wade until she received a typed letter in the mail on Thursday.

Lizzie was thrilled to have a letter from Wade, but its contents were less than exciting.

*I don't know how communications between Mesquite and Sagebrush have been compromised but trust that they have. Communicating by mail is effective but slow and impersonal. We still have to be careful. Mail carriers might notice frequent addresses. We also need to be careful about contents in case of interception.*

Lizzie put the letter away and began preparations for the Christmas party that evening. She thought about possible ways of communicating with Wade. The only solution she could come up with was to mix things up using every available method.

• • •

It was the third Tuesday of December, the beginning of the busiest week at the inn to date. Lizzie wasn't sure how they would manage three consecutive nights of events. She was going to do everything in her power to have a successful week.

Lizzie drove into town. She had arranged to have her hair cut before shopping for more party supplies. She had been invited to join Jan and Faith for lunch. She reluctantly agreed when Jan pointed out that she had to eat and would be in town anyway.

Wade had planned to take his lunch to go until he saw Lizzie's jeep in the parking lot. He knew he was taking a risk, but he wanted to see her. He parked his truck and went inside.

Lizzie was sitting with Faith and Jan, chatting as they enjoyed their lunch. Wade tipped his hat at the three women as he passed by. He chose a corner table positioned so that he could see Lizzie while he ate. He placed his order and tried not to stare. He cringed as the door opened, fearing Megan had tracked him down again.

It wasn't Megan. He wasn't any happier to see Drake Wagner sit down at the table with Lizzie and her friends. He was trying to hear what was being said without being too obvious when he heard a familiar, unpleasant voice from the doorway.

"Hi, Wade. Have you already ordered? I'm running a little late today. I had to do some shopping for this weekend. Would you like to see what I bought?" Megan turned to make sure everyone in the room had noticed her. She froze when she saw Drake sitting with Lizzie. A wide range of emotions played across her face as she seemed to be trying to decide how she should react.

Everyone in the room was watching Megan and Drake, except Wade. He was watching Lizzie. She was obviously uncomfortable. She looked in Wade's direction, rolled her eyes, and sighed deeply.

"How are you Megan?" Drake asked in an effort to break the tension.

Megan's face showed disgust as she replied, "Ugh, don't talk to me."

"Fine, I was just trying to be polite."

The waitress brought Wade's food in a container to go. He hadn't planned to take it with him but decided it was best. He desperately wanted to stay to see what happened next. Instead, he left money on the table and quickly made his escape unnoticed by everyone, except Lizzie.

Lizzie wished she could leave with him. She feared this was going to get ugly. She didn't want to be a part of it.

Megan looked at Lizzie. She smiled as if she were a cat about to torture a mouse. She turned toward the table where Wade had been sitting. Lizzie almost laughed out loud. Megan's expression was priceless. In an effort to save face, Megan sashayed to the recently vacated table and sat down.

Lizzie said goodbye to her friends, finished her shopping, and drove home. A typed letter waited for her in the mail. She opened it before doing anything else.

*Radio call for Musician from Guitar Man Tuesday at eleven p.m. Limit ten minutes.*

Lizzie was sitting by the radio when Wade called.

"This is Guitar Man calling Musician. Come in."

"This is Musician. Go ahead, Guitar Man."

"I can't talk long. I just wanted to hear your voice."

"It's good to hear yours, too."

"I heard a good story today. It's about two men and two women in a bar. The first man and the first woman are having a drink. The second man walks in and sees the first woman. He can't take his eyes off her. The second woman comes in. She creates a scene because she's not happy to see the first man with the first woman."

"I think I've heard that joke. The second woman was expecting to meet the second man. She was about to include him in the drama, but he had disappeared. She was very embarrassed when she realized the second man was gone. There was some laughter at her expense. I can't remember the punch line."

"I can't either."

"I know that the first woman had no idea that the first man was planning to be there."

"I'm sure the second man would be thrilled to know that," Wade paused before adding, "I hate to sign off, but our time is almost up."

"I understand. Goodnight, Guitar Man."

"Goodnight, Musician."

# CHAPTER 23

Carl Ellis was furious. He stormed into the house while yelling at his wife. "Where's my supper, woman?"

Brandy hurriedly placed a bowl and a pot of stew in front of her husband. She spilled a little on the table and moved quickly to avoid the blow that she knew would be coming.

Carl glared at her as she made him a glass of iced tea before sitting down at the table.

"I'm going hunting tonight. That cougar killed one of my calves last night. The bounty will do me no good if any more of my livestock are killed."

"The traps haven't worked?" she asked meekly.

"I'll check those while I'm out. Make me a thermos of coffee. I want to get started right after supper."

Brandy nodded and got up to make the coffee.

"Where's Hayleigh? Did she already eat?"

"She's in her room doing her homework. She'll eat when she's finished."

"You both need to eat more. You're skin and bones. I don't know why I have to be saddled with such ugly, skinny females," he said between bites as he ate the entire pot of stew.

Brandy didn't reply. She poured the coffee into the thermos and handed it to Carl.

"Where's my sandwich?" He yelled as he backhanded her across the cheek, knocking her to the floor. "You don't expect me to be out all night without anything to eat do you?"

"No, I'll make you one. All we have is bologna," she said as she got up and went to the refrigerator.

"Bologna! Why haven't you gone to the store, woman? You go tomorrow and get something that will make a decent sandwich. Do you hear me?" He yelled as he stood over her menacingly.

"I will. Is there anything else you want me to get?" she quavered. Her hands shook as she made his sandwich.

"No! Why are you always spending my money? Get the sandwich meat and nothing else. Have you got that?"

She nodded as she put the sandwich and a small bag of chips in a paper sack. He snatched the bag from her hands and stormed out the door.

Brandy sank into a chair and took a few deep breaths to calm her nerves. She didn't know how much more of this she could stand. She looked up to see her seven-year-old daughter standing in the doorway.

"Mama, are you okay?"

"I'm okay, baby. Are you hungry?"

"Yes, ma'am."

"Go wash up while I get you a bowl of stew."

"Okay, Mama."

Brandy looked out the window to make sure her husband had gone. It wouldn't do for him to come back and find that she had more food prepared. She often hid food away so that she could be sure that her daughter would eat.

Hayleigh sat down at the table. Her mother smiled at her and kissed her on top of her head as she placed the food on the table.

"Does it hurt?" Hayleigh asked, pointing at her mother's cheek.

"A little. I'll be fine," she assured her daughter. "Did you finish your homework?"

"Yes. Can we read *Curious George* before bedtime?"

"We'll see, sweetheart. If your Daddy is home, you'll have to go right to bed."

"I hope Daddy stays out all night."

Brandy laughed. "You'll still have to go to bed tonight. You have school tomorrow."

Hayleigh frowned. She ate a few bites of her stew before asking, "Did you mail my letter to Santa?"

"Hayleigh Ellis, I've told you every day this week that I mailed your letter. Why do you keep asking me?"

"Do you think he'll bring the book that I asked for? I didn't ask for anything else. A book wouldn't be too hard for Santa to bring would it?"

"Well, have you been a good girl this year?"

"I have, Mama. I promise."

"Then, I think Santa can manage to bring your book."

The little girl beamed at her mother. "I'm full Mama. Can I go play?"

Brandy brushed a strand of hair from her daughter's face. "You can play until bath time."

Hayleigh started toward her room. She stopped and ran back to her mother, giving her a big hug. As she pulled away, she gently kissed her mother's bruised cheek. "I love you, Mama."

"I love you too."

Hayleigh happily went to her room to play.

Before Brandy cleared away the dishes, she ate the stew that her daughter had left. She had scrimped and saved for months to have enough money for Hayleigh's Christmas gift. She had asked Dara to order it for her. It should have been delivered by now. Her next problem would be giving it to Hayleigh without Carl's knowledge.

Carl didn't know how often she went to Dara Preston's house. He had seen her there once. Dara had told her about Carl's visit the night of their dinner party. She was much more careful after that. What would he do should he ever find out what she was planning? She shuddered at the thought. He couldn't know. No one could know. It was a secret, a dream that she kept locked away inside her heart. There it would stay until the time was right. She knew that it needed to be soon.

• • •

Carl had been driving up and down farm roads for hours. He had seen no sign of the cougar. The traps he had set were untouched. His stomach grumbled as he bounced down a path near the river bank. He knew he was on the Preston's land, but he didn't care. All he cared about was killing that cougar. He stopped his truck and pulled out the sandwich that Brandy had made.

He rolled down his window and turned off the engine. He wanted peace and quiet while he ate. *I should eat all my meals out here. I wouldn't have to look at Brandy. I could enjoy my food for a change.*

He thought about how young and pretty she had once been. She was too skinny now. She looked old, too old for a man like him. He ate contentedly thinking about the kind of woman he deserved to have in his life.

Suddenly, he heard the cougar scream. He froze for a moment, listening before he stuffed the remainder of his food back into the bag and reached for his rifle. He got out of the truck and took a flashlight from behind the seat. He reached for his machete as well but decided against carrying it. He didn't want to be weighed down with anything else. He left it on the driver's seat for easy access just in case. The full moon was bright enough that he decided against taking the flashlight. He left it beside the machete.

The cougar sounded close by, but he couldn't be sure. Sounds like that could carry a long way. He thought he heard something ahead to his left. He crept into the trees, listening as he moved. Quietly, he moved a few feet, stopped, and listened. He repeated the pattern until he heard the cougar scream again. It was much further away than he had thought.

Carl stomped back toward his truck. He wasn't trying to be quiet now. He was tired and angry. He really wanted to get that cougar. He couldn't understand why everything he wanted seemed to be just out of his reach. The bounty on the cougar would make it possible to make some changes. Now, he'd have to wait a while longer. He'd keep hunting until that cougar was dead. He just hoped he was the one to kill it.

Carl was grumbling to himself while he walked. He could see the hood of his truck in the distance. All he had to do was get back on the road to make the walk a little easier. He'd hunt again tomorrow night.

He reached the road and noticed something was fluttering around the front of his pickup. He walked slowly, trying to focus on the object. It looked like someone standing by the driver's side door.

"Get away from my truck!" he yelled.

The person didn't answer or run. Instead, the stranger opened the driver's door.

"Who are you? What are you doing? Get away from my truck, or I'll shoot!"

There was still no response from the stranger.

"I warned you!" Carl snarled as he raised his rifle and fired toward the truck.

Not a sound could be heard. Carl could no longer see anyone. He crept slowly toward the pickup, looking all around him for the stranger.

As he neared the vehicle, he saw no sign of anyone in the area. *Must have run off when I fired that round.* He climbed in and turned the key. It wouldn't start. Carl cursed as he got out and lifted the hood. Realizing he would need his flashlight, he stomped and cursed until he returned with it to look at the engine.

He stared at the engine, trying to find the problem. He cursed as he wiggled wires until he noticed that one of the battery cables had been disconnected.

"What the hell?" he said under his breath. A piece of pink fabric was tied around the cable. He tore it away, dropping it to the ground, and replaced the cable. When he reached up to close the hood, a machete gleamed in the moonlight as it came down on its target.

# CHAPTER 24

Lizzie's alarm went off the next morning. She turned it off and reluctantly got out of bed. She had been dreaming about Wade and Drake. She would have liked to have finished the dream to see how it turned out.

She started a pot of coffee and got into the shower. After showering, she put on her bathrobe and went into the kitchen. She was pouring herself a cup of the morning wake up brew when the office phone rang. She carried her cup to the office and picked up the phone.

"Paradise Creek Inn," she answered.

"Lizzie, this is Maddie Clifton.

"Hi, Maddie. What can I do for you?"

"Is there any way that you could work with us today? There's been another death in Rayland."

"Oh, no! Who?"

"Carl Ellis was found this morning. We have a female inmate today, so I need to stay here. Would it be possible for you to meet the team at my place?"

"I'll be there."

Thanks, Lizzie."

Lizzie dressed quickly. She was about to call her parents when her grandmother walked in.

"Granny, I'm going to be working with the sheriff's department today. Carl Ellis was found dead this morning."

"Another death? Be careful. I'll take care of things here."

"Bye, Granny," Lizzie kissed her grandmother on the cheek before hurrying out the door.

She arrived at Maddie's house shortly after the sheriff's team. Wade motioned for her to get into the truck with him, and they were on their way to the scene.

Kent Preston was sitting on the running board of his tractor when they arrived. He stood when Wade and Lizzie got out of the truck. He was pale and trembling.

"Sheriff, I've never seen anything like it," Kent began.

"Don't think about that," Wade said as he led Kent toward the passenger side of his truck and opened the door. "Sit down in the seat of my truck; it's warm in here. Take a deep breath."

Kent sat down as instructed and took several deep breaths. He looked at the sheriff and nodded.

"Walk me through how you found him. I want every detail from the time you got up this morning until now."

"The alarm went off as usual at six this morning. Dara cooked breakfast while I got dressed. We ate and cleared away the dishes. Dara went to Wichita Falls to pick up Grandma Gail for the holidays. I planned to feed the cows. The trailer was already loaded with hay. I went outside and started the tractor. I was about to back up to the trailer when I noticed Carl's truck. I drove over to see what he was up to and found him. I called your office and waited until you got here."

"What time was it when you noticed the truck?"

"Probably around seven."

"Did you see anyone or anything else?"

"No."

"Did you touch anything?"

"No."

"Have you told anyone else about this?"

"No. I wouldn't want anyone else to see…"

"Don't think about that. Take another deep breath."

Kent obeyed.

"I need to take your clothing."

"Why do you need my clothes?"

"You have something on your shirt and pants that might be

evidence."

Kent looked down at his clothes. "Oh, I guess I threw up after I found Carl."

"Where were you when you vomited?"

"I think I was behind Carl's truck."

"Deputy Fletcher, look behind the back seat. You'll find a jumpsuit and a large evidence bag. Pull those out for me please."

Lizzie found the items and held them ready.

"Mr. Preston, Deputy Fletcher is going to stand in front of the truck with her back to us. I need you to take off your clothes. Put them in this bag and put on this jump suit."

Kent followed the sheriff's directions. When he was redressed, Wade asked him to remain in the truck until he returned.

"Fletcher, I think the doctor needs to check on Mr. Preston. Stay with him. Try to keep him talking about anything except the body. I'll send the doctor over before he takes the victim in for autopsy."

Yes, sir."

Wade could hear Lizzie talking about Kent's grandmother as he walked away. He didn't want Lizzie to see the victim either.

"What do we have boys?"

"No discernible shoe prints this time, sir. There's too much vegetation. We did find where someone vomited behind the victim's truck," Reed answered.

"Mr. Preston said he vomited after finding the victim."

"We're dusting for prints, but the prints we've found are mainly on the driver's side. We did find something different this time," Reed said, holding up an evidence bag with a long black hair inside.

"Maybe this one isn't connected to the others," Wade said doubtfully.

"It's connected sir," Dodson replied. He handed the sheriff an evidence bag containing a piece of pink cloth. "It was under the victim's body. This was beside it." Dodson held up another evidence bag containing a bloody machete."

"This one is much more gruesome than the other two," Doctor

Hughes said stating the obvious. "He has several wounds to his head and torso area. They all seem to be consistent with that machete."

Wade looked at the body. He could understand why Kent was having difficulty processing the sight. Carl's body was a bloody, mangled mess.

"Doc, I think Mr. Preston may need your attention. Would you mind stopping to talk with him before you go back into town?"

"I'd be surprised if he didn't. I'll go visit with him while Mr. Ellis is being loaded in the truck," Doctor Hughes said as he walked toward Kent and Lizzie.

Carl's body was being placed in a body bag when Wade noticed something.

"Wait just a minute. Pull his arms out again. I want to look at something."

The deputies complied. Wade looked at Carl's wrists. The left wrist had a band of lighter skin than the rest of his arm.

Wade sighed, "I'll bet we're missing whatever he wore on that wrist. Alright, let's get him in the truck."

Wade looked toward his truck. The doctor was talking with Kent Preston. He knew Kent didn't have anything on him that belonged to Carl Ellis.

"Mr. Preston, I think it would be wise for you to go home. Try to rest. Is your wife at home?" asked the doctor.

"No, she went to Wichita Falls. She should be back around noon."

"I'm going to my truck to see if I have something to help you rest. I'll be right back."

Wade watched the doctor walk to his truck and then joined him there.

"Is he alright?" Wade asked.

"He's having an anxiety attack. I'm going to give him some medication. It should calm his nerves. Unfortunately, it won't erase what he saw."

"Should he be left alone?"

"No, at least not today. I'll call his wife and explain the situation.

I'm sure Dara will postpone her plans and come back right away."

The two men walked together toward Kent and Lizzie.

Doctor Hughes gave Kent the medication, "I want you to take one of these pills every four hours. If you aren't feeling more like yourself tomorrow, call me. I'll give you a prescription."

"Okay, but I'm not sick."

"I know you're not sick now. They're to keep you from getting sick. Would you mind if I call Dara to tell her about your medication?"

"No, I don't mind," he answered and gave the doctor the phone number.

"Fletcher, the doctor doesn't want Mr. Preston to be left alone. I need you to go with me to inform Mrs. Ellis of her husband's death. We also need to get Mr. Preston to his house."

"He's worried about his livestock. Should we feed them for him? He said all he had to do was pull the trailer into the pasture and unhook it. The cows will eat from the trailer."

"Do you think you can drive that tractor?"

"Yes, sir," Lizzie grinned. "I've driven tractors most of life, sir."

Wade was a little embarrassed. "I'm sorry. I guess I forgot who I was talking to for a minute."

"Apparently so, sir," Lizzie joked.

Doctor Hughes returned. "Mrs. Preston is on her way home. She and Grandma Gail should be here within an hour or two. If there's nothing else, I'll take Mr. Ellis and get started on the autopsy."

"Thanks, Doc."

The doctor waved as he walked to his truck.

"Stay here with Mr. Preston until I come back. I need to discuss how we're going to get everything done with Dodson and Reed."

"Yes, sir."

"Lizzie, am I supposed to take one of these now?" Kent asked.

"Let me see what the directions say."

Kent handed the box to Lizzie.

"It says to take them with a meal. You should probably wait until you get back to your house. What do you have to eat there?"

"I think we have some cereal."

"I'll fix you some when we get back to your house."

The two talked about different cereals they enjoyed as children while they waited for Wade to return.

"We have a problem, boys. The doctor doesn't want Mr. Preston to be left alone. His wife is at least an hour away. Fletcher and I are going to get him home. Meet us there when you've finished here."

"Yes, sir," both men answered.

As Wade walked back to his truck, he nodded at Lizzie. She climbed onto the tractor. She was pleased when it started easily. She drove to the Preston's barn and backed up to the hay trailer. She hooked the trailer to the tractor and drove to the pasture where the cows were waiting. She had to get off the tractor to open and close the gate. The cows followed as she drove to the middle of the pasture. Unhooking the trailer, she drove back to the barn. Wade was watching with Kent from the back porch when she killed the engine and jumped off.

"Thank you, Lizzie," Kent said. "I didn't know you could drive a tractor."

"You're welcome. I don't drive them as much as I used to. It was kind of fun."

As promised, Lizzie got a bowl of cereal ready for Kent. He had changed into his own clothes. She made sure he took his medication and talked with him while he ate.

"Dara and I like to sit on the front porch in the evenings with a bowl of cereal. We sat out there last night just staring at the full moon. Did you see it? It was really beautiful."

"Yes, I did. I was looking out the window while talking with a friend on the," Lizzie hesitated. "On the phone. It was beautiful."

"We went back inside when we heard the cougar scream. We hadn't heard it for almost a month."

Dodson and Reed stopped in front of the Preston's house. Wade went outside to talk with them."

"Dodson, I need you to stay here with Mr. Preston while Fletcher and I talk with Mrs. Ellis. After that, you'll go with me to interview the neighbors. You'll ride back into town with me."

Yes, sir."

"Reed, take the evidence into town. Start processing everything."

"Yes, sir."

Reed drove away as Wade and Dodson walked into the house.

"Kent, my deputy Craig Dodson is here. He'll stay with you while Deputy Fletcher and I go see Mrs. Ellis. Your wife should be here soon."

"Okay, I'm sorry you have to babysit me."

"We aren't babysitting. We just want to make sure you're alright," Wade assured him.

Dodson struck up a conversation with Kent. Wade and Lizzie climbed into the truck and drove toward the Ellis home.

"You almost said radio in there didn't you?" Wade teased.

"Almost," Lizzie replied.

"Thanks for helping today. I know you don't really have the time."

"I won't be able to help again for a while. We have three parties this week."

"I understand. If our female inmate makes bail, Maddie will be free to help us," Wade said as he parked the truck. "I hate this part of my job."

"I know. There never seems to be a good way to say it does there."

"No," Wade sighed as he got out of the truck.

Lizzie followed and stood behind him as he knocked on the door. Brandy Ellis answered with wide frightened eyes.

"Carl isn't here," she said.

"May we come in? It's important," Wade said.

Brandy nodded as she reluctantly opened the door.

"Mrs. Ellis, do you know where your husband is?"

"He went hunting last night but hasn't come home yet."

"What time did he leave?"

"He left around eight I think. Is Carl in some kind of trouble?

"Mrs. Ellis, your husband was found dead this morning."

"Carl? Dead? Are you sure?"

"Yes, ma'am."

"What happened?"

"He was murdered. Kent Preston found his body near his truck this morning."

"Was it the same person who killed Paul and Nick?"

"We aren't certain, but we think so."

"I thought all this time that Carl killed them. Now, he's dead, too? Who could be doing this?"

"We don't know yet. Is there anything you can tell us that might help find the murderer?"

"I was so sure it was Carl. He's gone hunting almost every night. He said the cougar killed one of the calves, so he left earlier than usual last night."

"Do you know of anyone who had a grudge against Carl?"

"No one liked Carl. I don't think anyone will mourn his death, but I don't know who would have killed him."

"You won't mourn for your husband?"

"No, I won't. I've been planning to take Hayleigh away from here as soon as I had enough money saved."

"What will you do now?"

"I'm not sure. I'll have to think about it."

"Did Carl usually wear something on his left wrist?"

"A copper bracelet. He never took it off. He said it was his good luck charm."

"Is there someone we can call to come stay with you?"

"No, I'll be fine."

"Thank you. We may have to ask more questions later."

"Sheriff, I need to tell Hayleigh. Would it be possible to take our truck to pick her up?'

"Your truck is going to be processed for evidence. It may take a little while, but I'll see if I can arrange a ride for you."

"Thank you. I want her to hear it from me rather than someone at school."

"No one knows other than my office and the Preston's for now. As we conduct interviews, I'll request that no one talk about it until Hayleigh has been told."

Wade and Lizzie drove back to the Preston's house. Dodson and Kent were talking. Kent seemed to be recovering from the shock of finding Carl's body.

"How is Brandy holding up?" Kent asked.

"She'll be okay. Deputy Fletcher will stay here with you until your wife returns."

"That's not necessary. I'll be okay alone until Dara comes home."

"We're following doctor's orders. He doesn't want you to be here alone today."

"Well Lizzie, what should we talk about while we wait?"

Wade and Dodson left the pair talking and drove to see the Carson's.

"Mornin', Sheriff. You're out and about early this mornin'," Pearl said.

"Good morning, Mrs. Carson. This is Deputy Craig Dodson. We have some questions to ask you."

"Do you want to talk to Mack, too?"

"Yes, ma'am if it's convenient."

"He's workin' on a flat. I'll get him."

Pearl left the room, but the two men could hear every word spoken between the couple.

"Mack, Sheriff Adams and his deputy are here. They have more questions."

"Why didn't you just say Wade and Lizzie are here?"

"Cause it's not Wade and Lizzie."

"Well, who is it then?"

"It's Wade and another deputy."

"Oh, that young fella that was here last time."

"No, this one is Greg I think he said. Hurry up; they're waitin'."

"I'm comin'." Mack followed Pearl inside. "Mornin', Sheriff."

"Good morning, Mr. Carson. This is Deputy Craig Dodson. We need to ask you both some questions."

"Pleased to meet ya. More questions about Paul's death or Nick's death?"

"Neither. Kent Preston found the body of Carl Ellis this morning."

"Oh no!" Pearl exclaimed. "Was it the same person?"

"We think so, but we won't know for sure until the evidence is processed," Wade answered.

"I sort of thought Carl was responsible for the other deaths. Now, he's dead. I don't know what to think," Mack said.

"Do you know of anyone who might have wanted Carl dead?"

"I'd guess anyone who knew him would want him dead," replied Pearl.

"But we don't know anybody who would do the job," Mack added.

"When was the last time you saw Carl?"

"He was in here one day last week with a flat he needed fixed. I think it was Thursday," answered Mack.

"Where were you between eight last night and seven this morning?"

"Yesterday was our weddin' anniversary. We went to Wichita Falls for dinner and a movie," Pearl said happily.

"We left here after we closed the store at six. We went to the Texas Roadhouse and had us a steak," Mack said.

"Then we went to the movie theater in Parker Square. We saw Savin' Mr. Banks."

"We got home around one o'clock this mornin'," Mack informed them.

"We haven't done anything like that in years," Pearl added.

"We're goin' to start earlier next time we do it. We're too old to be out that late."

"Speak for yourself Mack Carson."

"Thank you folks for your cooperation. Hayleigh Ellis doesn't know about her father's death yet. Please don't discuss it with anyone until she's been told."

"That poor little girl. How is Brandy holding up?" Pearl asked.

"About as well as anyone would expect. She needs a ride to pick up Hayleigh. Would either of you be able to take her?"

"We would, but we're expectin' a truck load of groceries today. We need to be here."

"I'll find someone. Thank you again."

When they returned to the truck, Dodson said, "They're quite a pair."

"Yes, they are. They don't miss much of what's going on around here."

Wade dialed Lizzie's cell phone.

"Fletcher, has Mrs. Preston arrived yet?"

"No, sir. She called a few minutes ago. She said she would be here in half an hour."

"Dodson and I are going to do another interview. Maybe, she'll be back by the time we've finished."

# CHAPTER 25

Sheriff Adams and his deputy arrived at the Dylan's home. They knocked on the door several times before Morgan answered. It was clear to the officer's that she had just gotten out of bed.

"I'm sorry to disturb you, Mrs. Dylan. I need to ask you some questions."

"Of course, please come in," she said in her far away manner. "If you'll excuse me, I'll go splash some water on my face. It seems I can't wake up."

She left the room and returned within ten minutes fully dressed with her hair combed. "I'm sorry I was slow to answer the door. I haven't been sleeping well. When I do sleep, I have difficulty waking up. You said you have more questions?"

"Yes, ma'am. Carl Ellis has been killed. Had you seen him recently?"

"I've heard a lot about him, but I've never met him."

"Would you have any idea who might want him dead or why?"

"No, I'm sorry. How is his poor wife dealing with his death?"

"As well as expected," Wade said. "Their daughter hasn't been informed yet. Please don't discuss this with anyone until her mother has the opportunity to tell her."

"Of course. That poor child! It's terrible to lose a father, or a mother for that matter."

"Where were you and your husband between eight last night and seven this morning?"

"We were here watching a Christmas movie. We went to bed after the evening news. We were up at six this morning. Alex left for work at seven. Do you think it was the same person who killed the others?"

"We aren't sure, but it's possible. Thank you for your time. We'll be back if we have more questions."

"Mrs. Dylan, are you taking anything to help you sleep?" Dodson asked.

"Only warm milk before bed. I don't like to take medicine unless it's absolutely necessary."

"My sister drinks herbal tea. She says it works for her."

"I'll have to try it. Thank you.

"Goodbye, Mrs. Dylan."

"Goodbye."

Wade and Dodson walked to the truck. When they were inside, Wade asked, "What was that all about? Does Crystal really have problems sleeping?"

"I don't know. I had to come up with something. Mrs. Dylan acted like she'd taken a heavy dose of sleeping pills."

"That would explain the way she talks and moves. Her husband says she has nightmares and sleep walks. She doesn't rest when she does sleep."

"That would explain it, too. Sleep deprivation can do strange things to people."

"Everyone else we need to interview other than the Preston's are at work in town. Maybe Mrs. Preston is home now. We still need to see about getting Mrs. Ellis into town to pick up her daughter."

"Maybe Fletcher can do it. Her jeep is close by."

"That's a good idea. I was going to ask one of the Preston's, but Fletcher might be able gather more information for us."

Dara Preston met the sheriff at the door. "Thank you for taking care of things here."

"We were happy to do it. How is your husband? Is he able to answer some more questions?"

"I think so. He's a little woozy from the medicine, but he should be able to answer."

"What he saw this morning was something terrible. Anyone who isn't accustomed to seeing that would be affected."

"That's what Doctor Hughes said," Dara replied as she led the men into the living room.

"Kent, the sheriff needs to ask us some questions. Do you feel up to it?"

"Please, stop babying me. I'm perfectly capable of answering questions," Kent retorted.

"I'd say he's fine," giggled Grandma Gail.

"When was the last time either of you saw Mr. Ellis?"

"I haven't spoken with him in several days. I saw him drive down the road daily. The last time was yesterday afternoon," Dara said.

"I spoke with him Thursday morning," Kent said. "He was still trying to talk me into selling this place. I haven't seen him since then."

"Do either of you know of anyone who wanted him dead?"

"I don't know that anyone wanted him dead. I know a lot of people wished he'd go away," Dara offered.

"Most folks around here were afraid of him. They disliked him because of it. I can't imagine any of them would actually kill him," Kent added.

"Did you see or hear anything that was out of the ordinary between eight last night and seven this morning?"

"I thought I heard a gunshot while I was working in my office," Dara said.

"What time was that?"

"It was eleven forty-five. I looked at the clock when I heard it. I assumed someone was hunting."

"Where were you both between those times?"

"I worked in my office from six thirty until midnight. Then we went to bed. We were up at six this morning. I left before seven to pick up Grandma Gail," Dara replied.

"It was my night to do the dishes. We finished dinner at six thirty. After I cleaned up the kitchen, I watched television until midnight. I was up at six and found Carl just after seven," said Kent.

"Thank you both for your cooperation. Please, don't tell anyone about Carl's death until his daughter is informed. Mrs. Ellis wants to tell her rather than have her hear it from someone else."

Wade nodded at Lizzie. She followed both men out to the truck. Grandma Gail followed as well.

"Sheriff, I need to speak with you. It's very important, but I don't want Kent or Dara to overhear."

"Do you want to talk now or would you rather come to my office?"

"I'd rather come to your office, but I don't drive."

"I could send someone to pick you up."

"No, that won't do. How would I explain that? I'll give you a call when I've figured something out," she said as she turned to go back into the house.

The three officers climbed into the truck.

"Fletcher, I'd like for you to take Mrs. Ellis to pick up her daughter. Take her anywhere she needs to go. I'll let you know when we'll be meeting about the case."

"Yes, sir."

Wade stopped the truck beside her jeep, "Make mental notes about anything she says or does that might be important to the case."

"Yes, sir," Lizzie said as she got into her jeep. She drove to the Ellis home and knocked on the door.

"Yes," Brandy said apprehensively.

"I'm here to give you a ride into town if you still need one."

Her face brightened. "Yes, thank you. I'll just be a minute. Please, come in."

Lizzie waited near the door while Mrs. Ellis gathered her things.

"I haven't picked Hayleigh up from school during the school day before. Will they need to see my ID?"

"I don't know. It would probably be a good idea to have it just in case."

"You're probably right. I'm ready. Thank you for doing this."

"You're welcome. I don't mind at all."

The two women walked out to the jeep and climbed in. Lizzie was halfway to Vernon before Brandy spoke.

"I'm sorry I haven't been talking much. I'm so nervous about telling Hayleigh. I don't know how I should say it. I don't know how she'll react."

"I'm sure there's no easy way to tell someone her father died. How old is she?"

"She's seven. They weren't particularly close, but he was her father after all."

"I'd offer advice, but I'm not qualified. I don't have any children. I've never been in this situation either."

"If it were you in this situation, how would you want to be told?"

Lizzie thought for a few minutes before answering.

"I think I'd like to be told the truth. I'd want some of the details but not all of them. I'd want to know when, where, and most of all why. Of course, I'm much older than your daughter. She might not want more than just the basic facts, or she might want to know every detail."

"I think the basic facts would be all she'll need right now. I'll tell her more when she's ready. Thank you, Deputy."

"You can call me Lizzie."

Brandy smiled, "Thank you, Lizzie."

It was the first time Lizzie had ever seen Brandy Ellis smile. She looked beautiful.

When they arrived at the school, Brandy asked, "Will you come with me?"

"I will if you want but won't it frighten your daughter to see a deputy with you?"

"I don't think so. I'd like the moral support."

"I'd be happy to."

The two women walked into the school and found the principal's office. Brandy talked with a secretary at the front counter. She asked to check her daughter out for the day. When she informed the woman that Hayleigh might be out of school for several days, the secretary's attitude deteriorated.

"Did you know that students are required to be in school a certain number of days each year? You could be taken to court for your child's nonattendance."

"I didn't realize that. There's been a family emergency. I don't think she'll be able to focus if she is here," Brandy said meekly.

"Children are able to do much more than their parents give them credit for," the secretary said derisively.

"Excuse me, ma'am. May I speak with you privately?" Lizzie interjected.

"Who are you?"

"I'm Wilbarger County Deputy Fletcher," Lizzie said as she showed the woman her badge. Lizzie would have thought her uniform would have been enough.

"Well, alright. Follow me."

Lizzie followed the secretary into a small conference room. "Ma'am, I don't think you understand the situation. Mrs. Ellis doesn't want this information broadcast all over the school. She wants to be the one to give her daughter this news. It is a family emergency."

"Why would a deputy sheriff need to bring a woman to pick up her own daughter?"

"Mrs. Ellis has no means of transportation. I drove her into town so that she could check her daughter out of school. She asked me to come in with her. Right now, I'm very glad I did. You're making a very difficult situation much more difficult. Mr. Ellis has been killed. Mrs. Ellis would like to tell her daughter privately. Are children not allowed time from school to mourn the loss of a parent?" Lizzie asked angrily.

The secretary paled and stammered, "Oh my. I had no idea. I'm so sorry."

"I'm not the person you should apologize to."

"You're right. I'll apologize to Mrs. Ellis right away."

"Ma'am, Mrs. Ellis would appreciate it if you would keep this to yourself until she has had the opportunity to tell her daughter."

"Certainly. I understand completely. Oh, that poor child."

The secretary apologized to Brandy repeatedly. Finally, she went to Hayleigh's class to personally escort her to her mother's side.

"Mama! The little girl called happily, "What are you doing here?"

"We're going to have a special day off. We're going to take a ride in Deputy Fletcher's jeep. Would you like that?"

"Uh huh." The little girl beamed at Lizzie.

When they reached the jeep, Lizzie helped the little girl into the back seat. Brandy fought back the tears as they left the school parking lot.

"Lizzie, would you mind taking us to Allingham Park?"

"I'd be happy to," Lizzie answered.

When they arrived at the park, Brandy climbed out of the jeep and held her hand out to her daughter.

"Isn't Deputy Fletcher coming?"

"I'll wait for you right here," Lizzie assured the girl.

Lizzie watched as mother and daughter walked hand in hand to a park bench. Brandy brushed a strand of hair from Hayleigh's face as they sat down. She saw Brandy take a deep breath. She saw Hayleigh wrap her arms around her mother's neck and sobs wrack her little body. As she watched with tears in her eyes, she realized that Brandy was sobbing, too.

Lizzie couldn't imagine being in either situation. Her heart broke for them. She said a silent prayer while she waited.

Mother and daughter walked back to the jeep hand in hand. "I think we'd like to go home now," Brandy said as she climbed into the back seat with her daughter.

Lizzie nodded and drove back to the Ellis home.

Lizzie had not yet heard from the sheriff. She decided to drive to the office anyway. There might be something she could do to help. She also needed to tell Wade about her discussion with the secretary at the school. She was concerned she had overstepped her authority. She wanted Wade to be aware of what had happened.

Wade was talking with Sheriff Duncan when she arrived. He waved her in and indicated that she should sit down. She waited until he had finished his conversation.

"Did you get Mrs. Ellis taken care of?" Wade asked.

"Yes, sir. I took them home before coming back here."

"Thank you. Did you learn anything that might help our case?"

"Mrs. Ellis hardly spoke during the drive. She was struggling with a way to tell her daughter the news. They were both crying afterward. Mrs. Ellis could have been hurting for her daughter or she might have been mourning her husband. Other than that, she hardly spoke."

"I didn't know if she would talk or not. She was much more forthcoming this morning than in the past."

"I need to tell you something. I might have crossed a line at the school this morning."

"Oh? What happened?"

Lizzie told him the whole story. Wade said nothing for several minutes when she had finished. She worried that she had made a huge mistake.

"You did the right thing. I would have done the same thing. I got angry just listening to you talk about it. I doubt anyone will make a complaint, but if they do, I'll handle it."

"I'm sure everyone at the school knows about Carl's death by now."

"They probably do. I'm surprised we were able to keep it quiet as long as we did. Go get some lunch. We'll meet in the conference room at two."

"Is there anything else I can do to help?"

"We need someone to run the office while Maddie goes to lunch."

"I can do that."

"Come back here after you've had lunch."

"Yes, sir."

The meeting started promptly at two o'clock. Wade started the recording.

"This is Sheriff Wade Adams. Today is December 18, 2013.The body of Carl Ellis was found this morning at approximately seven o'clock this morning on land owned by Kent and Dara Preston. Mr. Preston discovered the body. Doctor Gerard Hughes, what did you find during the autopsy?"

"Mr. Carl Ellis was killed by a blow to the back of the neck with a sharp blade. It severed his spinal column between the C5 and C6 vertebrae. He was very nearly decapitated. Death was instantaneous. I estimate the time of death to be between eleven thirty and midnight. His other injuries were inflicted post mortem. All of the wounds are consistent with the machete found at the scene. Compared with the other two victims, the killer had a more pronounced hatred of Mr. Ellis. That's my personal opinion."

"I believe your right. Thank you Doctor. Deputy Gordon Reed, what do you have for us?"

"All of the fingerprints in the truck belonged to the victim. His prints were on the rifle found at the scene. It had been recently fired. There were no prints on the machete. The blood on the machete matched the victim's blood."

"Were you able to get DNA from that strand of hair?"

"No, sir. The hair is synthetic. It's from a wig."

"Deputy Craig Dodson, do you have anything to add?"

"The strip of pink fabric found under the victim's body matches those found at the previous crime scenes. We've interviewed everyone. No one is particularly upset about the demise of Mr. Ellis, but they have no idea who might have killed him. The Flynn's and the Dylan's said they had never met the victim. The Carson's alibi checks out, but we have not been able to verify the alibis of the rest of the neighbors or party attendees."

"Does anyone have anything to add?"

"Yes, sir."

"Deputy Lizzie Fletcher, you have the floor."

"Mr. Preston mentioned that there was a full moon last night. Didn't Mrs. Brinkman mention a full moon on the night that Deputy Brinkman was killed? Were all three men killed on a night with a full moon?"

"Someone pull up a lunar calendar. Compare dates of the full moon to the dates of our murders."

Everyone waited while Reed opened a laptop and searched to see if there was a full moon on the dates in question.

"Yes, sir. There was a full moon on all three nights."

Wade sighed, "This can't be a coincidence."

"What can't, sir?" Dodson asked.

"It's time I shared a piece of information with you that until now only Deputy Fletcher and I have been aware. We told you that there was a ghost story told at the party the Preston's had in October. I'll tell you that story now." Wade summarized the story of Ruby's ghost.

"Now we have the bodies of three men. They were all murdered on a night with a full moon. They all had a piece of pink fabric on or near their bodies. We have a strand of long black hair. All consistent with the ghost story," Wade pointed out. "However, the actual deaths are different. These men didn't die by accident or suicide. They were murdered with something that belonged to each particular victim. Our killer also took souvenirs. The tag from Mr. Randolph's sheep shears, Deputy Brinkman's name tag, and Mr. Ellis' copper bracelet."

"Are you saying the killer is a ghost sir?" Lodge asked jokingly.

"No, I'm not," Wade grinned. "I'm saying the killer would like for us to think so."

"The killer has established a pattern. We can be pretty confident that, if another person is murdered, it will be on the next full moon," Dodson said.

"When is the next full moon?" Wade asked.

Reed searched quickly. "January sixteenth, sir."

"I said before that I think the killer knows the victims well. He watches them. He knows their routines. He somehow lures them alone out into the open and then strikes. No witnesses, no evidence left behind other than what we are meant to find."

"How are we going to stop him, sir?"

"There has to be a connection between the three victims. I know they were in high school at the same time. They lived in the same area. There has to be something else. Is it because they are men? If that's the case, every man in the Rayland area is in danger."

"That makes it look like a conspiracy among the wives to get rid of their husbands." Reed pointed out.

"It might be," Wade replied.

"If I may," Doctor Hughes began. "I don't believe any of the women in the Rayland area would have enough strength to do the damage done to Mr. Ellis."

"I agree with you, Doctor Hughes. Carl Ellis was a big man. If the wives are responsible, they may have hired someone. That would mean that the clues left behind are meant to confuse us."

"They're doing a damned good job," Dodson said under his breath.

Wade tried to hide his smile as he continued, "I want everyone working to find a connection between our three victims. Search everywhere you can think to search. Talk to anyone who might have an idea. I'd like to think our killer is finished, but I'm afraid there will be more deaths if we don't figure this out."

The meeting was adjourned, and Lizzie went back to the inn. She couldn't help but wonder who the next victim would be.

# CHAPTER 26

Wade was working at his desk the next morning when Lodge tapped on his door.

"Come in."

"Sheriff, there's a woman here to see you. She says you're expecting her."

"Who is it?" Wade asked warily.

Lodge grinned. "It isn't Miss Ford. She said to tell you Grandma Gail is here."

"Show her in," Wade smiled with relief.

Lodge escorted Grandma Gail to the Wade's office. "Would you like some coffee, ma'am?"

"Yes, that would be lovely. Thank you."

"Would you like cream or sugar in it?"

"No, thank you."

Wade pulled a chair out for her. They chatted while waiting for the coffee.

"How is your grandson feeling today?"

"He's having a hard time with this. He had nightmares last night."

"I thought you were going to call me before coming to the office," Wade teased.

"There wasn't time. Dara decided that Kent needed to see the doctor. I tagged along, saying I needed something from the store across the street. She dropped me off a few minutes ago. I'm supposed to meet them there in a little while."

"I see," Wade said as Lodge brought two cups of coffee. He closed the door on his way out. "What is it that you need to talk about?"

Grandma Gail took a deep breath and a sip of coffee.

"I lied to you, Sheriff Adams."

"Oh? When?" Wade asked as he leaned forward.

"Do you remember asking me if there was any truth to my ghost story?"

"Yes, I do. You said there was a family named Lawrence whose house burned down. Was that the lie?"

"No, it's true. The lie was that it was just an old story going around. The entire story was true."

"That really happened?"

"Yes, it did."

Wade was stunned. "All of it? The deaths of the Lawrence family, the men killing themselves or dying in an accident, and the death of Ruby are all true?"

"All are true, except the death of Ruby."

"Ruby is alive?"

"Yes, I added that part to make it a ghost story."

"Where is she? What happened to her?"

Grandma Gail took another deep breath and another sip of coffee. "She's sitting across the desk from you."

"You're Ruby Lawrence?" Wade asked astonished.

"Yes, my full name is Ruby Gail Lawrence Preston."

Wade stared at her in disbelief. "I'm speechless. I don't know what to say or ask you."

"I told the story that night because I had been trying to find a way to introduce the information to my grandson. I saw an opportunity and thought the guests would enjoy a ghost story. Kent has been researching our family history. He has thoroughly researched the Preston family. He's ready to begin researching my side of the family now. That night at the party was the first time I've told anyone what happened back then."

"Why did you change your name?"

"That was my Uncle Ward's idea. After George Parker died, my uncle and aunt were afraid that someone would blame me. They sent me to live with another relative out of state. They suggested that I use the name Gail instead of Ruby. I used the last name of my relatives as an extra precaution."

"If it was an accident, you wouldn't have been charged."

"They weren't concerned about any legal blame. They were concerned about the Parker family. They're vindictive people."

"Don't you mean were?"

"No, there are still some of them around. Do you remember that I told you Carl Ellis reminded me of someone from my past?"

"Yes, I do. Are you saying he reminded you of George Parker?"

"Yes. That's what I'm saying. I'll say a little more. George Parker had an illegitimate son. That boy's last name was Ellis."

"Carl Ellis was descended from George Parker? Wow!" Wade exclaimed.

"George Parker wanted my family's land, and so did Carl Ellis. I don't know why they wanted it so badly. I can only guess that some story about it has been passed down through the generations."

"Are you saying that the land Kent and Dara live on belonged to Woody and Dorothy Lawrence?"

"It's the same land, but they didn't own it. They rented it from the Preston's. When my husband and I decided to live there, I couldn't bear the thought of building a house over the place where my family had died. I encouraged him to build where the house stands now."

Wade leaned back and shook his head, trying to take it all in.

"Sheriff, I've told you the truth. Now, I need the truth. Is my story responsible for the deaths of those poor men?"

"The person responsible for these deaths already had the idea of murdering those men. I think your ghost story gave whoever it is an idea to camouflage his or her identity until the job is completed. There are some similarities in the evidence and your story. There are more differences."

Grandma Gail sighed, "Thank you for telling me the truth."

"Thank you for blowing my mind," Wade teased.

Grandma Gail laughed, "I'm an old woman, Sheriff. I know the time I have left is short. I didn't want to die with that lie or those deaths on my conscience."

"I understand. I have one bit of advice for you."

"What is that?"

"Keep your family inside at night, especially on the night of a full moon. Don't go anywhere alone after dark."

"I understand. Is this common knowledge or just for us?"

"It isn't common knowledge yet. Keep it to yourselves for now. I hope we catch the person responsible before anyone else dies."

"Thank you, Sheriff. I'd better get going."

Wade escorted her across the street before returning to his office. He needed time to process what he had just learned.

The days turned into weeks. Still, nothing pointed the sheriff and his team toward the killer. Nothing could be found that linked the three victims other than what had already been discovered.

If the wives of Rayland were responsible for the deaths, there were only four possible victims left. Wade felt in his bones it was someone else.

• • •

The holiday parties at the inn had been successful. Lizzie and her family were looking forward to a quiet Christmas at home. Lizzie had hoped they would be able to include Wade. Instead, Drake came to visit with Eli, Jan, and Jan's parents.

"Lizzie, I have to go back to Colorado in a couple of days," Drake said while they sat on the front porch together. "If I'm able to come back in a month or two, will you have dinner with me?"

"That could probably be arranged, depending on how booked the inn is then."

"What if I booked a room one weekend?"

"Why would you book a room here?"

"So that I could spend all of my time with you, silly."

"Oh," Lizzie answered in surprise.

"I'd like to try again, Lizzie. I know it's been a long time. I know I hurt you. Can't we put that all behind us and start over?"

"Drake, I don't know what to say."

"Say yes."

"I don't think I'm ready for another relationship yet. I'm still getting over the last one."

"You mean with Wade Adams?"

"Yes," she replied. I also have some concerns. What if we do try again? What if we decide we want to be together? What happens then?"

"We'd get married."

"What then?"

"I don't know what you mean."

"Are you going to give up your career and move back here? Will you expect me to give up my career and move to Colorado?"

"I hadn't thought of that."

"I have."

"You have?" Drake asked grinning at her.

"Oh, it's not like that. I've thought about it in general. I love being so close to my family. I love running this inn. I've put a lot of work into this, and it's finally starting to pay off. I'm not ready to give it up for you or anybody else."

"I see," Drake said clearly disappointed.

"I'm sorry, but that's how I feel. I care about you; I always have. You were my first love after all. I'm just not ready for what you're offering."

"I'm hearing not now but maybe later," Drake teased.

Lizzie laughed and hugged him. He held her for a long time before they went back inside.

• • •

It was New Year's Eve. Wade was hungry. He wanted a good meal for a change. He was tired of eating takeout food. He was tired of hiding at home. Tonight he was going to the steak house. He planned to eat until he could hold no more.

He drove to the steak house and parked his truck. As he was getting out, he noticed that Megan Ford was parking at the other end of the parking lot. He was tired of this, too.

He went inside and asked for a table in the center of the restaurant. He ordered his meal and waited.

As if on cue, Megan entered the restaurant. She walked straight toward Wade.

"Hi, Wade. This is a great place to have dinner tonight isn't it?" She began to sit down.

"I'm sorry, Miss Ford, but I'm expecting a guest. I'd appreciate it if you would sit somewhere else."

"Expecting a guest?" She looked around to make sure she had an audience. All eyes were on the two people in the center of the room. "I thought I was your guest?"

"No, Miss Ford. I have not invited you to be my guest tonight or any night. I never will. I request in front of all these witnesses," Wade said looking around the room, "that you stop this harassment."

"Harassment? What are you talking about?" Megan was struggling to hold back her rage.

"If you choose to continue to follow me into restaurants, to my home, and while I am working, I will be forced to file charges against you."

"You wouldn't dare," Megan spat at him.

"Oh yes, I would," he replied calmly. I'll throw every charge at you that I can possibly find applicable to this situation. I'll make sure you're prosecuted for each and every one of those charges. I have plenty of witnesses to corroborate my story. You could spend years in jail just because you want to cause someone grief."

Megan glared, grunted, and growled. Unable to find the right words for a scathing reply, she turned on her heel and stomped out of the restaurant.

The restaurant patrons applauded. Wade stood and bowed to the crowd. Tires screeched outside and applause erupted again.

"It's about time somebody put her in her place man," someone called from the crowd.

As the patrons returned to their meals, the waitress brought Wade the biggest steak he had ever seen.

"The owner says it's on the house. Happy New Year," she told him and smiled as she walked away.

Wade enjoyed every delicious bite of his first peaceful meal in months.

• • •

Lizzie and her family were busy preparing for a luncheon. The ladies from the Vernon chapter of the Red Hat Society would be there at noon. The dining table was covered with a white lace table cloth over a red table cloth. The places were set with the inn's best china and silverware. Crystal glasses accompanied each place setting. The room had been decorated with flowers and red hats of various shapes and sizes.

Twelve women arrived promptly and took their seats at the table. They chatted while they ate. They complimented the food. They complimented the décor. They discussed chapter business. When dessert was served, they began to talk about things happening in the community.

Two women who were retired teachers were very interested in what Lizzie could tell them.

"Lizzie, you've been working with the sheriff's department haven't you?" Mrs. Brewer asked.

"Yes, ma'am. From time to time."

"Were you working for them when those three men were killed at Rayland?" Mrs. Hite asked.

"Yes, ma'am."

"Does the sheriff have any idea who killed them?" Mrs. Brewer asked.

"I don't think so."

"It's such a shame. Those boys were thick as thieves when they were in high school. Then that terrible accident happened," Mrs. Hite observed.

"What accident?" Mrs. Brewer asked.

"I thought you knew this story. I don't remember all the details, but they were at Lake Kemp. They were all on a boat. Something happened with another boat. I don't remember exactly what it was, but a young person skiing behind the second boat drowned."

"That's so sad," Lizzie interjected.

"Yes, it was. There were no charges filed against our boys because it was ruled an accident, but I understand their friendship suffered because of it."

"I think I do remember that," Mrs. Brewer said. "Wasn't there another boy with them?"

"I believe there was, but I can't remember his name?"

"When did this happen?" Lizzie asked, trying to keep the excitement out of her voice.

"Oh, I'm not sure. Our boys were either juniors or seniors. The accident happened during summer break."

Lizzie did her best to concentrate and be a good hostess. She desperately wanted to tell Wade what she had learned. There would be a full moon tonight. They didn't have much time.

As soon as the luncheon was over and the ladies had gone, Lizzie called the sheriff's office.

"Sheriff's office. How may I help you?" Lodge answered.

"Lodge, this is Fletcher. Is the sheriff available? It's urgent."

"He's not in right now. Do you want me to call his cell?"

"Yes, please. Tell him I know how our victims are connected.

There is a fourth person we need to worry about. I don't know who it is yet. I'm going to try to find out."

"Where will he find you?"

"I don't know yet. Have him call my cell."

"I'll let him know."

Lizzie disconnected and called the high school.

"Vernon High School."

"Could I speak with someone in the library, please?"

"Please, hold while I transfer your call."

"Library."

"Hi, I'm trying to find copies of old year books. Do you keep any there?"

"It depends on how old you're talking about?"

"Middle to late nineties."

"Yes, we have all of the yearbooks from the nineties."

"This is Lizzie Fletcher with the Wilbarger County Sheriff's department. Would it be alright if I come by to look at those in a little while?"

"Yes, just check in with the office. I suggest you get here before school is out. The parking lot is terrible at that time."

"Thank you, I'm on my way."

Lizzie quickly changed into her uniform and grabbed her badge. She rushed to the jeep and hurried to the high school. She found one vacant parking space in front of the building near the street. She hurried into the building and went to the office.

A secretary smiled and greeted her, "May I help you?"

"I called earlier. The library is expecting me."

"Do you know where it is?"

Lizzie smiled, "Yes, ma'am."

She should remember where the library was located. She worked in there as an aide when she was a senior. She opened the door and walked inside. It looked just like it had years ago.

"Deputy Fletcher?" A young woman asked.

"Yes, ma'am."

"I'm Sierra Mason, the librarian. The old yearbooks are on this wall over here," she said leading the way. The ones from the nineties are on the last bookshelf near the top."

"Thank you."

"Let me know if I can help with anything," she said leaving Lizzie to her search.

Lizzie talked herself through her plan. *Those guys were ahead of me in high school. They probably graduated the year that I finished seventh or eighth grade. That would mean I need to check 1996 or 1997 first.*

She pulled out the two yearbooks. She searched through the seniors of 1997 first. They weren't there. She looked through the juniors, still no luck. She opened the 1996 yearbook and saw Nick Brinkman. *He was senior class president? I never would have guessed that.* She found the other two men also listed as part of the senior class. She looked through all of the names but didn't recognize anyone who now lived at Rayland. She browsed through the entire book, looking for photos of the three victims together but found none.

She made some notes and returned the two yearbooks to the shelf before taking out the 1995 book. She searched the junior class for names of people who currently lived at Rayland and for photos of the three victims together. She found no one's name but did find a photo with the three victims.

"Excuse me. Would you make a copy of this for me, please?" She asked Ms. Mason.

"Sure," she looked at the photo and looked at Lizzie. "Aren't these the men who were killed recently?"

"Yes, we've been trying to find a connection between them. We didn't know they had once been friends."

"I'll be right back."

She made the copy and gave it to Lizzie. I'll put this up for you. You seem to be in a hurry."

"Thank you. I am. Do you happen to know where I could find old newspaper articles?"

"As a matter of fact, I do. The newspaper office keeps them for people to use for research."

"Thank you so much for your help."

"You're welcome."

Lizzie hurried to her jeep and drove to the Vernon Daily Record. She was about to go inside when her cell phone rang.

"Hello."

"Lodge said you had something urgent to tell me."

"I do. I know how the victims are connected. There's someone else connected to them. I'm trying to find out who that fourth person might be."

"Where are you?"

"I'm at the newspaper office. I'll fill you in when you get here."

"I'm on my way."

Lizzie went inside and explained what she needed. She was led to a room with volumes of bound newspapers. After being pointed in the right direction, she began searching through newspapers from the summer of 1995.

Wade arrived and was directed to where Lizzie searched. She explained what she was doing and why. Wade began helping in the search. They didn't know the date of the accident. They weren't even sure it would be in the newspapers they searched, but they had no other leads. They searched through every page of every newspaper until they found an article on the front page of a Sunday paper dated July 30, 1995.

Wade looked at his watch, "We're running out of time. You read, and I'll see if we can get a copy of the article."

The article read: *Seymour youth drowned on Lake Kemp. Boating Accident to Blame. Sonny McCoy, aged twelve, died Saturday while boating with his family on Lake Kemp. McCoy was skiing behind his family's boat when another boat crossed their path. Mr. McCoy veered out of the way causing the boy to fall. He became entangled in underwater vegetation and drowned. Four Vernon students were driving the second boat. Names are being withheld pending investigation.*

Lizzie found nothing in the next day's paper about the incident.

Wade returned and indicated which article they needed to have copied.

"It didn't give the name of the students on the second boat. We know the name of the boy who drowned but nothing else."

"Keep looking. There has to be something about the students being indicted or exonerated."

They searched until they found an article on the third page of a newspaper dated August 18, 1995. The article read: *No charges to be filed against Vernon students. Four Vernon students involved in a boating accident that claimed the life of twelve-year-old Sonny McCoy on July 29 of this year will not face charges. The incident was ruled an accident by authorities. Vernon High School students Nick Brinkman, Carl Ellis, Paul Randolph, and Vernon Regional Junior College student Andrew Clifton were involved in the accident.*

"It's Drew!" Lizzie said as she looked at Wade in surprise.

# CHAPTER 27

"Let's go. It's dark and the moon is already up."

Wade and Lizzie hurried outside. "Ride with me. We've got to get everyone available out there. I'll call the office. You try to get in touch with Drew or Maddie."

Lizzie frantically dialed Maddie's home number. When she got no answer, she dialed her cell. "They aren't answering."

"Keep trying. Lodge, get everyone available to Maddie's place immediately. Drew may be the next victim. No one is answering the phones at their house."

Wade hung up. Lizzie heard the call go over the police ban radio. She continued to dial the phone numbers she had for the Clifton's.

Maddie's house was dark when Wade and Lizzie arrived. They could hear the baby crying from somewhere inside. Wade signaled for Lizzie to stay behind him. He drew his gun and crept up to the front door. As he touched the knob, the door opened slightly.

"Wait here," he whispered to Lizzie.

Wade crept through the door holding a flashlight over his gun. He scanned the room until he saw Maddie lying on the floor. Her hands and feet were bound with duct tape. Another strip of tape was stretched over her mouth.

"Maddie, is anyone else in the house?" whispered Wade.

She shook her head.

"Fletcher, you can come in," Wade called as he went to Maddie. He pulled the tape from her mouth.

"She took Drew."

"Where did she take him?"

"Outside somewhere."

"Do you know who it was?"

"No, she's wearing a Barbie doll mask."

"Fletcher, cut her loose. Both of you wait here."

Wade went outside to search for Drew. The remainder of his deputies arrived shortly after he reached the barn.

Drew stood facing Wade with his hands raised. In front of him, stood a woman in a torn pink dress and a long black wig. She was pointing a gun at Drew. He was trying to reason with her when he saw Wade.

Wade signaled that he should keep her talking.

"You don't understand," she said. "My whole world began to fall apart that day. It's your fault. You and your friends ruined everything."

"I tried to save him. Don't you remember? I tried to save him."

"But you didn't, did you! My big brother is dead! My father blamed himself. My mother found him in our garage with the car running two days after the funeral. My mother tried to drink away the pain. She's been drunk twenty-four hours a day for most of my life. She may as well be dead. She's in a mental hospital and probably will be until she dies."

Wade and his team were moving into position.

"I'm so sorry. It was an accident. None of us meant for it to happen."

"You were drunk and driving a boat."

"I wasn't driving, and I wasn't drinking."

"I swore that one day you would all pay. I never dreamed I'd find you all living in the same little community. When I heard that ghost story, it was as if God had planned it all for me. I saved you for last because you did try to help. Don't worry; your death will be more merciful than the others. I'm going to let you choose how you're going to die."

"But I tried to help…"

"You didn't stop him! You let him kill my brother!"

"I tried! There was nothing I could do. Carl wouldn't listen."

Lizzie and Maddie arrived at the barn door and took cover.

"This is Sheriff Adams. Drop the gun and put your hands behind your head, interlocking your fingers."

"No! He has to pay like the others."

"I'll investigate that accident. If he's guilty, he'll go to jail. Drop the gun."

"What will be different this time? No one did anything about it then. Why would you now?"

"Drop the gun. We'll all go somewhere quiet to sort this out."

Wade's voice was calm and reassuring. The woman seemed to relax a little. Wade kept talking as she lowered the gun.

"No one else has to die. We can work this out," Wade told her.

Suddenly, she turned around and raised the gun, pointing it at Wade. Drew ducked behind bales of hay as a bullet struck the frame of the barn door. Wade returned fire and hit the woman in the right shoulder. The impact caused her to drop the gun and fall to the ground.

Wade kept his gun on her as he approached cautiously and kicked her gun out of her reach. Dodson rushed in and cuffed her. They helped her to her feet.

"Drew? Are you alright?"

"I'm okay."

Maddie rushed to her husband, and they held each other tight.

"Are you okay?" Drew asked his wife.

"I'm fine."

"Let's see who this is," Wade said as he pulled the mask from the woman's face.

Wade stared in surprise for a moment before saying, "Alex Dylan, you're under arrest for the murders of Paul Randolph, Nick Brinkman, and Carl Ellis and the attempted murder of Andrew Clifton. Dodson read him his rights. Someone call an ambulance."

"Yes, sir!"

Lizzie watched from outside the barn door until Wade looked at her. Then she ran to him and hugged him close as tears ran down her face.

"I'm alright, Lizzie," Wade whispered into her hair. "Deputy Fletcher, this is conduct unbecoming an officer of the law. I may have to fire you."

They both laughed as they went to check on Drew and Maddie.

"Are you sure you're okay?" Wade asked.

"Yes, we're fine, now," Maddie answered.

"I'm so glad this is over," Drew added.

"Is your baby alright?" Wade asked.

"Yes, he hadn't been crying very long when you arrived. He needed a diaper change. He went right back to sleep."

"I never would have guessed it was Alex," Drew said.

"I was sure it was Carl until he was killed," Wade confessed. "After that, I suspected everybody."

"How did you figure it out?" asked Maddie.

"I didn't. Lizzie did."

"It was luck really. There was a luncheon at the inn today. Two of the ladies were teachers when the victims were in school. They were talking about the deaths and mentioned the accident. The rest was finding the right information."

"We almost didn't find it in time," Wade added.

"I, for one, am thankful that you did," Drew said.

"Me, too," Maddie chimed in.

"How did he get the drop on you Maddie? Wade asked.

"I was putting Brody down for the night. When I came out of his room, there stood a masked woman pointing a gun at me. She threatened Brody if I didn't cooperate."

"When I came in, I saw the same thing, but the gun was pointed at Maddie. I followed orders to keep her and the baby safe."

"Drew, how did you end up on that boat with them?" Lizzie asked.

"I was living with my uncle while going to college. The boat belonged to him. I met Nick at work. We worked together at Coy's Supermarket and became friends. I invited him to the lake. He asked if he could bring his friends Carl and Paul. I didn't see any of them again until we moved to Rayland."

The prisoner was taken to the hospital for treatment. Wade dropped Lizzie off at the newspaper office to get her jeep.

"I need you to write up a report about what you found out and how you did it. You can do it at the office or at home. If you do it at home, email it to me."

"If it's all the same to you, I'd like to write it up at the office while it's still fresh on my mind."

"We'll still have to be professional for a while longer, maybe until the trial is over."

"I understand. I'm sorry for my lapse of judgment earlier," Lizzie joked.

"I'll see you at the office," Wade said smiling down at her.

They drove to the office and finished their reports. Lizzie was proud that she had been able to help put the murderer in jail.

• • •

His real name was Alexander Dylan McCoy. He dropped his last name the day after his eighteenth birthday. He met Morgan while they were in college. He had told her that he was an only child whose parents had died in a car accident during his first year of college. She never knew about the boating accident.

A search warrant was issued, allowing the sheriff's department to search all of Alex Dylan's property and his classroom. Evidence was found that he had been videotaping and photographing the activities of his victims for months. A key to a storage locker was found among his belongings. In that storage locker was an old Dodge pickup. Carpet fibers were collected from the truck bed that matched the carpet found in the ditch. In the glove compartment of the truck, receipts were found from thrift stores in Wichita Falls for a pink dress, women's shoes, and a wig. The victims' missing belongings were found in his office at the middle school. He had hidden them in a coffee can beneath of stack of sheet music.

Alex Dylan used his one phone call to contact his wife. When she arrived, Wade led her to his office.

"Mrs. Dylan, I'd like to ask you some questions before you see your husband. You may have an attorney present if you'd like."

"Thank you, Sheriff. I don't mind answering your questions. I know that Alex is innocent."

"Have you been having nightmares and sleep walking lately?"

"No, why do you ask?"

"You said you've been having trouble sleeping."

"Yes, I have."

"Do you have any idea why?"

"I'm prone to insomnia when I worry. Our finances are in bad shape. I haven't been able to find a job."

"You said that you drink warm milk before going to bed. Do you prepare it yourself?"

"Alex makes it for me. Why?"

"Your husband told me that you have been having nightmares and sleep walking. He said he found you standing in the middle of the road in front of your house."

"When did he tell you that?" she asked in confusion.

"He asked me to meet him for lunch after Nick Brinkman's death. It was the day before Thanksgiving. He told me that you had been very upset by the murders. He implied that he found you sleep walking on the night that Nick Brinkman died."

"Why on earth would he say such a thing?"

"It isn't true?"

"No, it isn't true," she answered obviously upset.

"When my deputy and I visited you after Mr. Ellis' death, he commented that you seemed to be heavily medicated. Are you taking medication?"

"No. I don't like taking unnecessary medicines. I prefer natural remedies. I don't understand why you're asking these things."

"Mrs. Dylan, I suggest you that go see Doctor Hughes as soon as possible."

"What for?"

"I believe your husband has been drugging you. Doctor Hughes can tell you for sure."

"Why would you think that?"

"Your speech is one indication. Your movements are sluggish. You seemed to be exhausted every time we spoke. You had great difficulty waking up to talk with us the last time we visited you at your home."

Morgan Dylan looked down at her hands. "Yes, I remember that."

"I believe your husband drugged your warm milk at night so that he could spy on the victims. He'd go to bed when you did. He'd leave when you fell asleep. He'd be back in bed beside you when you woke up. When the bodies were found, you truthfully provided him with an alibi."

Mrs. Dylan said nothing.

"Do you recognize these?" Wade asked showing her the dress and wig.

"No, I've never seen those before."

"You may see your husband, now."

"Thank you."

Wade led her to the visitation room. Alex Dylan was staring at the wall and rocking in his chair. She looked at her husband. He did not look at her. She spoke to him. He did not answer. She touched his hand. He did not respond. Sadly, Morgan Dylan left the jail and contacted a defense attorney.

Wade called Sheriff Duncan immediately after the arrest to let him know that his deputy's killer had been caught. The following morning, he left the office and drove to Rayland. He wanted to visit with each of the people he had gotten to know over the past few months. He wanted to tell them that their nightmare was over. He went to see Irene Cutter first. He tapped lightly on her door and waited with his hat in his hand.

"Well hello, Sheriff," Mrs. Cutter smiled happily.

"Good morning," Wade smiled back. "I hope I'm not disturbing you."

"No, I'm glad to see you. Come in and sit down for a while."

Wade sat down and said, "I see that you're free from that cast."

"Yes, and I was never so glad to get rid of anything in my life." She looked at him for a moment and then asked, "Is this a social call or business?"

"A little of both. I wanted you to be the first to know that we caught Nick's killer."

Irene listened as Wade told her the story.

"I never would have guessed it was Alex Dylan," she said. "I met him once at the Carson's store after he first moved here. He didn't seem the type."

"I know what you mean, but looking back on the investigation there were some indications that something wasn't right. I didn't pick up on them at the time."

"The important thing is that you got him. Our little community can be peaceful again."

The new friends visited for a while before Wade said goodbye. "I'll stop by from time to time to check on you. Call me if you ever need anything."

"There is one thing you can do for me," she winked. "I hear you've been keeping company with a little red haired girl. I'd like to meet her."

Wade laughed, "If I can convince her to go out with me again, I'll bring her to meet you."

It was determined after a psychiatric evaluation that Alex Dylan was not competent to stand trial. He was to be housed at the state hospital for the criminally insane until he was deemed competent.

Morgan Dylan took Sheriff Adams advice and went to see Doctor Hughes. She learned that she had indeed been drugged. When the truth was revealed about her husband, she filed for divorce and moved out of the area.

Brandy Ellis moved from the farm in Rayland to a small town in Oklahoma. She found a new life with her daughter Hayleigh. She had a good job and was able to provide quite well for her daughter. They were both healthy and happy.

April Randolph stayed on the farm in Rayland. She eventually received the money from the life insurance policy and hired someone to do the farming. She donated Paul's antique collection to the Red River Valley museum in his memory.

Emily Brinkman moved into Vernon and lived next door to Dan Hayes. She continued to work at the Farm Bureau Insurance office.

Kent and Dara Preston inherited the Preston family farm after Grandma Gail passed away peacefully in her sleep. Kent began researching the Lawrence family tree.

Mack and Pearl Carson closed the Rayland Farm Store and retired. They remained residents of the Rayland community.

Brian and Kelly Flynn were able to keep their home. They continued to work full time while farming on weekends.

After Alex Dylan was taken to the state hospital in March, Wade waited two weeks to call Lizzie.

"Lizzie, would you consider having dinner with me tonight?"

"I'd love to Wade, but is that a good idea?"

"The case is closed. There isn't going to be a trial anytime soon. You're no longer employed by the sheriff's department. It shouldn't be a problem."

"Then, yes. I'll have dinner with you."

"I know it's been months, but I'd like to start again if that's okay with you."

"I'd like that, too."

"I'll pick you up at six."

"I'll be ready."

# THE END

CPSIA information can be obtained
at www.ICGtesting.com
Printed in the USA
FSOW01n0401070616
21161FS